TALES OF AN URBAN WITCH

Robert Williams

South of the River Collective

Copyright © 2023 Robert Williams

All rights reserved. The characters and events portrayed in this book are
fictitious. Any similarity to real persons, living or dead, is coincidental and
not intended by the author.
No part of this book may be reproduced, or stored in a retrieval system,
or transmitted in any form or by any means, electronic, mechanical,
photocopying, recording, or otherwise, without express written
permission of the publisher.

ISBN-13: 9798870588742

Cover design by: Robert Williams
Printed in Great Britain

CHAPTER ONE

BAD MAN

My name is Margaret, although most people call me Mags, and I am an Urban Witch. There, that's the difficult part out of the way. Introductions are so hard, aren't they? I'm a witch who lives in a tower block in a part of southeast London that has yet to be discovered by celebrities, hipsters, or goths. It's quite popular with vandals, but that's another story.

There are more of us about than you might think, but we try to stay in the background and not make a fuss. You won't see us on the covers of newspapers or magazines or on television. And none of us are influencers, whatever they are. By our nature, we tend to avoid the limelight, and in any case, the Witch's Council frowns on that sort of thing.

You wouldn't even be able to tell that I was a witch of any sort by looking at me. In fact, many people think I'm a librarian or a nurse. Both are sort of true. Modern witchcraft is a vocation that requires many skills.

***

It had been a long day, not helped by the weather suddenly realising the calendar had flipped over into July a few weeks ago and it was trying to make up for weeks of rain and wind by coming up with the hottest day for decades. Everything was an effort, and I just wanted to melt into a little puddle.

Despite that, I shivered, and I could see goose pimples rising on my bare arms. My flat had turned unnaturally cold, unnaturally quickly, and that could only mean one thing: a ghost.

Ghosts are an occupational hazard for witches, and more so for urban witches. We attract them. It's like we're some sort of supernatural ghost magnet. It's part of the job to guide lost souls to the afterlife, although some of us are better at it than others. You should meet my friend Agnes. She was so good at ushering the dead to their eternal rest that … Well, we'll meet Agnes later.

Urban witches draw more ghosts than their rural counterparts simply because of population density. There are more people living in towns and cities than in the countryside, and obviously more people die there. London has been rumoured to have more ghosts than living people, but you should never listen to rumours. That one wasn't true, although there are a lot of ghosts in London, and now and then one finds its way to my flat on the sixth floor of Talltree Towers.

I put the kettle on and sat down to wait for it to boil. That gave me time to put myself in the right state of mind to receive the ghost. Some witches describe this as opening ourselves up to the psychic plane. Those are the witches that go in for dark clothing and dancing naked in the woods before dawn. The more sensible of us think of this state as just becoming calm enough to listen.

As I said, it had been a busy day. I'd cleared up someone's asthma and found a cat that had become locked in a shed on the allotments. I'd also visited poor Jake on the fifth floor. He was as fit as a fiddle, but in a bad way, emotionally. I saw his ex-wife coming to visit just as I was leaving, so I expected more trouble later. She was a drunken waste of space with a face that would curdle water.

I had hoped to put my feet up with a large, cold gin and to make a significant dent in my boxed set of *Downton Abbey*. Although no one thing had been taxing, taken as a whole, and with the heat, the day had drained me. An evening off would have been fantastic, but my visitor changed all that.

When the kettle boiled, I made tea – a bag-in-a-cup job. I preferred a pot of loose leaf, but I felt lazy, and it was only for me, after all. The ghost wouldn't want one.

I took a sip and, sufficiently calmed, started to speak.

"What do you want, love?" I asked in my gentlest voice. I wasn't expecting an answer. It can surprise ghosts when people take notice of them, and it might take them a little while to realise they are being addressed.

I gave it a minute, then spoke again. "My name's Mags, love. I'm a witch. I can hear you if you want to talk to me."

"I killed him." I barely heard her.

"Killed who, dear?"

Well, there was no need to guess what she wanted. The guilty ones always wanted absolution. It didn't matter who gave it. Confession is good for the soul, especially when you're dead.

"I killed him." She was louder and stronger. The vaguest of shadows was forming in front of my cooker.

"Who, dear? Who did you kill?" I sometimes worry my professional voice makes me sound like Claire Rayner.

"Bad man."

I sighed. This was going to take a while. I eyed the boxed set of *Downton* and knew I wouldn't be watching any of it tonight.

"Who is the bad man, love?"

"Husband. Bad man."

"Why was he bad? Did he hit you?"

She was silent for a long time. I thought maybe she'd gone, but the room hadn't warmed up and the shadow was still by my cooker.

"I don't remember," she said at last.

Ghosts lose track easily. We call it the death trauma. From what I've heard, death can be a bit like changing gear without a clutch while wearing a blindfold. I guess that might make you forget a few things.

The shadow now had the vague shape of a woman. I directed my words toward it.

"When did it happen? When did you kill him?"

"Just now."

I cursed myself for being stupid. Spirits have no sense of time. It was always *just now* to them. It could literally have been just now, or, more likely, decades ago.

The shadow had gained a little more substance. I could see the outline of a woman now, and she was wearing a dress of some sort. Or it could have been a coat. It was difficult to tell. There was still no colour or texture to her.

I was getting nowhere, so I tried a different tack.

"Why have you come to see me, love?"

"I don't know." There was a pause before she spoke.

My main theory — my only theory — was still that she wanted to be forgiven. She'd killed her husband after he'd hit her one too many times. I'd seen it so often on the estate, although most times the wife was still alive. He must have dealt her a fatal blow before she'd killed him.

"It's not your fault, you know. You were only defending yourself."

"Bad man."

That confirmed it. He'd been hurting her, and she lashed out in self-defence.

"Yes, dear. Bad man. What did he do?"

She was silent.

"Did he hurt you, dear?"

"Yes. Hurt. He hurt me."

"Did he hit you?"

"No."

I sighed. She was really the most difficult woman.

"You need to tell me a little more before I can help you, dear. You do want my help, don't you?"

"I don't know."

Curious. Why else would she be here?

"How did you die, dear?" This was a risky question to ask. Often ghosts have no idea that they have died. It was a truth they sometimes couldn't handle. Even just mentioning their death can scare them away.

TALES OF AN URBAN WITCH

"I ... I fell. Tripped. Cat. Stairs. Railing. Running. Fell."

She probably died here in the block. Spirits rarely wander far and quite a few people have met their end on the stairs. The crap lighting, the worn steps, the low railings. It was a recipe for disaster.

"Why were you running?"

I thought back to all the deaths on the stairs I could remember in the years since I moved into this block. The old woman who tried to escape a mugger but didn't spot the skateboard. The little girl running away from home. The man who'd stayed too long at the pub and was late for his dinner.

None of them matched the shadow taking form in front of me or the voice I could hear. She was a three-dimensional shade with a vaguely familiar voice, but I couldn't put a name to her. She was a woman I knew but not well enough, and she was triggering a memory that tickled at the back of my mind. The lack of colour didn't help.

"I needed to see you."

"Were you coming for my help, dear?"

She wouldn't have been the first person to come running to me. Many people around here think of urban witches as another emergency service. We know things, and we're local. On this estate, I'd be on the scene much sooner than an ambulance or the police. I've delivered more babies than I can count and there were several local boys that I'd scared back onto the straight and narrow. I'd be no good in a fire, though, and no matter how cute your cat, you'd never find me up a tree.

"No." She'd frowned before answering. I could see her shadow-brow crinkle with concentration. Who was she? I nearly had it. I think she'd lived in the block but wasn't a client herself. A client's mother? A wife, maybe?

"Then why did you want to see me?"

"Bad man."

This made no sense.

"Bad…" she paused, brow furrowed again. "Bad woman."

Bad man. Bad woman. What could that mean? Unless… "Am I

5

the bad woman?"

"Yes."

"Why?"

"Bad man."

The bad man made me a bad woman?

Oh no! The pieces fell together all at once. I could see her face properly for the first time. I did know her!

"Veronica! It's you, isn't it? I saw you going to see Jake when I was leaving him earlier. I thought you looked cross."

"Bad man."

"Wait! That was only an hour ago, and he was fine then. When did you kill him?"

"Just now."

Typical! This was the one time when *just now* really meant *just now*. Bloody ghosts!

I ran out the door and headed for the stairs that would take me down to Jake's flat. It would be quicker than the lift. I could see Veronica's body in the courtyard below. How she had fallen over the railing on the way up was a mystery, but it was one I couldn't be bothered with right now. Her ghost, now coloured properly, stood by the body, and looked down at it mournfully. I took the stairs down quickly, but carefully.

The door to Jake's flat was open – she hadn't bothered to close it in her mad dash to exact whatever twisted revenge she'd had in mind for me. As I charged in, I found Jake on the kitchen floor, a large pool of blood around his head and his favourite cast-iron frying pan on the floor beside him. He had a pulse, however. He was still alive.

"Bad man." Veronica had followed me in, but I ignored her while I called for an ambulance.

"You didn't kill him," I said after I'd hung up. I was getting Jake's blood on my jeans, but that wasn't important.

"Bad man."

"No. He wasn't bad, Veronica. He loved you, but you were impossible to love. Impossible to please. You left him. Remember?"

"Bad man."

"Yes, you justified leaving him by saying he was bad. He was lazy, you said. He hit you, you said. He saw other women, you said."

"Bad—"

"No! You always said that, but you lied. You were the bad one. You beat him. I saw the bruises. I saw him cooking and cleaning and washing dishes while you slept on the sofa surrounded by vodka bottles. He was too bloody knackered for other women. You probably put him off women for life."

I ignored her for a minute to make sure he was comfortable. The 999 operator had told me not to move him. I couldn't see anything to suggest a broken neck or a fractured skull, but I didn't want to take chances.

"Jake? Jake? Can you hear me?" He stirred but didn't wake. "It's Mags, love. I'm here. Don't worry, I've called an ambulance. They'll be here soon. Stay with me, won't you?"

"I killed him," Veronica said.

"No, you didn't."

"Blood."

"Head wounds bleed a lot. You've hurt him quite badly, but he's not dead."

She looked at me, confused. She didn't know what to do.

"You thought I was having an affair with him, didn't you?"

"Bad woman."

"Oh, bugger off. I saw him to fix his bruises and set his arm that time you broke it. He was always too embarrassed to go to a doctor, so he got me to deal with his injuries. Lucky, he heals well. You'd have killed a lesser man a dozen times over. When you left him, I came to rebuild his self-esteem, to tell him he wasn't the waste of air you said he was. I was, still am, his friend."

"*Friend.*" She managed to say the word in italics. Sarcasm? From a ghost? She blinked at me.

"Yes, friend. You could have been his friend if you'd tried. Your marriage would have lasted longer for a start. I doubt you know how to be anyone's friend. You attacked him for nothing, you hear? Nothing."

What was keeping her here? She knew now that she hadn't killed Jake, and she thought she was in the right. She wouldn't want to apologise, and she didn't need my forgiveness.

I laughed then as the reason hit me. She still wanted me to admit I had been having an affair with her husband. She wanted to punish me like she had been going to do when she was still alive.

"You wanted to hurt me, maybe kill me like you thought you'd killed Jake. That's why you were running."

She nodded slowly.

"And now you're dead and you blame me for that."

"Bad woman."

"You still want to kill me?"

She nodded again, and I laughed.

"Well, good luck with that, sister. You're a piss-poor ghost, you know that? You've hardly enough watts for me to see you. You're never going to get enough strength to even touch me, let alone kill me."

Her lips pursed, and she glared at me.

"You know what? I'm going to let you stick around for a while to see if you can give yourself a break and move on. I know of at least seven ways to disperse a ghost and all of them are painful."

She looked smug at that point.

"Painful for the ghost. Notice I said I'd disperse you. I didn't say I'd help you pass over. I said disperse. Like a sugar lump in a cup of tea. You'd be dead forever."

Her gloating smile faded as her fate suddenly became real to her. She knew she would float around me for a while until I died or got sick of her. There was a chance she'd change her ways, of course, but I wouldn't hold my breath.

I ignored her and reached over to grab Jake's hand and held it. I stroked his hair with my other hand as I waited for the blue lights to arrive.

CHAPTER TWO

LOVE POTION

As an urban witch, people come to me with problems, problems they can't take to anyone else, and I do what I can for them. Most of the time, they just need sympathy, a cup of tea and a nudge in the right direction. Sometimes, they need a little bit more.

I hadn't decided what Bruce and Jenny needed yet. A kind word, perhaps, or maybe Relate's phone number or the address of the swingers' club that everyone knows about, but no-one has visited. Allegedly. Time would tell me what Bruce and Jenny needed.

Bruce looked like a stereotypical used-car salesman with his sharp suit, shaven head, and bright shiny eyes that darted around the room as if looking for something to sell. He had dressed carefully and well. Nothing he wore was cheap, but he had stopped short of flashy. He let himself down, however, by looking me in the eye too often and using my name in every other sentence. Old salesman tricks. He spoke in that incredibly earnest tone that politicians use when they are lying. You know when politicians are lying? When their mouths are open. Old joke, but oh so true.

"Mags, this is a lovely cup of tea."

"Thanks. It's just Sainsbury's. Nothing special."

"It really hits the spot. You sure you've not put anything extra in it?" He laughed in that way people do when they think they've said something funny, and they want you to know. Or maybe he was nervous. People find witches intimidating for some reason.

"I'd charge you more if I had."

Jenny looked like a trophy bride, a gorgeous woman who was so far out of Bruce's league that people must have wondered why they were together. It was a question on my mind, for sure. I guessed he had married her because she would look good on his arm. Goodness knows what she saw in him. She could have done a lot better.

Whatever his reasons for marrying her, he seemed to have no interest in her as a person now. His body language – witches are fluent in body language – told me his attention was on me, completely. She didn't register on his radar at all, but his indifference didn't matter to her. She just smiled. She smiled a lot, but the smile looked genuine, pleased. Pleased to be with him. Pleased with who she was. Pleased to be here. That last one had me foxed. Her designer clothes and handbag were very out of place in my kitchen. I tried to hide the hole in my second best cardy whenever she looked in my direction.

"More tea, Jenny?"

"Thank you, yes. That would be delightful." Her accent was odd, and that was one more thing that intrigued me about the couple. It wasn't right. It sounded very landed gentry and enormously fake. It would have been ideal for a TV costume drama. Her accent was exactly like Lady Mary's from *Downton Abbey,* but it didn't suit her.

"Another biscuit?"

"Oh no. I couldn't. I've got to watch my figure." She glanced at Bruce with a knowing smile. She thought he preferred her slim, but I could see he couldn't give a toss.

What was wrong with this couple?

I talked about my services but kept to ones I knew they wouldn't want, such as finding missing cats and curing gout. I just wanted to watch them some more. People let down their guard when they are listening, and they think no-one is watching.

Bruce, I could see, was waiting for an opportunity to speak. His eyes darted furiously as his brain tried to frame questions he could ask. I could see him become frustrated, time and again, as I fed him just enough information to come up with something to ask me, only for me to supply the answer a few seconds later. It didn't matter. He had his own questions to ask. That much was obvious.

As I spoke, Jenny smiled in a distracted way, yet she was listening intently. Her eyes never left me the whole time I was speaking, not even when she blinked.

What did she want?

"Are you okay, Jenny, love?" I used the opportunity to lean in closer to her and looked into her eyes. As any good witch will tell you, eyes are not the windows to the soul that everyone believes, but they are an infallible indicator of someone's state of mind.

"Of course. Everything is absolutely fine. I couldn't be happier."

This wasn't a case of Jenny's smile not reaching her eyes. Jenny's ever-present smile did reach her eyes, and she looked as happy as she claimed. At least, she believed she was. She believed it with *almost* every ounce of her being.

Almost.

There was a tiny part of Jenny that wasn't happy. I could see it in her eyes. Deep inside, she raged. I didn't let on that I knew, but I could see that she'd noticed. Her smile didn't waver, but the rage intensified. I nodded to show that I would try to help her but, as to how, I didn't have a clue.

"How can I help?" I asked, directing my question at Bruce.

His salesman-smile faded, and his eyes lost their twinkle. For the first time, I noticed the fine wrinkles around them and the dark shadows underneath. He was exhausted.

"Well, it's tricky," he began.

"If it were easy, you wouldn't be here."

"You're not wrong, Mags. You're not wrong." He looked in Jenny's direction, but not at her. Why was he hesitating? Had it anything to do with her inner anger?

"Jenny and I have been married a long time," he said.

"How long?"

"Three years."

"Three years?" I was incredulous but tried not to show it. I couldn't believe he thought three years was a long time.

"Three blissfully happy years," Jenny said, still smiling.

"Happy. Yeah," Bruce added, without conviction.

"Then, what's the matter?"

His eyes properly focussed on Jenny for the first time since they had arrived, and her face lit up. Bruce's face showed nothing except weariness. Then he took a long look at me.

"I know it doesn't sound like it, but three years can feel like a lot longer. You know?"

I nodded. I think I knew where this was going.

"Every night," he said. "Every sodding night."

"Sex?"

He nodded.

"We make love every night," Jenny added. "Bruce is such a beast."

He shook his head and then buried his face in his hands.

"Three hours every night. Three hours! I can't do it, Mags, I really can't," he said. He was almost crying. "I just want to sleep."

I patted him on the shoulder, and he jumped. He looked up and relaxed when he saw it was me.

"You want me to calm her down?"

"Or give me something."

"What?"

"I don't know. Energy. Stamina. Will-power. The ability to say no."

"Have you tried your GP?"

"He just laughed and wished he was so lucky."

"You can buy Viagra over the counter these days."

"I don't need it."

"Little Bruce is always ready to perform," Jenny said with a giggle.

TALES OF AN URBAN WITCH

"It's the rest of me that's knackered, Mags. My todger has a life of its own. Even though I'm ready to drop, it still springs up as soon as we're in bed."

That didn't sound right. There was more to this than just nymphomania. Something else was at work.

"Let me try something," I said and got up. "More tea?"

They both nodded, so I put some water on to boil and stared at my distorted reflection in the kettle. It looked thoughtful. My best theory was that Jenny and possibly Bruce as well were under the influence of love spells, but I needed to be certain. I left the kettle to boil and went in search of my dowsing rod.

The law doesn't officially recognise witchcraft. There is a sort of liaison officer at the local police station, but as his role is unofficial, there is nothing about magic or the craft in his title. He works with us when someone commits a crime using magic, but can't do anything if they've broken one of our laws. He couldn't do anything about a love spell unless it had caused a law to be broken.

The Witch's Council had a stronger view about them and had banned love spells and love potions in 1974. We think they are evil. We always have. It just took us a long time to make the attitude formal. They were as close to being illegal as you could get in the witching world.

That led me to think that this wasn't a spell cast by a witch. Whoever had cast this spell had truly messed it up. A love spell is basic stuff. A first-year trainee would have been able to mix a simple love potion from ingredients they'd bought from Lidl. There was literally no scope for getting it wrong. Jenny should have loved Bruce with all her being. Body and soul. The angry spark I saw in her eyes should not have existed.

I found my dowser, a Y-shaped willow branch, tucked away in my DIY cupboard. I knew I had left it in the kitchen, but willow has a habit of migrating. The dowser likes my screwdrivers.

"The kettle has boiled," Jenny said, when I returned. "I tried to make the tea, but I'm afraid I didn't know where you kept everything."

"Don't worry. I'll make it in a minute. Let's do this first. Close your eyes and relax."

I sat down and grasped the rod loosely, one branch of the Y in each hand, my fingers finding familiar grooves and notches in the wood. I cleared my mind and concentrated on the roughness of the bark, the weight of the branch in my grasp, and the way the rod seemed alive and about to dance on its own.

Then I spoke to it. Not out loud, of course. That sort of behaviour, talking to a stick, makes the punters feel uncomfortable. I just thought at it, and I told it I wanted to find evidence of witchcraft, and at once the rod pulled my arms wildly, describing a circle, and pointing at every part of my kitchen. My dowsing rod has a sense of humour.

So, I told the rod to ignore anything of mine and it pulled to my left, towards Jenny. A definite spell at work in that case.

Now, what about Bruce? I told the branch to ignore Jenny, and it drifted slowly towards him. The reaction wasn't as strong as with Jenny. No, that wasn't right. The reaction was just as intense, but it was as if the dowsing rod were scared of him. That puzzled me, but I let it lie.

"Well, that's all in order," I said, putting the rod down. "Let's get that tea made."

I clattered about in the kitchen making preparations, my kettle-reflection looking shifty this time.

"Why did you come to me?" I called out to them.

"I just told you," Bruce answered.

"Yes, I know, but why me? Me in particular. You don't look like locals."

Bruce laughed. "I used to live in this block. On the ninth."

"Ah. The penthouse flats." Property developers had bought all the top floor and converted from eighteen bog-standard flats into six 'stunning luxury apartments' with two dedicated express elevators. Gullible pretentious idiots had bought the apartments like the estate was going to be the next Clapham. They didn't know the area very well. They sold the apartments almost immediately – for a third of their value – when it emerged that the estate wasn't the best place to be parking cars that cost more than the average local family earns in a decade. Not if you wanted to keep your tyres, anyway.

"I loved that flat. Stayed there two years. I only moved when I married Jenny."

I raised an eyebrow. Most people hadn't stayed long enough to unpack.

"I even got to know some of the locals," he continued. "They all spoke highly of you, Mags. Everyone knows you. Good old Mags."

Old? I'm forty-eight. Bloody cheek!

"Here you are," I said, with a flourish as I laid the tray on the table in front of them, then poured each of them a cup.

"Thanks, Mags," Bruce said.

"Tell me about when you first met."

Bruce looked at Jenny and shrugged. He took a sip of the tea and grimaced before speaking.

"Back then, Jenny and I didn't really get on."

"Really?"

"I hated him," she said. The spark in her eyes still did.

"Mags, back then, I wanted Jenny more than anyone, anything. I could think of nothing other than her, and I vowed I would stop at nothing to get her."

"He kept at it. Persistence pays off," Jenny said.

"It came on gradually. As I kept pressing my case, she began to tolerate me, then accept me and then, finally, love me."

Ah, a cumulative spell. Probably a potion administered to her over a few months.

"How long did this take?"

"I don't know. Six months, I think."

"And she's been like this ever since?"

We both glanced at Jenny, who was looking at Bruce as if every word he'd said had been poetry. Bruce nodded.

"Does it ever change?"

"How do you mean?"

"Does she have off-days where she isn't so much of a puppy?"

"No, I don't think …" he said, slowly. "No, wait. Yes. She does. She gets snappy with me every month. I thought it was … you know."

I rolled my eyes. Men rarely get to grips with the concept of menstruation, and few could talk about it easily. This wasn't the time to educate him, however.

I decided it was time to drop the bombshell.

"I think you are both under the control of love spells."

"What? How?" Bruce said, shocked.

Outer-Jenny just smiled while inner-Jenny burned brighter.

I patted Bruce's hand and muttered reassuring words in his ear. He looked distracted for a few moments.

"Most likely, someone fed you a potion," I said in a louder voice. "In Jenny's case, it was a substandard potion that wears off every month and has to be refreshed."

Jenny's eyes raged so brightly that I was surprised that Bruce didn't see it.

"Who on earth could do that to her?"

"I don't know, but I intend to find out. Love spells are against the Witch's Code. Unless there was a good reason for it, the witch who did this is in big trouble."

I patted Jenny's hand and muttered reassuring words in her ear. The rage in her eyes dimmed briefly.

"Can you turn it off?" Bruce asked.

"Sort of."

"Sort of? What do you mean by that?"

"It's unorthodox, but I could give you a love potion myself."

"You said that was illegal." I was glad Bruce had been paying attention.

"It's against the Witch's Code. Not illegal, as such. We can use them, but if there's a good reason. Countering another love potion is a good reason."

"How will it help?"

"My potion will kill the existing spell and put another in its place, but it will be a spell I can control. I'll be able to change its actions and cancel it, for instance. What do you say?"

"We'll be normal?"

"Whatever that is for you, yes."

Bruce thought for a minute and then nodded his assent. I turned to Jenny.

"Will I still love Bruce?" she asked, eyes blazing.

"You'll love him more and he'll love you with all his heart." Temporarily. It would end when I cancelled the spell. I didn't tell her that. Outer-Jenny would hate the idea.

I suddenly doubted myself. Should I do this? I was planning on casting a spell that would eradicate outer-Jenny's personality. In effect, I would kill her. She was as innocent as a puppy, and she would be gone when I had finished. Inner-Jenny would be back in control.

I took in a deep breath, making up my mind, and then exhaled. There was no Inner Jenny and Outer Jenny. There was just Jenny, albeit one who's personality had been hamstrung.

"Very well," I said. "I have already given you the potion."

They both jumped.

"I thought that tea tasted funny," Bruce said. "I don't feel any different, though."

"You won't. This isn't the fourteenth century. Things have moved on as far as spells are concerned. I've primed you both with a code word. The potion won't take effect until you hear me say the right word. Are you ready?"

They both looked at me with a solemn intensity, daunted by what was about to happen. Jenny's eyes blazed. In unison, Jenny and Bruce nodded.

"Look at each other, please." I didn't want them falling in love with me, although I had the counter-spell ready, just in case. I didn't want to use it. My mum brought me up to not waste spells.

The soothing words I had muttered in their ears earlier had primed them for the code word I was about to use.

"Marigold." Not the most original of code words, I must admit, but my washing-up gloves had been in view when I was speaking into Bruce's ear.

The effect was immediate. Bruce's eyes, which had previously looked at Jenny's left ear, locked onto her eyes, which in turn lost their spark. Lustful grins split both of their faces and they lunged for each other.

"Sleep," I said, and the lunges ended gracelessly on my kitchen table. Love potions double nicely as sleeping potions given the right code word, and I had primed them with both.

I made Bruce comfortable and then sat Jenny up in the chair. I needed to talk to her alone.

"Jenny! Jenny! Can you hear me?"

She groaned.

"Good. Listen to my voice, Jenny. Can you do that?"

"Bruce…"

"He's right here, love. Don't worry. Now listen. I'm going to count down from three and click my fingers. At that point, the love potion will cease to work for you, Jenny, and you alone. You, Jenny, will wake up. You got that?"

She groaned again, but nodded slowly.

"Three … two… one." Click.

"Jenny. You're back to your normal self. Tell me, who has been doing this to you? Was it Bruce? Has he been—"

"You stupid meddling bitch!"

I have to admit that was not the response I was expecting.

"What?"

"You couldn't leave well enough alone, could you?" Her accent was now less *Downton Abbey* and more Deptford Market.

"What?" I know I'd repeated myself, but I had no idea where this conversation was going.

"I administered the love potions, you idiot. Me! And they weren't substandard, either."

"But why? You hate him. I could see that in your eyes."

"You saw me hating being dragged here. You saw me hating you poking your nose in where it wasn't wanted. You saw that!"

"No. That wasn't it."

"Yes, it was. Not only that. You are undoing years of work."

"What?" I said again. My vocabulary isn't the best when I am confused.

"Look at him."

I looked. Bruce was sleeping peacefully.

"What do you see?"

I saw Bruce, a man in his late thirties, asleep. His smooth head needed a shave, I suddenly noticed, and so did his face.

"A sleeping man."

"You're supposed to be a witch. Look properly."

His hair and his beard were growing noticeably, and I could see the gap between his eyebrows was narrowing.

"He's a werewolf?" I had met a few of those over the years, but Bruce didn't fit. I could usually spot a werewolf a mile away, but Bruce wasn't one. Bruce was something else.

"No, he's a satyr."

"A satyr?" I may have laughed. "And what are you? A nymph?"

She gave me a pitying look.

"I'm as human as you. I'm his Keeper."

The Keepers. I'd heard of them.

"Bugger."

"Indeed. Thanks to you, we've got a sex-crazed time bomb ticking away in your kitchen."

"Sorry."

"I had him under control. My control. I fed him a potion that made him interested in me and me alone every night and another one to myself every month to convince me I wanted him."

"But only enough so that the real you were still able to watch over him. That was why I could see that spark in your eye. The spell wasn't crap at all. It was meant to be like that. You had to watch. And so you watched, and you hated. Don't say it was me you hated. I couldn't tell much from that spark, but I could see it was old."

She sighed, her anger against me spent. I had found the truth.

"Of course, I hated him, but I hated myself more. He found it exhausting. That was nothing compared to how I felt. Night after night, making myself be used by that thing and the biggest part of me thinking I enjoyed it."

"But why do you do it?"

"Who else? Me or a member of my family has to wear him out or he'd be shagging most of London and wouldn't be asking permission."

I knew Keepers worked in families. Women and men allowed themselves to be used to keep supernaturals from preying on all the poor humans. We owe them. We all owe them.

"It's all I've known. We've been Keepers for generations. Satyrs, nymphs, werewolves, centaurs. We've kept them all, and more. Our whole reason for existing is to keep things like him in check. My mother was a Keeper, and all my aunts. I took over on Bruce when my Aunt Sarah wanted to get married and have a family. Before her, it was my Great Aunt Maureen and so on. Can you imagine the carnage if one of these things got loose in London?"

I stared at Bruce. "Oh no. Jack the Ripper."

She sighed. "Well done. Yes. The Ripper was a satyr. My many-times-great-grandmother got him under control eventually, but we lost three others along the way.

I continued to look at Bruce. His beard and hair had fully grown out. Horns poked out from his locks and his shoes had fallen off, exposing neat hooves.

"I could keep him asleep."

"He'll wake up. We've tried that with them in the past. We're just going to have to reinstate the spells I had in place."

"But you'll be trapped again. There has to be another way."

"There isn't. You're going to have to help me set this up. We don't have much time."

I nodded reluctantly and reached for my kettle in order to prepare another potion. I caught sight of my hand reflected in the shiny surface.

"Wait!" I said, "I have an idea."

***

Half an hour later, Jenny led Bruce away, blindfolded. The spell had done its work, but we didn't want to take any chances. He went as meekly as a sedated satyr.

"Thanks, Mags, this is going to change my life. Both our lives. You have no idea. We can get some sleep at last."

"I'm glad I was able to help."

"Oh, here." She reached into Bruce's pocket and pulled out his wallet, then thrust a large wad of fifty-pound notes into my hand.

"That's way too much," I said.

"It's not enough, believe me."

I kissed her goodbye in answer and watched as she led him away. As they started walking down the stairs, I raised my hand to wave and realised I was still holding my mirror.

The thing about love potions is that the person under the spell falls in love with the first person they see. When I activated the second potion, Bruce was staring at his own reflection.

I laughed as I shut the door behind me. She was going to have a terrible job of getting him out of the bathroom.

CHAPTER THREE
WAITING

People think that witches hold the medical world in disdain. Natural ways are the best and that sort of thing. There's a bit of truth in that, of course, or I would be a doctor and not an urban witch. Witches are, however, a bit more pragmatic than that. While I can cure your warts with a few carefully chosen herbs, I would be the first to send you off to A&E if I thought you had a fractured skull.

Unfortunately, there are people who are beyond any kind of help. They have illnesses that are too aggressive for both the craft and medical science. All that anyone can do is to make the patient comfortable until the end.

One of my friends, a dear, close friend, had reached a point where that end was in sight and nothing more could be done for her. Ethel had originally been a client but had long ago become a friend. She was such a nice woman and was so unrelentingly helpful. I'd lost count of the number of babies she'd helped me deliver, or the times she'd volunteered to clean or cook for some of the more unfortunate people I looked after. All for no reward. She brushed away their offers of money, although she accepted a cake now and then if it looked especially tempting.

She had been admitted to St Roland's the previous week by her consultant. The cancer in her lungs had spread and flourished, and she was about to die. The hospital and I had done all we could. I was sad because she was dying, and I was sad because I'd failed her. I'd come to apologise as much as to say goodbye.

St Roland's was a 'modern' hospital, built with lots of glass and steel. It was an odd-shaped building with a roof that had a meandering twisty wave built into it and several wings that suggested that the building would look like a snowflake if viewed from above. Or a flower of some sort. Or maybe someone's initials in Mandarin.

The shape also suggested that the architect was more interested in winning design awards than in helping people get better. I'd heard rumours of people dying on their way from one part of the building to another, with the ghosts of patients trapped within its labyrinthine corridors. They weren't. I'd checked, but it was a good story I could have easily believed.

I was expecting Ethel to be unconscious but, to my surprise, she was sitting up, wide awake, and was telling a nurse on the other side of the ward that she was making the bed wrong.

"No, dear," she was saying. "You need to fold that bit under the corner. That way it will – Oh hello, Mags!"

Her voice carried well for all that it was weak. My face broke into a spontaneous grin, and I almost burst into tears out of relief.

"Eth, you're looking so well!"

She laughed.

"I've taken them all by surprise. They'll be sending me home tomorrow!"

The nurse caught my eye and shook her head. Ethel didn't see her.

"Let's take it slow, eh? Have a nice rest here and we'll see about getting you home when you're good and ready," I said to her, in what I hoped was a reassuring tone.

They'd hooked her up to a dozen different machines, each tracing a bodily function in lurid green lines and beeping in different pitches and rhythms that in combination sounded like an early eighties one-hit wonder.

In addition to those screens, a small LCD television was

showing an episode of *Downton Abbey* – one I'd missed by the look of it – and I could hear tinny dialogue from the headphones Ethel had discarded on the bed. Lady Mary was looking as pensive as ever.

I sat beside Ethel and took her hand in mine. I lay my other hand on her forehead for a few seconds and listened. Listening wasn't the right word, of course, as I could hear nothing useful with all the beeping. Instead, I listened with another sense and let her body tell me how it felt. It didn't have good news. Despite how she looked, she didn't have very long.

This was her lightbulb moment. Lightbulbs, the old kind, the ones with jingly bits of metal inside them, used to shine brighter just before they burned out. It sometimes happens with people. They would have their lightbulb moments, just before they passed away, and there would be a day, or even just an hour or two, where they were stronger and fitter than they had been for months.

"How am I, Mags?" Ethel had seen me work plenty of times and knew what I'd been doing.

"You'll outlive us all."

"You're a terrible liar," she said with a laugh, which turned into a wracking cough that lasted too long and left her visibly weaker. The nurse placed an oxygen mask over her face, and her breathing gradually settled.

"Ooh! Don't make me laugh, Mags. It hurts."

"Sorry."

By the nurses' station, in the corner, a familiar figure sat on one of the visitors' chairs. Agnes. She nodded at me but didn't attempt to move. She was knitting. I'd known Agnes for decades, and every time I saw her, she'd been knitting.

"I see you're still watching *Downton*," I said to Ethel, just to make conversation. If Agnes was here, I knew there wouldn't be many opportunities to talk with Ethel in the future.

"It's all I could find," she answered, sinking back onto her pillows. "I prefer *Hotel Hellada,* but they don't have it here."

"What's that?" I rarely have time to keep up with television.

TALES OF AN URBAN WITCH

"One of those Scandi things," she said. "Or Greek. Foreign anyway. Dead good. The men are so dishy. What I wouldn't give to be fifty years younger."

I promised to look it up when I had the chance.

"D'you know," Ethel yawned. "I'm feeling very sleepy all of a sudden."

I had seen the dose of diamorphine she was on, and I was amazed she was awake at all.

"I might have a little nap. Do you mind, Mags?"

"You go ahead, Eth. I'll be here when you wake up."

"Just five minutes. Then I'll be as right as…" She fell asleep.

Without me noticing, Agnes had moved from the nurses' station and was now sitting in the other bedside chair. She was still knitting.

"She won't wake up, will she?" I asked her.

She shook her head.

The nurse, seeing Ethel had fallen asleep, came over with a cup of tea.

"Hello, I've made you a tea. It's got milk and sugar. Is that okay?" She hadn't brought one for Agnes. I wasn't surprised. The nurse couldn't see her.

"Perfect." I usually had it black and unsweetened, but I needed the sugar.

"Are you a relative?"

"An old friend."

Ethel only had one living relative. She'd outlived two husbands and most of her siblings. There were no children, but there was a younger brother who lived in Australia. He was on his way but would get here too late.

"Well, I'm glad someone's here."

"She's not doing well, is she?" I asked. It wasn't really a question, just something to say.

She hesitated before speaking. I knew what she was thinking. I had been in this situation many times myself. Should she answer with the truth or some sugar-coated fluff?

"I'm afraid she won't be with us for very much longer." I

ROBERT WILLIAMS

apparently looked strong enough to cope with the truth.

"It's her time," I said in a resigned voice. "Don't worry. I'll stay with her until … you know."

She put an alarm button near me, patted my arm, and bustled off.

"It's a shame about Andrew," I said to Agnes, once the nurse was out of earshot. "But Australia is so far away."

She nodded.

"I called him yesterday. He's coming. I should have called him sooner."

Agnes tilted her head, listening. She could see I needed to speak.

"He was her favourite, you know. More like a son than a little brother. She hated it when he had to move away."

Another tilt.

"Different times then," I said. "He could be himself there. He couldn't here. She understood, but it broke her heart."

Agnes's knitting needles clacked softly in a tiny percussive tune of comfort. It formed a counterpoint to the beeping of the machines. I lost my thoughts in the clicking for a few moments.

She smiled at me and nodded towards the door.

"No, I'll stay, thank you. I promised. I want to say goodbye."

Agnes nodded, unsurprised, and carried on knitting.

"I'm going to miss her," I said.

The rise and fall of Ethel's chest had slowed and become shallower since she'd fallen asleep. "She will go soon."

Agnes nodded.

The clicking of her needles and the beeping of the machines claimed my thoughts again. The heart monitor's traces were becoming erratic and weak. Blood flowed through the vein in Ethel's neck in discrete pulses. One, two, three. It really wouldn't be long.

"She's a special one, isn't she?" I said when I was able to think again. "She gave so much and expected so little."

And suddenly, I was blinking back tears, sad that such a wonderful woman would be taken from the world and out of my life.

The traces on the monitor were barely more than a flat line now. The visible pulse in Ethel's neck faltered, as if the blood were uncertain which way it needed to go. Up or down?

"I'll call the nurse over. They like to feel involved."

I pressed the alarm just as the heart line flattened and the machine screeched Ethel's demise to the ward. The nurse arrived and promptly called for help. I moved to one side while a frantic group of doctors and nurses hid Ethel behind a curtain and tried to bring her back to life. We all knew it was a futile exercise, but they had to try. For someone as ill as Ethel, it was only a token attempt.

Agnes and I listened with interest, and presently, Ethel's ghost joined us.

"Mags?"

"Hello Ethel."

"Am I dead now?"

I nodded.

"I'm feeling a lot better for it."

She looked amazingly good. People react to death in different ways. Veronica, a pathetic woman who'd died trying to kill me, had taken half an hour to manifest herself. She'd also had trouble speaking and even now, months later, she could barely string a sentence together. But that was another story.

Ethel, however, was coherent and looked solid. She even looked younger.

"You look amazing," I said.

"I should die more often," she said with a laugh in her voice, then turned to Agnes. "I know who you are."

Agnes smiled and cast off the last line of what she was knitting.

"This is for you," I said as Agnes handed Ethel the finished product. She took it and gave it a shake before holding it up.

"What is it?" she asked. "A onesie?"

"Try it on and find out," I said.

We could hear the doctors and nurses still trying to restart

ROBERT WILLIAMS

Ethel's heart. We knew they wouldn't succeed. There was some swearing. They liked Ethel.

Ethel shrugged and climbed into the garment. There were obvious holes into which she pushed her head, arms, and legs and, in moments, she was wearing it.

"This looks ridiculous. What are these extra bits at the back?"

Agnes continued to smile and, as she did so, the garment, smoothed itself out into a loose robe. It fitted Ethel perfectly. The parts at the back stretched themselves into large white wings.

It figured. Ethel had been a churchgoer all her life, and Agnes always knitted to suit.

"It's time for you to go, Ethel," I said.

Ethel nodded and gave her wings an experimental flap.

"Thank you, Mags," she said. "You've been a real friend to me all these years."

"And you to me, Eth. I wish I could have done more for you."

"You did enough."

"But—"

"You did enough," she insisted, and so I nodded.

"Be good," I said.

"I don't think I could be anything else now," she said and laughed. A halo glowed itself into existence above her head and I smiled. Ethel was enjoying herself.

"Any chance you could come for Veronica soon?" I asked Agnes.

She shook her head.

"You couldn't knit her something in red?"

Agnes smiled an admonishment, and I sighed.

"Hello?"

I turned to see the nurse I'd spoken to earlier walking toward me, a sad expression on her face.

"I'm very sorry," she said. "We did everything we could, but we lost her."

I looked over my shoulder. Ethel and Agnes had gone.

I wiped a tear from my cheek. I knew Ethel was okay, but I would miss her.

"Don't worry," I said. "She's in a much better place."

CHAPTER FOUR

CHANGES

My job as an urban witch usually doesn't take me very far from my flat. Most times, it normally doesn't take me all that far from my kitchen. People come to see me and have a cup of tea and tell me their problems. I try to help them. It usually isn't much more than common sense and an external point of view. Witchcraft is mainly common sense, if truth be told.

Then there are the cases where I need to use a bit of magic and then common sense just goes out the window. I had a feeling that would happen with Dorothy.

Her problem seemed simple to begin with.

"Oh Mags," she said, after I had poured tea and pleasantries were out of the way. "I've been getting these terrible headaches."

"Have you been to your doctor?"

"He's no good. He either just gives me pills or wants to send me to a home. I might be old, but I'm not ready for that."

I agreed. Dorothy was older than she looked, but she had the appearance and constitution of a healthy woman in her late fifties. She looked run down at the moment, however. Her eyes were sunken, and she had dark rings under them. Her headaches obviously stopped her sleeping well.

"Oh, yes. I can't sleep for more than a couple of hours. The pain wakes me up and then gets worse because I can't sleep. Your plant has seen better days."

Dorothy had a habit of switching track mid-flow. It made conversations with her difficult. She was right about my plant, though. It was supposed to be a begonia with large, variegated leaves and masses of flowers. The leaves were large but hung limp from the stem and gave the plant the appearance of an exotic lettuce that had been in the fridge too long. It had been a present from Dave and Beth, a couple of my regular clients, for my continued help in their efforts to try for a baby.

I'm no good with houseplants, however, but I resisted the urge to ask Dorothy for her advice about it. I had to get her back on track, or I wouldn't be able to help her.

"Tell me more about the headaches. Where do you get them?" If I could identify which part of her head ached, I should be able to make her something for the pain and help her sleep.

She thought for a moment before answering and idly stroked the begonia's leaves.

"On the bus," she said, eventually.

I laughed. "No, I meant where in your head?"

"Oh, all over. It's like a tight band."

It sounded like a tension headache. I nodded sagely and made a note on my pad.

"Although sometimes it feels like someone is stabbing me."

That definitely did not sound like a tension headache. I made another note and added a few question marks. Dorothy's fingers continued to stroke the begonia.

"Let's go back to the bus. Why did you say that?"

"I always get a headache on the bus."

Perhaps it was some type of travel sickness, but if that was the case, why did she get headaches in bed in the middle of the night?

"Your lift brings it on as well."

"My lift?"

I made another note about claustrophobia and added some more question marks. Large ones.

"Yes. As soon as the doors close, my headache comes on really badly. I've still got it now. It won't go away until I get home, but it will hang around in the background until I try to sleep. Then it's back with a vengeance."

"Sorry," I said, out of reflex, as if I were responsible in some way for my building giving her a headache. This obviously wasn't travel sickness. "Have you tried using the stairs?"

"To the sixth floor? Sorry, love, no."

I smiled weakly at her. She had a point.

"I'm at a bit of a loss at the moment, Dorothy." I was struggling to think of a common denominator. "Where don't you have a headache?"

She looked distant for a couple of seconds. "Well, I'm fine at home, during the day and in the park. And most of the shops in the precinct." That was our local shopping centre, a row of 1950s shops, each of which had a flat above. Over the years, developers had wanted to bulldoze them and replace them with something newer, but planning permission had been rejected repeatedly.

What did buses and my block of flats, especially the lift, have in common that the local shops didn't? I couldn't think of anything.

"How about I get you to call me when you feel a headache coming on?"

"Call you, dear?"

"Yes, you've got a phone, haven't you?"

"Oh no, Mags. I've never had one of those."

I rummaged through my cupboard and found an old Nokia. I keep old phones for just this sort of situation so that people who need one in an emergency can call me. The phones are all fully charged and have pay-as-you-go SIMs.

"To tell the truth," she added, "I've always been frightened of them. You know. Energy."

The Witch's Council discourages us from using the 'E' word. Not in the sense that Dorothy was using it, anyway. We use it in very specific ways, none of which would apply here. I pretended she meant microwave energy.

"I know. They can be damaging over time, but it's difficult to escape them these days, and small amounts won't hurt."

"If you say so, dear."

I laughed. "I don't know any other witch who doesn't have one. If we think they're okay for us, then they're probably okay for you." I know that was a sweeping statement and full of fallacies, but reassurance doesn't necessarily have to be truth.

I handed her the phone, and she held it in her hands, looking at it doubtfully.

"What do I do with it?"

"You need to turn it on."

At her blank look, I pointed at the little red button on the side. After another blank look, I pressed it for her, and the tiny screen flared into life.

I was expecting a polite "ooh," so I was a little surprised when she screamed and threw the phone on my sofa. I rushed over to turn it off as she clutched at her head.

"I'm sorry," I said, wondering what had happened. The phone seemed to have given her an instant headache. Either that, or she was the best actress in the world.

She whimpered.

"I'll get you something to make you feel better."

"Thank you."

I made her a tea. Well, tea is a very broad label. In truth, I couldn't tell you what I made. There was no recipe. I was operating on instinct. I threw in some chamomile and some dried lavender flowers. I probably added some turmeric and crushed willow bark. Yes, I know I could have just given her an aspirin, but I know what I'm doing with the raw ingredients.

I watched Dorothy as I made the tea. She'd sat back on the sofa and was resting her head with her eyes closed. I could see she was still in pain, but it was fading. The infusion would help it fade faster.

"Dorothy?" I said in a gentle voice when I'd finished. I knew she wasn't asleep, but she looked fragile. "I made you this. It should help with the pain."

"Oh, thank you Mags. You are kind."

I should have put the mug on the coffee table in front of her, but she reached up for it and so I handed it to her. It could have been that her hands were too dry and had no grip, or maybe the headache had affected her coordination, but she didn't have a good hold of the mug as I let go of it and it fell out of her hand.

But then something weird happened.

I am a witch. I'm used to odd things happening, so for me to say something was weird, it had to have been *very* weird indeed.

It was weird because the cup fell like it was in slow motion. No. It wasn't *like* slow motion, it *was* slow motion. It was hanging in the air, the infusion leaking out of it like a naked lava lamp.

"Silly me. Sorry," Dorothy said, and grabbed the mug out of the air, scooping up the tea as she did so. She placed the mug on the table a moment later with not a drop out of place. "I'm so clumsy."

"What was that?" I asked.

"What?"

"The cup."

"I didn't have hold of it properly. I dropped it. No harm done, though."

"But…" I couldn't make any words come out. The cup didn't … no… the cup was floating… How? Why? Nothing I could think to ask her would make any sense.

"Drink your tea before it gets cold," I said eventually. "It will help with the pain."

I sent her home after I told her I would investigate what I could do about her headaches. After she left, I noticed that my begonia now had luxuriant foliage and was smothered with flowers.

***

I needed information. Dorothy's ability to hold mugs of tea in the air without touching them had to be related to her headaches, whether she acknowledged it or not. No-one could possibly think that was normal and yet that was exactly how she'd reacted. To her, stopping a cup from emptying itself mid fall was not unusual.

Was she a witch? Was she telekinetic? Was she something else? My guess was something else, especially when I figured in the begonia. I'd better find out. I looked for my dowsing rod – my first line of investigation for pretty much everything – but it wasn't where I would have expected to find it. It wasn't where I'd left it, but then it never was. It was also not with my screwdrivers, its favourite spot. It had to be hiding, which was not a good sign.

I would have to use the crystal ball. I don't use it very often. It looks nice on the sideboard and gives me a bit of credibility with the clients, but I am, to be honest, scared of it. I picked up the ball carefully and grabbed the velvet cloth it had been resting on so that I could give it a polish to remove finger marks. The ball had to be clean. This was the part that scared me. I wasn't at all worried about what the ball would show me, but I was terrified of dropping it. They're not cheap, you know.

Some witches, the showy ones, you know the type, will insist on washing their crystal ball with pure water gathered from a mountain stream at dawn by thirteen virgins dressed in white, but that is just part of the show for the punters in my book. Using it in anger, or even, as I was all too ready to admit, in a blind panic, even though I didn't know why, all I needed was to give the ball a careful polish with the cloth.

Then I put the cloth on my table with the ball roughly in the centre and put the kettle on. I still had some of Dorothy's tea mixture left. It would calm me down quite nicely.

When I was ready, I lit some candles, turned off the light, and sat down at the table.

People often ask witches what they see when they look into a crystal ball. Witches give a variety of replies, but my answers often disappoint them.

"It depends," I would say.

The trick to a crystal ball isn't magic. It looks like magic, of course, but the trick is in letting the mind run free so that it can form images. Something in my head knew what Dorothy was and what she'd done. At least it had a fairly good idea, but to bring that idea to the surface, I needed something to focus on and a relaxed frame of mind. Having a nice cup of tea helped with that part, and the crystal ball helped with the other.

I stared into the depths of the ball. The reflection of my own face was barely recognisable in the strange light, my nose enormous. I ignored it and concentrated on the reflected candle flames.

My crystal ball wasn't made of glass. Some years ago, I'd gone through a bit of a hippy phase and bought a real crystal ball made of real crystal. It was a perfectly polished sphere of something that is known as clear quartz. That is a bit of a misnomer, of course. Looking at it, it was obvious it was anything but clear. Most of it was perfectly transparent, but it was shot through with white crystalline deposits that looked like clouds trapped in solidified air. They flickered in the candlelight, appearing to twist and turn like living things.

I fixed my gaze on part of one of the white layers and watched as it appeared to jump on its own, dancing like some wild sixties go-go dancer or the 'lady' from *Tales of the Unexpected*. My thoughts drifted and flickered in time with it, and gradually the shapes in my mind merged with the shapes I saw in the crystal. I saw people and animals dancing around a campfire, an abstract Busby Berkeley spectacular without music.

The shapes gradually became more mundane and took on meaning. I could see myself, my flat, friends, clients. None of them stayed long in my sight for long and I knew they weren't what I was looking for. My mind was just calibrating itself.

An image tried to form but fell into the parade of familiar shapes without my mind getting a good grasp of it. Every time it started to form, it slipped away. I was trying too hard.

I took a deep, calming breath and tried again. The faces and images flitted in front of my mind's eye, too fast to follow. I grabbed at the ones I knew were irrelevant and threw them out. More shapes replaced them. The shapes I wanted danced away before I could recognise them, giving me a tantalising glimpse.

I saw Dorothy dropping the cup, and it fell an inch, maybe two, before stopping. Then the image dissolved to show me something else.

There was a sense of something round. A circle. The sun? No. The moon? No. What? Ah! A clock. The image stabilised once I had the concept locked down and I could see it clearly. It was not a clock I owned.

It looked like a clock you'd find in an old railway station. Victorian or Edwardian or something like that. It was a solid clock, large and round, with a white porcelain face and cast-iron hands and numbers. It was ticking, the second-hand marching around steadily, clonk, clonk, clonk. One tick every second.

Then it stopped. No, not stopped. The hands were still moving, but they were crawling. Dorothy's mug reappeared and I could see it wasn't floating in the air but still falling. Slowly, like the hands of the clock.

I gasped. She hadn't held the cup in the air. She had slowed it down. No, that wasn't it. She had slowed down time, but only for the cup.

A warning bell sounded at the back of my mind, and a theory began to form. It wasn't a theory that sat well with me. It gave me the same feeling as knowing I was in a locked room with a wasp. Or a lion. If my theory was correct, no wonder my dowsing rod was hiding.

I gave my crystal ball another wipe. It was going to be a long evening.

***

Dorothy's house was in Bodmin Street, one of the last surviving brick-built terraces on the estate. It had somehow escaped the various slum-clearance schemes and gentrification by waves of eighties yuppies and twenty-first century hipsters. Dorothy and her neighbours lived on a tranquil island in a turbulent sea of change. She was probably responsible for that, even if she didn't realise. Same as the local shops.

Her house was in the middle of the terrace and, structurally, was no different to any of its neighbours, although it was obvious which one was hers. Dorothy clearly took great care of the place; the tiny front garden was bursting with flowers and a climbing rose surrounded the front door. It may only have been a terraced house in southeast London, but it was a country cottage in its heart.

She didn't have a doorbell – of course – but had a large ornate brass knocker. Brass. My knocks sounded surprisingly loud.

"Oh, hello Mags, dear."

I hadn't arranged to see Dorothy, but she was home. I'd never called on her before, but whenever she called on me, I was home. Always. I hadn't thought anything of that before, but now I nodded as another piece of an already solved puzzle fell into place. Reality arranged itself around Dorothy. I could see that now.

"Hello Dorothy. I thought I'd come to check on you. How's your head?"

"Oh, you know how it is, dear," Her weak smile showed me the infusion had worn off.

"I think I know what's the matter. Can I come in?"

Dorothy's house was as neat and comfortable as her garden. Her kitchen would not have looked out of place on *Emmerdale*, not that I watched it. She had a range, a real working range, with a copper kettle that was coming to the boil.

"Tea? I was just making some."

"That's a nice range," I said. "Unusual design."

She beamed at me. "My father made it. He was very good with his hands. It's bronze."

"Impressive. Very clever." I let her make the tea without further questions and waited for her to sit down.

"So, these headaches. How long have you had them?"

"Oh, now there's a question." She frowned at the memory of pain. "Years. Decades, probably."

"Did you have them as a child?"

"Oh, no." She smiled at me, as if the memory of her childhood had taken away the memory of the pain. "I was a very healthy child. Well, I was after a while. I was sickly to begin with, but

I grew strong. Didn't even catch colds. My brothers were always sick, but I was full of beans. Even when…" she began. Her eyes were distant, as if she was remembering something from a long time ago.

"Even when what?"

"When my mother died. It was a sad time."

I'd seen that in the crystal. Her mother's death had affected the family badly. I wondered if anyone had ever bothered to tell Dorothy that her mother had taken her own life.

"Do you remember it very well?"

"No. I knew my mother had been sad and cried a lot. She'd always looked like the world had been too much for her. Then one day I'd come home from school, and she was gone. I wasn't allowed to say goodbye."

"People don't like to expose children to death too early." Especially when it was their mother hanging from a beam.

She nodded. "They sent me to live with an aunt for a while. She wasn't happy about it, but dad couldn't cope, and my brothers were angry."

They had blamed her. She was a little girl whose mother had just killed herself and yet they blamed her for the death. The crystal had showed me that. It was hurtful and painful to watch, especially as the boys had been correct. Dorothy hadn't killed her mother herself, but ultimately, she was the reason she had died.

"I was still happy, though. Children are so resilient, aren't they?"

I nodded. She had been a very self-centred child. It was her nature. She wasn't to know that now. It was too long ago. Over a hundred years.

"When did the headaches begin?"

"Not until I was a little older. My brothers had left for the war by then. I missed them terribly. I was still a child." They hadn't forgiven her for their mother's death, but they had forgotten. She'd made them forget without even knowing she'd done it. She couldn't help herself.

"These were your older brothers?" I knew the answer to the

question. The crystal ball had told me.

"No. I was the oldest."

"Yet you were still a child?"

"Yes," she answered in a matter-of-fact manner, as if it were self-evident. She couldn't see that it was strange that she would still be a little girl while her younger brothers had become grown men. The same as she couldn't see it was strange that she could catch a falling cup of tea by slowing down time.

"And that's when the headaches came?"

She nodded.

"You have one now?"

"A little. I've got used to it. I don't notice during the day normally, unless it's really bad, but you asked."

I nodded. Her defences were lower at night. "That's what I thought. Before I tell you what I think is wrong, I want to try something. Is that okay?"

"What?"

I reached into my bag and pulled out a hat. I'd made it from small squares of fabric and resembled something like a woolly hat crossed with a tea cosy. It was larger and thicker than you would find in the shops, and it crinkled as I handled it. It didn't look good, but then sewing isn't one of my talents. I'm a witch, not Coco Chanel.

"Put this on."

"What is it?"

"It's a hat."

"I can see that, Mags, dear, but why do you want me to wear it?"

"It's an experiment."

"Is it enchanted?"

I gave her a look. "Just put it on."

She took it from me and examined it, making it crinkle again.

"What's inside it?"

"I'll tell you later."

With the same wariness as someone putting their head in a lion's mouth, she carefully lifted the hat up and placed it on her head.

"What's it meant to do?"

"Do you feel any different?"

"No, I can't say I ... oooh! The pressure. It's gone. Mags, it's gone!" She was smiling and her eyes were wet.

"Well, that confirms what I thought. You are sensitive to radio waves. I lined the hat with foil, which blocks them."

"Foil?"

I nodded. "I know. It sounds barmy, but it works."

"I'll never take it off."

I laughed. "You'll have to at some point. This one isn't very durable. I can make a better one for you. It would be more useful to have one of your rooms lined with foil."

"When can you do that?"

"I have a friend who can help me. He can do it next week."

The foil-lined room would allow her to be pain free without the hat. It would also allow me to confirm my bigger theory and then find a way to deal with it.

***

Have you ever tried wallpapering an attic room with kitchen foil? It wasn't easy. Don't forget that we had to put foil on the inside of the roof, as well as the walls and the floor. There were no windows, fortunately. It's a shame Dorothy didn't have a cellar.

I had help. Dave was there. He and Beth were the couple who'd given me the begonia. I'd helped them conceive a few times, but I hadn't been able to help her bring the babies to term. Sometimes biology is too difficult to master. So now I was helping them with the adoption papers. In return for all that, he'd redecorated my flat when it had been necessary, and didn't ask too many questions. Don't get me wrong. I don't have anything to hide, but sometimes, when witchcraft is involved, accidents happen, and a little tidying up is needed. A wall needs repapering here and dried ectoplasm sanding off there. That sort of thing.

He took my request to help me line Dorothy's attic with foil without batting an eyelid. When we had finished, no radio waves were able to get in or out of the room. It was time to bring Dorothy in.

"I don't feel any different," she said, after I'd led her into the room.

"Remove your hat."

She did so and grimaced. "I can feel it more than ever."

I nodded. "You've got used to the hat. Now, let's see what happens when I close the door."

Dave was waiting outside. He winked at me, and I nodded in return. It's amazing what you can say with a wink and a nod. The conversation, such as it was, took a moment and I could close the door with no apparent delay.

Dorothy gasped. She was euphoric, her grin almost wider than her face. "This is amazing. I can't feel anything. I mean, I thought the hat was good, but this…"

"You don't remember when you first came here, do you?"

"Of course, I do. Dad drove us here in a big van. A charabanc, he called it."

"No. Not here. When you first came to this world."

"When I was born? Ha-ha, no. Who remembers that?"

"A few people do."

"It was a long time ago."

"One hundred and thirty years."

"That long?"

"And yet you don't even look sixty."

She looked even younger now. The pressure from the radio waves had aged her. Now that it was gone, she was losing years.

"Clean living, I suppose."

"I have another theory."

"Oh, yes?" She wasn't really listening. The euphoria from having the radio waves cut off was a distraction.

"My theory explains why you are sensitive to radio waves and why you get headaches on the bus."

"Why's that then?"

"Iron. You can't touch iron. You can't be near it. You can't tolerate radio waves because of it. You can't be inside anything made of iron or steel, like buses or cars, or lifts, or modern buildings with iron rods inside the concrete."

She laughed. Not the heh-heh-heh of an old woman, but the gleeful peal of laughter from a young girl.

"Who's allergic to iron?"

"That's the other part of my theory. It explains why you look so young and why you looked younger than your little brothers."

"They had hard lives."

"You are a changeling."

"A what?"

"A changeling."

"What's a changeling?"

"A fairy child substituted for a human baby."

Dorothy laughed. "I'm sorry, Mags, but that's ridiculous. A fairy?"

I shrugged. "You don't age the same as the rest of us. You are allergic to iron. You can slow time. You can make plants grow."

"Still doesn't mean I'm a fairy. That's daft."

"If I reopen the portal to fairyland, you will remember—"

"Go ahead! Open it up. I've never heard of such nonsense."

Before I'd let her into the room, I'd prepared a spell. It was a spell that few of us had ever cast, and no-one had needed to attempt it for more than a century. It was long and complicated and only needed a few words to finish it.

"Let the wall between our worlds thin and a doorway open!"

The rest of the spell had taken a good hour to recite and used up most of my stock of herbs. Their smell masked the smell of the glue Dave and I had used to hang the foil.

A patch of air in the middle of the room glowed faintly, a thin rugby ball in shape, about twelve inches tall by three wide and pulsing faintly. With each pulse, the patch grew in height and intensity so that within a few seconds, it was about seven feet tall and two wide. It had become too bright to look at directly.

"Well, that's very impressive, Mags, but I still don't remember anything."

I frowned. She should remember her earlier life now that the doorway had opened.

"Perhaps you need to go through," I said.

"You've got to be kidding. There's no way I'm going anywhere near that thing."

I fumbled with an answer. I was sure she would remember if she were to step through the portal. I couldn't think of the words to persuade her to do it. As it turned out, I didn't need to.

"What's that?"

"What?"

"That noise, can't you hear it?" she asked.

"What noise? I can't hear anything."

"Singing. I can hear someone singing. Lots of voices."

I could just hear something now. A choir, their voices blended into the most bewitching song I had ever heard. I tried not to listen, but I had to. Suddenly, I wanted to join them and add my voice to theirs. I stepped further back, so that I had the wall against my back.

"And look, Mags, I can see through it now. It's beautiful."

I looked at the floor. If I looked through the portal, I would be lost.

"Someone's coming!"

I could hear footsteps and then a new voice.

"Who has opened a doorway to the Kingdom?"

I looked up to see the most attractive man I had ever seen. I couldn't take my eyes off him. I can't tell you what he looked like. His features just didn't register, but there was something about him that mesmerised me.

"Me," I said. "I opened it."

"I shall reward you, witch. Now that a door has opened, my people can visit your world once more. You are ours."

"I don't think so. I only opened it so one of your people could go home."

"One of my people? There were none of my people in your world when the last portal collapsed. There were only the sick and the elderly. We sent them there to die."

Nice caring society.

TALES OF AN URBAN WITCH

"I got better, Father." So, *now* she remembers.

"Daughter? You live. How can this be? You were so ill when I left you here."

"You left your own daughter to die?" I asked, amazed that I could question this man.

"It's our way," Dorothy answered. "The Kingdom remains strong by eliminating the weak. I was weak and I could not stay in the Kingdom."

"But—"

She ignored me and spoke to her father. "You left me with good people. They cured me and made me strong."

"I will reward them."

"Alas, they are long dead."

He laughed. "They live such brief lives."

"This world ages you, father. I was old, myself, until just now."

I risked a glance at her, avoiding looking at the door. Dorothy looked like a teenager now.

"You must come home."

She walked over to the door and stood next to him.

"And your friend must come as well. She has saved you, and we must reward her."

"No!" I nearly screamed my answer. I definitely did not want to go to fairyland. "Thank you, my lord, but I should remain here, if it's all the same to you."

"You will be one of us. Not a slave. One of us. You have my word on that."

I knew he was telling the truth. The Witch's Council's library said that fairies were true to their word. If he said I wouldn't be a slave, then I would be free. They were slippery creatures, though. There would be some other way that I would suffer.

"My place is here. I will remain."

"I insist," he said, and there was no arguing with him. His voice was enchanting, but in a very real and very dangerous sense, and it was a command. "You must come with us," he said.

Dorothy passed through the portal and her father took a step so that he was half in the Kingdom and half out. I could feel my

45

feet obeying his command, moving me towards the portal.

I still had control of my voice, however.

"Dave! Now!" I shouted and immediately the wooden door in the wall beside me burst open. I could see Dave outside, his eyes tightly closed and the chain around his waist as I'd told him. The fairy portal dimmed but didn't collapse. Radio waves from outside were making their way in. Dorothy's father clutched at his head and cried out in pain.

"I remember now why we stopped visiting your world. It is evil. We will cleanse it one day."

My treacherous feet started listening to me again and stopped where they were.

"But not today," I said. "Go home."

With one last grimace, he stepped through the doorway, and it shrank. It didn't disappear, however. It just stayed as it was, a glowing rugby ball of air, safe to look at.

"Bugger," I said. "I'd hoped it would close completely."

"Are you okay?" Dave asked. "Can I open my eyes yet?"

***

The portal showed no sign of closing, either on its own or with the limited supplies I had with me. The spell I'd used to open it had a simple counter spell that should have closed it in five minutes, but it remained stubbornly rugby-ball sized. Perhaps the King had done something to it. I would have to come back another time with a stronger spell and a stronger me. This had drained me.

I decided to lock the portal inside the foil covered room. As soon as we closed the door, however, we heard the portal spring into action, the fairy choir's seductive voices audible outside the room. This time, however, they weren't enticing us. Neither of us felt any need to go into the room, and the choir seemed to sing a sort of lament. It was beautiful but sad. It felt like a farewell.

"Maybe that's Dorothy saying goodbye," I said, although I had no idea. It could just as easily have been the entire fairy race missing our world. I doubted that and knew that Dorothy's father would make good on his threat someday.

The voices suddenly went quiet, and the attic was silent once more.

"Let's lock up and go make a cup of tea. I'll arrange something with the Witch's Council for security." I was hoping they would say that I could live in Dorothy's house. It was larger than my flat and I wouldn't need to climb six flights of steps to get there when the lift was broken.

We heard it just as we'd put the last padlock in place. A thin, wordless wail that could only be one thing. We quickly undid all the locks and the bolts and pushed the door open. On the ground, wrapped in a woollen blanket, was a baby. It wasn't happy.

Dave went to pick it up.

"Wait!" I said. "It could be another changeling."

He stepped back, and I picked it up. "It just looks like a baby to me," he said, a smile in his voice.

"They all do. Come on, let's take it outside. We'll soon know if it's real or not."

It was a little girl. The blanket was rough and old in style, even though it appeared quite new. I carried her carefully out of the room and into Dorothy's back garden. The sudden sunshine had no effect on the child. She even fell asleep. That was a good sign.

"Have you got that chain nearby?" I asked Dave.

"No. I left it outside the room."

"Go and get it, there's a love. I need to test her properly. While you're there, lock the door again."

He ran back into the house, and I sat down on a low wall.

"Now, missy. While Dave's out of the way, let's see if you are human."

Witches are quite well equipped in the field. I didn't have my crystal ball or my dowsing rod. That was still hiding. I did, however, have a pin, quite sterile and made of stainless steel. You never know when you need such a thing.

My test resulted in a tiny drop of blood on her little finger and a lot of tears, most of them mine.

"There, there, poppet. That's done and out of the way. You're human, aren't you? Clever girl!"

Dave returned with the chain.

"What happened?"

"Oh, nothing. You know babies." I grabbed the chain off him and made a show of touching it to her bare skin. There was no reaction. Obviously.

"Not a changeling then?"

"No."

"Where did she come from?"

"My guess is that she's the baby that Dorothy replaced."

"Shouldn't she be older?"

"Time is a funny thing in the Kingdom," Their name for it sounded a lot better. Fairyland made it sound like some sort of jolly theme park. The Kingdom gave it more gravitas and made it sound appropriately threatening. "Sometimes minutes go by in there and centuries pass out here. Other times it's the other way round."

"What will you do with her?"

Before I answered him, I asked a question of my own. I'd need to approve it with the Witch's Council, of course, but it would mean no effort on their part, so I was sure they'd approve.

"Do you think you could live in this house?"

"Yes, but—"

"You and your wife could be quite comfortable here … and you could keep an eye on the portal for me. Could you do that?"

"Yes, of course. You know I could."

I handed him the baby. I would sort out the paperwork later.

"Meet your new daughter," I said. "Her name's Dorothy."

CHAPTER FIVE

MANHUNTER

One of the things I do, as an urban witch, is relationship counselling. I'm a lot cheaper than the so-called professionals and I use straight talk. No business-speak, no clichés and no kumbaya-style group-hugging. I help husbands and wives understand each other a little better and help them both get on with their lives, with no one getting hurt.

I wish I'd been able to help Simon and Anna.

***

It surprised me when the police called. I'd had some dealings with them in the past as I had somehow been nominated as the local police liaison witch (not my official title) while Gavin, a poor young sergeant had been lumbered with the job of being the local paranormal liaison officer (not *his* official title either). He not only had to work with me, but with any Tiffany, Dawn, or Hesta who walked in claiming to have foreseen a murder in their cornflakes.

We got on quite well, all things considered. He'd realised, fairly quickly, that I knew what I was talking about, and we had been able to help each other occasionally. Growing up on the estate helped, as he knew about urban witches. I think my mum delivered him.

"Mags," he said, his voice loaded with sadness, even over the telephone line.

"What's the matter, Gavin?"

"We've had a death. Someone from your block." Something in his voice told me this wasn't just someone being stabbed in the pub.

"Who is it?"

"We were wondering if you could come and help us." He ignored my question. Interesting.

"Why?"

He hesitated. The paranormal liaison officer had called me about a murder and was hesitating before telling me why he thought I would be able to help. This could not be good.

"This isn't a normal death, is it?" I asked.

"No. It isn't. I … I… I can't talk about it over the phone."

I didn't think he wanted to talk about it at all.

**

Gavin arranged for a police car to pick me up at the Taunton Street entrance to my block. He needn't have bothered. My destination was one of those nondescript economy hotels and was about half a mile from Talltree Towers. I'd scarcely worked out how to fasten the seatbelt before we'd arrived.

Gavin was waiting for me as the car pulled up.

"Thanks for coming, Mags," he said, shaking my hand. His face was pale. He was obviously shaken by what he had seen.

"This hotel. Some sort of knocking-shop, is it?" I asked him.

A surprised laugh escaped from his mouth, caught off-guard by my question.

"No, not a knocking-shop. Too expensive for a start."

I looked at the building. It was a generic chain hotel, one of many instantly forgettable establishments that spring up in towns all over the world when no-one's looking. Ugly, bland and utilitarian.

"So, this was a private liaison of some sort that had been organised in advance."

Gavin nodded again.

"And the poor girl tricked into coming here came to regret it?"

"No, not quite." He looked uncomfortable. Something was

bugging him about this case, and it wasn't just what was waiting in the room upstairs.

"It was a man, then. And he was meeting another man."

"That's about the shape of it."

"There's something more, isn't there? You're holding something back."

"He was married." He'd hesitated before speaking. There was still more.

"Oh no. It's Simon, isn't it?"

It could be no one else. I knew Simon. He was married, but I knew he liked men. It could only be him. He'd come to me a few months ago for a little chat. That had been him coming out to me, although there had been more to it than that.

I'd felt uncomfortable about it, to be honest. Oh, not about him liking men. I didn't care two hoots about that, but I didn't like keeping it a secret from Anna. Secrets are part of the job, of course, but in the few months Simon and Anna had lived here, I'd grown to be friends with them in a nodding-on-the-way-to-the-shops sort of way with the occasional lengthy chat. I'd discovered Anna was another rabid fan of *Hotel Hellada* and I'd begun to think of her as a friend. Keeping a secret of this magnitude from her had left a nasty taste in my mouth.

"We haven't told his wife yet," Gavin said.

"Why not?"

"We need your professional opinion first."

"As a witch?" An irrelevant question.

He nodded. "Then I'll need your help as her friend. I wondered if you would be able to tell her."

I sighed. "No, you need to tell her, but I will help. How about that?"

He nodded, but didn't look me in the eye.

***

The hotel room was basic and modern and exactly what you would expect in a chain hotel. You would have to look out of the window to work out where you were. The rooms were the same from Basildon to Honolulu and from Sydney to Skegness.

The only furniture in the room was the bed, a desk and an uncomfortable-looking easy chair that no-one would ever want to sit in. Standard stuff. Wardrobe space – no door – was next to the bathroom. A suit hung there, and an overnight bag was on the floor beneath it, unopened.

Simon lay on the floor beside the bed, face down, with his jogging bottoms around his ankles and his bare bottom in the air.

"Not the most dignified of deaths," I said as I arrived.

"No," he said, the word strangled. Gavin was clearly upset by this case. Why? His reaction bothered me almost as much as seeing Simon dead.

"Was he found like this?"

"Nothing has been touched, including … the b-body." He stumbled over the word.

"And the door was just left open?"

"No. Locked from the inside."

"Windows?"

"They don't open. There's air-con." Modern hotels don't like windows that open. They don't trust people to not jump out of them. Dead guests cause problems. I bet they were cursing Simon for this.

"A classic locked-room mystery." I'd read a few in my time.

Gavin nodded agreement but was tight-lipped. I looked at Simon's body. There was something odd about it, but I didn't know what.

"How did he die?"

"The pathologist says massive blood loss but won't commit himself until … until—"

Why was he struggling?

"Until the autopsy?"

He nodded.

That's why Simon looked odd. The blood loss. He was very pale.

"Where's the blood?"

"We don't know," he said, staring fixedly on the body. "Can you

TALES OF AN URBAN WITCH

tell us?"

And then I saw them. Two tiny puncture marks on Simon's neck.

"Vampire."

"That's what I thought. Is there any way to confirm? I have to be very careful about this in my report."

"Give me a few minutes."

***

Dead people fall into three groups, broadly speaking, with subtle variations. There are the ones who know they are dead and happily go trotting off to the afterlife with next to no hanging around. You'll remember Ethel had done that.

The second group are the troubled souls, like Veronica, trapped by their own misperceptions of the world, convinced they have wrongs to be righted and a purpose to fulfil. They are often confused. It takes them a while to work out that they are dead and even longer to come to terms with it. Veronica has been haunting me for the last few months and still hadn't worked it out properly.

And then there is the third group. These are the ones who know they are dead but will go to the afterlife when they are good and ready. They aren't necessarily troubled souls, but they might have something they want to do. Simon was in that third group. I could tell because he was surprisingly cool about being summoned.

I knew he hadn't been to the proper afterlife yet. It would have taken a lot more effort to reach him, had he been there.

This worried me.

"Hi, Mags. Good to see you."

"Hello, Simon. I'm sorry you're dead." There was no sign of my friend Agnes. She only ever appeared when the journey to the afterlife was about to begin. It wasn't Simon's time. She would lead him to his particular afterlife later.

This also worried me.

He laughed. "I always knew this thing would be the death of me." He slapped the erect penis his ghost was sporting. "Will I be stuck with this for all eternity? Not that I'm complaining."

"For a while, but not forever. The way you look as a ghost is pretty much the way you looked as you died."

"Trackie bottoms around my ankles and a huge stiffy?" he asked, with a laugh in his voice. "Shame I wasn't holding my phone when I copped it."

"You wouldn't get a signal."

"Didn't think so."

"Things will be different when you move on."

"I get a working phone?"

"No."

"And where will I go? As if I couldn't guess." He laughed.

I shrugged. As far as I could tell, there were many variations of the afterlife. Some ended up in something as close to heaven as most people imagine it. Some were poked by red-hot pitchforks. Others seemed to go on an eternal holiday or a never-ending party, or hung out in a celestial shopping mall.

The dead are always vague, and I hadn't spoken to that many who had passed beyond the veil. It took too much out of me to do that too often.

"I'm here with a policeman who is investigating your death," I said to Simon.

He looked around the room, but Gavin had gone out to the street to make a call. At least, that's what he'd said. I got the impression he was avoiding seeing Simon's ghost. He hadn't struck me as the squeamish type, but he had been acting strangely today. Perhaps it was the thought of the vampire. In all honesty, however, I was glad he'd left me in peace. Casting spells to summon the dead needed concentration.

"What happened?" I asked before he could ask me about Gavin. I had a few gay friends, and I knew what they could be like about men in uniform. I didn't want the distraction. "Who did this to you?"

He opened his mouth to speak, and his lips formed themselves into a word, but then stopped. He frowned.

"You don't remember his name?" I asked.

He tried again.

"No. I do. I just can't say it. It slips away."

"Try harder."

As I say, ghosts can have trouble remembering details like names or, in Veronica's case, everything, but that wasn't Simon's problem. He obviously could remember the name, but he was prevented from saying it. Vampires have a knack for hiding. That trick with mirrors goes a whole lot deeper than you think, even to the extent of keeping their names secret.

Ghosts can't sweat, but Simon gave the impression that he was about to as he struggled to say the name. Eventually, it came. "Augustus. His name was Augustus."

"You'd arranged to meet him?"

"Obviously. I haven't done this for ages. Since … you know."

I nodded.

"What changed? Why see this one?"

"He's got a silver tongue. Could charm the straightest of men into bed and convince them it was their idea."

"You didn't know him?"

"No. I never met him before. I just met him online."

"What does he look like?"

He shrugged. "I can't remember. I can only remember the sex. I was having the best sex of my life when he sank his teeth in my neck."

"And then you died."

"Not straight away. For a while, the sex got even better. And *then* I died."

He laughed at that, and I joined him for a few moments until the laughter dwindled. We looked down at his body.

"You need to move on soon," I said. "You know that, don't you?"

He nodded. "I know, but I can't. Not yet."

***

Anna looked puzzled when she answered the door to us. She wasn't expecting me, and I'd never called on her before. She didn't know Gavin, of course, but even if he wasn't in uniform, his bearing screamed *police*. And it was subtle, but it also hinted at *guilty*.

"Mags? What a surprise. I wasn't expecting you." She looked at Gavin.

"Hello, Anna. This is Gavin, a … friend of mine." Slight exaggeration. "He's with the police. I'm helping them with a case. Can we come in?"

"Police? What's wrong? Is it Simon? What's he done?"

Gavin and I exchanged a glance.

"Nothing, but, well, we need a chat with you."

"About Simon?"

"Yes."

She led us to her sitting room, and we sat on one of her sofas. Her flat was the same shape and size as mine, but it had been decorated to feel a lot bigger, a trick mainly achieved by using furniture that was slightly too small. Gavin and I perched on the edge of the sofa. There wasn't room for us to sit further back. Anna sat on a matching sofa opposite ours, also perched on the edge, but more out of anxiety than for comfort.

"What is it? What's happened?"

I looked at Gavin, expecting him to speak. He looked back at me with frightened eyes.

"You're right," I said, glaring at Gavin. He should be doing this. He was the policeman. I'm just the hired help. "It's about Simon. I'm afraid we've got bad news."

"What is it?"

"There's been an … incident," I said. How do I break this to her?

"He's dead." Gavin's words were abrupt. I glared at him again, but he wasn't looking at me. What was he thinking? What happened to sensitivity?

"Dead? What do you mean, dead? I mean, he can't be. He was fine yesterday when he left for Milton Keynes."

I raised an eyebrow. "I'm afraid it's true, Anna. That's why Gavin wanted me here. To help tell you."

"That's right," Gavin said. "Ms Hammond – Mags – is

consulting on this case."

While she was looking at Gavin, I muttered the words of a spell to help her accept his statement without question. It wouldn't do for her to ask why I was involved. We didn't want her to know about the vampire.

"They found Simon found dead in a hotel earlier today," I said.

"In Milton Keynes?"

I looked at Gavin, who looked back at me. This was it. This was when Simon's secret would be exposed. I answered Anna in a whisper.

"No. It wasn't Milton Keynes."

"Then where?"

Gavin stared back at me with eyes that were full of fear and sadness. Was he normally like this?

"He was in a local hotel," I said.

"Local? Local to where?"

"Local to here. It was the one on Market Street."

"But what was he doing…? Oh."

She crumbled. Her face, previously shocked but composed, dissolved in a mass of grief.

I moved to her sofa so I could put my arm around her and let her sob for a while. Gavin looked at the floor and seemed to be about to cry as well.

"I thought he'd stopped." I could barely hear her.

"Stopped what?" I asked, but I already knew her answer.

"The men."

"You knew?"

She sat up straight and sniffed, her dignity restored.

"He told me he was bi before we were married, but it was okay. I didn't mind. He was mine. He married me."

"Oh, Anna…"

"But after a while, there were all those business trips, the gym, rugby practice. None of them were genuine. Two, three, four times a week, he'd make some excuse to go out, but the squash kit in the laundry basket would be clean."

"I'm so sorry," I said, although I wasn't sure if I was

sympathising or apologising for not helping.

"And then something changed. A couple of months ago, he suddenly stopped. He would only go out once a week. He was my husband again. Fun to be with. He was happy."

That was about when he'd seen me for advice. I wondered if now would be a good time to say anything and I opened my mouth to speak, but Gavin caught my eye and shook his head. No? Why? How did he know what I was going to say?

"And now, here he is dead," Anna said, not noticing our wordless conversation. "I've lost him all over again."

***

We drove away in silence. We'd taken Anna to her mum's house, as it didn't feel right to leave her on her own. On the way back, I thought about what had been said and what hadn't. Eventually, I spoke.

"He came to see me, you know."

"Oh, yes?" Gavin kept his eyes on the road ahead.

"He told me he liked men."

"Uh-huh."

"He wanted to know what to do about Anna. He still loved her and didn't want to hurt her, but he was falling in love with a man."

Gavin answered with a strangled sound. I took a breath before saying more.

"I told him he needed to tell Anna and be true to himself. He shouldn't string her along anymore and he needed to make a go of it with this man."

Gavin stared at the road ahead.

"I guess he ignored my advice about Anna, but that man must have become his boyfriend."

Tears were streaming down Gavin's face, but his gaze didn't deviate from the road.

"It was you, Gavin, wasn't it? You are that man."

***

I took Gavin back to my flat. He was in no state to return to work. He could hardly string two words together without bursting into tears. After a couple of cups of tea, he was a lot calmer. It wasn't tea, however.

"It's been three months," he said. "Three of the happiest months of my life."

"You loved him." It wasn't a question. It was obvious. "And he loved you."

"We never said it, though. I knew it and he knew it, but we never said it. I loved him."

"I'm sure he loved you."

"It was just a bit of fun. I met him online. He had a thing about me being a copper." Told you. "And I liked the attention."

"But he was married."

"Oh, I know. Don't tell me. It was stupid. At least there were no kids, and the sex had dried up long ago."

"They loved each other."

"Yes, they—" Gavin yawned. It surprised him. "Oh, I'm so sorry," he said. "This has been a long day."

I smiled. My 'tea' was working. "Don't worry about it. You were saying about Simon."

"Oh yes. They loved each other, but he needed more."

I didn't pursue the argument. It was what Simon had told me. He shouldn't have married Anna.

"Anyway," he said. "One date – sex, of course – led to another, and another, and before we knew it, we'd become friends—"

"With benefits."

He yawned again.

"Sorry. I hadn't realised I was so tired. We'd become friends with benefits, I suppose. I hate that phrase but, yes, that's what we were, and then we realised we were seeing each other exclusively. That was three months ago."

"I'm sorry," I said and patted him on the shoulder.

"It's okay," he said, relaxed.

"It's not. It's far from okay,"

"But what can I do? I can't even go to the funeral. How do I say goodbye?"

The funeral worried me, but for a different reason. Funerals all over the country were being delayed. Industrial action. I felt very uneasy.

"What are your plans?" I asked.

Gavin smiled at me, his eyes half-closed.

"That's simple," he said. "I'm going to find Augustus and kill him."

Veronica was getting agitated about something in the kitchen. I could hear her saying "Bad man" repeatedly. I had to ignore her. She was, no doubt, remembering some innocent thing her husband had said or done.

"Maybe you should take a little nap first." I was using my professional voice. Gavin was nearly under. A few more seconds and he would be ready.

"A nap? Nap sounds good." Gavin's eyes closed and his breathing became steady. He was asleep.

Veronica was getting louder. She was heading my way.

"Bad man! Bad man!"

I turned to look at Veronica, preparing to banish her to the courtyard, but then realised she wasn't alone.

"Hello, Mags," Simon said.

"Bad man!" Veronica said, pointing at Simon's penis.

"I know," I said in a quiet but firm voice. Gavin wouldn't hear Veronica or Simon, but my own voice might rouse him. I doubted it, however. He was exhausted and had had two cups of tea. "Don't worry about it. Just go for a walk."

"Bad man."

"Veronica. He's gay and you're both dead. I think you'll be okay. Go."

"Bad man," she mumbled and left the room, her eyes the last of her to go, staring at Simon's penis.

"She's fun," he said.

"She's an acquired taste. What are you doing here?"

"You're planning to stop him."

"Stop who? What?"

"You want to stop Gavin avenging me."

I took a breath before answering. The fact that Simon knew,

bothered me. There had to be some sort of connection between them. Strong feelings, love, in particular, linger after death, but he shouldn't have known. I wanted to ask him how, but I knew he wouldn't be able to answer.

"You need to move on, Simon."

"I can't. Not yet. Gavin needs closure. He needs to see Augustus die."

"That's dangerous. Augustus killed you."

"Gavin's different. He's strong. If anyone can resist Augustus, he can. Besides, he's got you to help him. Augustus doesn't stand a chance against the pair of you."

I looked at Gavin, his eyes closed and looking more rested than I had seen him all day. For all that he was the supernatural liaison, he'd never had to deal with a vampire before. Most of his work was dealing with the fallout of spells cast by amateurs who didn't know what they were doing.

In my thirty years as a witch, I'd never encountered a vampire before. They cropped up occasionally in the Witch's Council's library, but more as rumour than fact. I felt ill-equipped. An imposter.

"Augustus stands more than a chance against us. You know that."

"What can you do on your own? Pass it on to the Witch's Council and let them deal with it? That's not really you, is it?"

How did he know about the Council? Again, I had a bad feeling.

He had a point, however, and a plan started to crystalise.

"Very well. I'll work with him to find Augustus."

He faded away and left me looking at a sleeping Gavin. I didn't want to, but I knew I would have to wake him. We would have to move fast. It was possibly too late already.

***

Simon could not have been the only victim. He just couldn't be. Vampires live a long time, and they kill. It's in their nature. There ought to be a string of bodies leading to Simon, but, as far as we could tell, there wasn't.

That didn't mean there were no bodies. It just meant we couldn't see them. Vampires are the chameleons of the supernatural world. The intrinsic magic that hides their reflections also does a good job of hiding them in other ways. Any evidence leading to them fades away. Nothing is more invisible than something the eye is persuaded to ignore.

It took a lot of effort. Effort, police databases, Google, and the Council's Library. The evidence was all there. We just needed to dig deep to find it and force ourselves to see it.

We found three victims in a five-mile radius. No-one had thought to link them. No-one had been allowed to think to link them. That didn't seem like many, so we expanded our search, then expanded it again. And again. Then, suddenly, there were lots of them. London, Manchester, Liverpool, Glasgow. Every city in the UK and most small towns had at least one victim, but none of them had been connected to any other until now. Some had been labelled as vampire fetishist or vampire wannabes in the local press, but the stories never made the nationals. Such was the level of magical camouflage at work.

We found two hundred and fifty-seven deaths in total in the last year.

***

The Council's library suggested two potential ways of dealing with Augustus. One was a denaturing spell. In effect, this would be a spell that took away the vampire's ability to, well, vamp. It was a long shot that it would work, but it was my preferred option. I don't like to kill, even if I have to.

The book that gave me the spell said that it was about fifty per cent effective. It came from an old book, so the language was less analytic than that. The prose was a bit flowery, to be honest, but most authorities agree it meant that if two witches try it out, then only one would succeed. Let's not think about the other witch.

The spell worked well on young, underpowered vampires but was less effective on the older ones. We had no idea how old

Augustus was, but he had to be old. The further back we looked, the harder it was to associate reports with him. Further back than five years and it was sheer guesswork.

The other option, in which I had much more confidence, was charging in the courtyard. Gavin viewed it with suspicion.

"I should sharpen some more stakes," he said.

"You're not Buffy the Vampire Slayer, you know. Do you realise it takes more than just a jab in the chest with a pointy stick? You have to find his heart and then hammer the stake into it. And you need to cut off his head. Both of those things are harder than you might think. Especially if he's trying to stop you."

"I've got to do something."

"Go online and find him. Leave this part to me. If the denaturing spell doesn't work, then I'll use this."

"And if that doesn't work?"

"We're dead."

***

The world of gay internet dating is bewildering. At least, it was to me. Gavin had spread a variety of screens across my mum's old sideboard and had propped up a selection of phones and tablets using an array of books and coffee jars. Each device had something on it that was designed to give men access to other men.

I watched over his shoulder as he talked to a man called Stuart, whose online name was something rather explicit and anatomically unlikely. They'd already been talking for a while. Gavin seemed engrossed.

The men Gavin talked to seemed to choose such ridiculous names. Some told him their real names, eventually. Well, real-ish names. The married ones thought that hiding behind a *nom-de-shag* and using their middle name instead of their first name, when pressed, would stop their wives from finding out. It wouldn't. Not that any self-respecting wife would dirty her eyeballs in any of these places.

Gavin typed slowly. Although he was younger than me, he was really not as *au fait* with technology as he could have been.

Had this been a legitimate operation, there would have been a squad of young eager constables clicking and swiping like good little internet natives. This was, however, not something that Gavin could put through the books. It was difficult getting senior officers to become interested in the case – the vampire's cloaking defence at work – and, in any case, the purpose was to kill the vampire, unless the denaturing spell worked. Officers ruling themselves as judge, jury, and executioner were on the wrong side of the law, even if the criminal was not human.

Gavin was technically on leave. Semi-official, semi-compassionate leave that would probably be withdrawn if his bosses knew what he was really doing.

We were doing this because we had to. There was a vampire to catch. He wasn't Stuart, the man Gavin was talking to, however. Nor was he any of the filthy-mouthed scoundrels he'd already blocked. None of them fit the profile the police psychologist had drawn up and, besides, the police tracking software had not shown any more obfuscation on their part than using the 'invisible' mode on their browser. Like that works.

U had any luk? Gavin typed. I groaned. I'm no writer but I hate to see English being massacred. The person Gavin was pretending to be, however, spoke like that, unfortunately. He was in character.

Oh, you know. The usual time-wasters typing with one hand with their pants around their ankles. Although I'd only been watching for ten minutes or so, I decided I liked Stuart. He used proper words, correct spelling, and had some idea about punctuation. Other men on here seemed to type with their penises and I don't think any of them had ever been to skool.

Haha, Gavin typed. Not *lol*. That's so last year. Keep up. *So, nothing?*

Well … Stuart was teasing him like a tenth-rate celebrity, compering *Croydon's Got Talent.*

Yeah?

There was a really nice bloke on here earlier. Sounded great.

Sounded?

No photo.

Y not?

Said he didn't have any to hand.

Dodgy.

But he was so polite. Old school. You know? My eyebrow shot up. This sounded interesting. *He talked to me like I was a person and not just an arse with legs. He took an interest.*

Sounds like you're in lurvvvvvve.

Don't be soft.

Y U here and not at his?

He wanted me to invite him round tomorrow, but I can't. The wife will be in.

I sighed and shook my head. Poor clueless woman.

Shame. Who he? #AskingForAFriend. I made a mental note to ask Gavin what that meant.

Oi! I saw him first.

I can sing your praises.

Hahaha. Sure. He's calling himself Augustus.

Gavin and I looked at each other in excitement. Augustus!

I'll look out for him, Gavin typed.

Tell me how you get on. Or rather don't. I'll get jealous.

If it was our Augustus, then Stuart's wife had saved his life.

***

Gavin slept on my sofa that night. I left him there while I made a cup of tea, and when I returned, I found Simon watching him.

"We never had the luxury of spending the night together," he said. "He looks like a baby. I loved him, you know. I just never said."

Simon, however, looked sick, something I'd never seen in a ghost before. I knew why.

"You need to move on," I said. "Before it's too late."

"I know, but I need to make sure he's okay," he nodded towards Gavin. "And that means making sure Augustus is dead."

"You think we've got a hope?"

"I've been watching your preparations. The denaturing spell won't touch him, but you knew that."

ROBERT WILLIAMS

I nodded. "What about—"

"It has a chance. You need to make sure it is ready."

"It will be."

There was a companionable silence while we both watched Gavin sleep.

"You know what you risk by hanging around?" I asked.

Simon nodded, but showed no inclination to leave.

***

It was a fine sunny day, and we made our final preparations. My surprise gained another day's charge and Gavin sharpened more futile stakes. I didn't try to convince him otherwise. My arguments would have been just as futile.

Sunset fell in its usual vague London way. The sun disappeared behind the other blocks in the estate and the sky gradually darkened until it was technically night. We checked online for the correct time.

"It's the seventh night since Simon's death," I said. "Augustus will be hunting."

This wasn't vampire lore. We had noticed a pattern in the death reports. He fed once a week, a creature of habit.

The website where Gavin had talked to Stuart was busy, but there was no sign of Augustus.

"Are we too late?" Gavin said, worried.

"No. Give him a minute. He's only just got up."

He fretted for a few seconds until —

"Got him!"

I looked around for Simon. There was no sign.

Gavin, in the meantime, was typing.

Hi, he said, careful to keep himself in character.

Good evening, Augustus wrote back.

What U looking for?

Who knows? Let's chat for a while.

There was a predictable pause.

Do you have a pic? Gavin typed. We knew he wouldn't have one, but we had to play the game.

I'm afraid not, Augustus had written. *I don't take a very good photograph.*

We laughed at that.

Y? Gavin typed.

I'm just not good with technology. I try to take my picture and I manage to get the wall behind me. I've been told I'm good-looking though, bewitching even.

What U do? Gavin asked, changing the subject.

I am independently wealthy. That ticked another box. Vampires are good with money.

Wow! Rich family?

In a manner of speaking. I made some wise investments in my youth.

Good for you. What were you planning for tonight?

I don't know.

His vagueness was irritating me, so I grabbed the keyboard from Gavin and slipped out of character. *Come on, mate. You must have had something in mind when you logged on. Chat/Sex/What?*

There was no reply.

"We've lost him," Gavin said. "Shit."

"I was too impatient. I'm sorry, Gav—"

"Wait! Look. It says Augustus is typing."

His words appeared soon afterwards.

I have needs…

I nodded to Gavin.

Who doesn't? he typed.

It's like a hunger. I have to satisfy it, or I will die.

"Drama queen," I muttered. Enough soul searching. "Tell him you have needs too," I said. Gavin nodded and typed my words.

I feel like I'm treating men like cattle, Augustus replied.

Gavin sighed. "Now he has a conscience! Bit late if you ask me."

"Can you persuade him otherwise?"

He nodded and typed, *Moo.*

There was a pause before Augustus started typing.

Hahaha. Moo. You make me laugh. I like you.

"Okay," Gavin said. "I think he's hooked. Time to reel him in."

I'm sure I could make you like me a whole lot more, he typed. *Let's meet.*

Well, I am tempted. Do you want me to come over?

Sure.

I won't come unless I am invited.

Huh? Gavin typed.

I'm fussy. Indulge me.

Gavin looked up at me, and I nodded. This was it. We were about to invite a vampire to come and visit us. I hoped we were ready.

Okay then. I invite you. Come to me.

I will be with you in a few minutes.

But I haven't told you where I live.

It doesn't matter. I will be there.

Gavin picked up the crucifix and one of his stakes.

The screen turned black, a strange three-dimensional, inky black that churned like smoke. Then the black smoke was somehow in front of the screen and expanding. Its outlines remained sharp and clear while twisting like a captured waterfall.

Gradually the smoke separated from the screen and shaped itself into a man. Although the word 'man' was an insult applied to him. He was a god, beautiful yet manly, rough but not ugly. He was irresistible. I could see how Simon had been trapped. If Augustus had been straight, I would have been tempted. As it was, part of me regretted I wasn't male.

"Oh, how delicious!" he said, a laugh in his voice. "A pining lover and his tame witch."

I opened my mouth to utter the triggering words of the denaturing spell, but nothing came out.

"You think that would work against me? I am too old and too powerful to be regressed by your pathetic spell."

"What will you do with us?" His power allowed me to speak. I just couldn't say the words of the spell.

"My dear! You need to ask? I will kill you, of course. I will drain you of your life and drink your blood."

"Both of us?"

"Of course. I will grant Gavin his wish to die so that he can be with his Simon, and then it will be your turn."

"You can manage that?"

"I don't have to drink all your blood to kill you."

My eyes drifted to where the surprise was concealed in my spare teapot.

Augustus laughed once more.

"I don't think I will let you get near to that, either."

So, my surprise was no surprise to Augustus and was therefore useless. We were done for.

At that point, my doorbell rang. An unusual occurrence. Friends knew I never locked the door, and I wasn't expecting any clients.

I glanced at Augustus and hated myself for it.

He laughed, showing me his fangs.

"Go on, let them come in. It will make no difference."

Knowing I was damning one of my neighbours, but having no control over my voice, I called out to them.

"Come on in," I shouted. "It's not locked."

The door opened and closed, and I could hear slow, deliberate footsteps in my hall. They stopped and my living room door pushed open to reveal Simon, fully clothed in his best suit. His funeral suit. The one he was supposed to be cremated in.

"Hello, Mags."

"Simon. I told you to go before it was too late."

"And you were right. It is too late."

"Simon?" It was the first time Gavin had spoken since Augustus arrived. "Is that you?"

"Yes, matey. It's me. I've come to take you away from all this."

Simon had become a vampire. It had been too long since his death and his spirit had returned to his body. This was what I'd been afraid of. If he'd gone on, or if the body had been destroyed, this wouldn't have happened.

"Youngling! You presume too much. I will feast first."

"Oh no, you won't. Not on my Gavin. He's mine."

"You will follow the precedent set down by the ancients. I am your sire—"

"Yeah, right," Simon said and stood beside Gavin. He put an arm around the two of us. I still couldn't move. "They're mine."

"You will defer to me. It is my—"

Simon turned to Gavin and kissed him.

"I love you," he said. Then he looked at me and winked. I had no idea what he was going to do. "Look after him," he whispered.

Before I could stop him, or even before I knew what he was doing, Simon's spare arm reached for my teapot and brushed it off the counter. The teapot smashed on the floor between him and Augustus, releasing my Plan B spell, and it flooded my kitchen with sunshine.

Augustus gasped.

I'd done my research. The best way to kill a vampire was to expose them to broad, bright daylight, but that, normally, is quite hard, involving digging up their coffins and prising off the lid. And that was only after weeks of detective work finding where they'd hidden themselves away.

That was why the book had recommended a sunshine bomb. It was a simple thing. A growing plant of some sort, a few herbs, and an invocation to Helios. Allow to cook for a day or two in daylight, preferably in bright sunshine. Serve as a surprise.

Augustus turned, trying to run back to the laptop and the safety of the internet. He even managed a few steps before he collapsed on the floor and, in seconds, was dust. Simon, however, remained where he stood, not trying to avoid the light. I could feel his arm around us until he became dust as well.

Agnes waved as she led Simon's spirit away.

CHAPTER SIX

HOLDING OUT FOR A HERO

Witchcraft is a calling. It isn't a job you choose from the situations vacant column of the local paper, it's something that chooses you. You must want to help people and have an openness to the weird, the otherworldly, the downright odd.

That cuts out most of the population straightaway. There are a lot of caring people, but few of them have enough of an appetite for the weird to allow them to cope with all that being a witch would throw at them. It helps if you have the craft in the family, but it's no guarantee. I know as many witches who followed their mothers as I do those who stumbled into it.

To be an urban witch, you have to be able to cope with all that, the caring and the weird, as well as the pressures of living in a city. For the craft to find you, a needle in a London-sized haystack takes everything I've mentioned, as well as a good dose of luck.

So, to sum all that up, urban witches are compassionate, weird and lucky. We also have a whopping great dollop of intuition on the side.

Well, that sums me up at any rate.

That intuition was why I was sitting in front of my television, the next episode of *Hotel Hellada* highlighted and my finger hovering above the play button but nowhere near pressing it. It

ROBERT WILLIAMS

had been there for five minutes. Were I a comic book fan, I would say my Spidey-sense was tingling. I'm not, but I'll say it anyway.

In layman's terms, something was going to happen. Something big. I couldn't tell if it was good or bad, but it was big.

Precognition is the least developed of my senses. My sense of the future is a bit like listening to someone speaking in the next room with the door shut and cotton wool in my ears. I would know they were saying something but wouldn't be able to make out the words. For me to know that something was going to happen, therefore, it would have to be huge, and it would have to be happening soon.

I turned off the TV. There was little point in me trying to watch *Hellada*. The way my anticipation was growing, chances were that I would pause it before the chef's bombshell exploded. Unfortunately, he would have to wait. He'd still be potentially the father of the sous-chef's daughter tomorrow, but the immediate future had something else planned.

A cup of tea seemed like a good idea, so I stood up and headed for the kitchen. Tea always helps in this sort of situation, whatever this sort of situation turned out to be. To my surprise, however, I found I had walked to the front door. My subconscious, not content with giving me bad vibes, had hijacked my journey to the kettle. So, no tea just yet. Obviously, the huge imminent thing was a lot bigger and rather more imminent than I'd thought.

As if on cue, there were a series of urgent knocks on the door, so I looked through the spyhole. With all the build-up, I was expecting someone, or something, more imposing, but there was just a man. He was short, dressed in black, and had a determined expression on his face.

He looked harmless, so I opened the door.

"Margaret Hammond?" he asked.

"Yes," I said. He knew my name, but he didn't know me. Nobody calls me Margaret and even fewer people used my surname. "Who are you?"

"I'm here to help you," he said, without answering me. "Let me in. There isn't much time."

"I didn't know I needed help," I said, but I let him in, anyway. "You'd better tell me what's going on. Start with your name."

"That's not important. You need to listen to me. I—"

I glared at him. He resisted for a couple of seconds, but few can resist my stare. It's not witchcraft. I've been able to glare like that since I was six years old.

"Ptarmigan Gillespie," he mumbled, and I intensified my glare, forcing him to repeat it clearly. "My name is Ptarmigan Gillespie."

"What?"

"My mother," he said with a shrug, as if that were explanation enough. I ignored it.

"Why do I need your help?"

"They are coming."

"Who?"

"The Dark Witches of Alabama."

"And who are the Dark Witches of Alabama?"

"Necromancers."

"What?" This really didn't sound at all right. I knew of no witches that were necromancers. Not even Americans.

"There's no time for this. They'll be here soon. They want your wand."

My what? "But—?"

He ignored me.

"Barricade the door," he said, gesturing at a heavy chair near the front door. "They won't come in that way, too obvious, but do it anyway."

"Now, wait a minute. Who are you to come here and order me about?"

"I told you. I'm Ptarmigan Gillespie."

"And? Should I know you?"

He sighed.

"There's no reason you should know me, no."

"You sound like I should."

"No, don't worry about it. I just try to help where I can. People always seem to need my help." He contrived to look wistful but failed. "Anyway, let's get cracking, shall we?"

"Are you going to help with this?" The chair was a heavy thing my mother had left me. It wasn't very comfortable and didn't go with my other furniture, so I kept it in the hall as somewhere to sit when I was putting on my shoes.

"No, I'm going to run a security sweep of your flat. They could get in anywhere."

I doubted it. I live on the sixth floor and have windows painted over so many times that I've never been able to open them. I played along, however, and struggled to shift the chair to a new spot behind the front door. It took me a good few minutes but, if anyone tried to break in that way, it would hold them back for a while.

I went to find Ptarmigan.

He was standing at my living room window, a cup of tea in his hand. I glared at his back. He'd had time to make himself a cup of tea while I was struggling with that sodding chair? Where was mine?

"Does this open?"

"It hasn't in the last twenty years. Sealed shut."

"Good. Well done. Level one or level two warded?"

"What?"

"You've applied standard warding spells?"

Never heard of them. "This is the sixth floor. I have never felt the need." Also, and I know I am repeating myself here, but it is important, I have never heard of them.

"You've not heard of broomsticks?"

Broomsticks? Most witches I knew used the bus. Witches in north London rode the tube. I knew a few rural witches who might have flown broomsticks in their youth, but I knew for a fact that at least one of them drove a Range Rover. Conceivably, these necromantic American witches could have flown on broomsticks, but why would they? There are much easier ways to get about. Uber, for one.

"Yes, but—"

TALES OF AN URBAN WITCH

"Oh, never mind. I'll do it myself. Barricade the bedroom."

He took a small plastic box out of his pocket and set it down on the windowsill. A small light flashed weakly on its top side.

"What's that?"

"Mechanical warding. Not as good as a spell, but it will help. Why not take a closer look?"

I studied the box. It looked very professionally made, although obviously not something you'd buy off the shelf. The light seemed to flash a little more brighter than it had earlier.

"Impressive. Where did you get it?"

"A friend made it for me."

"A friend?"

"Someone I helped."

He seemed to help a lot of people. I wondered if they knew they needed help before he turned up. I didn't think I had, but then I didn't know about necromantic American witches. I've led a sheltered life, obviously.

"Anyway, we're wasting time. They mustn't get that wand. The Witch Parliament depends on you keeping hold of it. The world is depending on you."

Witch Parliament? Had there been a re-organisation of some sort? Had I missed an email? There had been nothing in the last newsletter. We still had a Council as far as I knew, but we are a very closeted group. There could be changes in the highest echelons and I wouldn't know.

I shrugged. The question would keep. I felt like I was reading a book with most of the pages missing.

I ran to my bedroom and locked the door. The bedroom had a small window, but anyone trying to get through it would have to be supermodel thin. No witch was that skinny, not even a necromancer.

Clouds were gathering in the sky outside when I returned to the living room, and I could see occasional flashes of lightning. Rain started pattering on the window. Heavily. Some foolhardy birds circled high in the sky in the distance, freeloading on the powerful thermals.

I noticed Ptarmigan had helped himself to another cup of tea and a plateful of my chocolate digestives.

"Nasty weather," I said, trying to distract myself. It had been a perfect summer evening earlier.

"Weather? That's not weather. That's them! They're here."

I didn't see anything other than black clouds and the dark specks circling beneath them.

"Are you sure?"

"I've seen them before. It's them." He stared at me for a couple of seconds. "Why don't you take a closer look?"

Looking up at the clouds, the dark specks I had taken for birds resolved themselves as each black dot dropped lower. They were people. Specifically, they were women. Even more specifically, they were witches, but not witches in the sense that I knew them.

These were witches borrowed from every clichéd fairy tale and movie from the last century, from their impractical pointy hats to the pointy-toed black slippers. Black cat familiars sat improbably on the broomsticks alongside them. Nothing fell off. Cats stayed on broomsticks and hats stayed on heads.

Who were these charlatans? They certainly weren't witches. Have you ever tried to make a cat sit anywhere? And who, outside of someone at a Goth convention, would wear that much black? Black was, of course, the new black, but witches never follow fashion. Our clothing choices are governed by comfort and not style. Sally in Boadicea Tower, for instance, wore more pastel shades than the old Queen Mother and Lucy in Juniper House was never seen out of a onesie, even now.

One of the witches flew at the window, her mouth open in laughter. Was that a cackle?

Honestly, cackling?

She had green skin, and yes, there were warts. If she'd been any more of a cliché, she would have been a cartoon. This didn't seem at all right. What was going on?

She touched the window and there was a sort of explosion. It was a larger version of a fly hitting a supermarket bug-zapper.

She flew back, losing her broomstick and her cat in the process. All three tumbled out of sight and I worried vaguely about the cat. An innocent casualty or a thwarted agent of evil?

The warding box, or whatever it was called, squealed electronically. "It can't take much more of that," Ptarmigan said. "I've seen this lot at work before. They're vicious. Get ready to fight them off!"

"With what?" I had no idea. I'm an urban witch. People come to me to get warts removed or for some help to register a baby. This is southeast London not Hogwarts.

"Think of something or you'll be saying goodbye to that wand."

I started to answer, but he carried on.

"When they get hold of it, the Witch Parliament will be in danger. Haven't you got anything over there?" He nodded at something behind me, then added with careful slowness. "Take a closer look."

I turned to follow his nod … and saw my display shelves taking up most of the wall. There was my dowsing rod propped up against an Ordnance Survey map with my pendulum draped carefully over one corner. On the shelf below was my crystal ball, glittering in beams from the tasteful recessed spotlights.

The wand, however, took centre stage of the entire display and glowed with its own hidden power. I felt a surge of pride as I looked at it. This was *my* wand, the source of *my* power, *mine* alone to use as I wanted.

And yet, something felt wrong. I didn't know what it was, but there was a thought, an elusive thing, slipping away just as it formed. I'd nearly had it in my sights.

A crash shook me from my thoughts. Another witch had just been zapped off the window. She tumbled to the ground and was quickly out of view. The warding box was squealing again, but it didn't sound healthy and quickly cut off.

"That's it for the box. They'll be through the window next time. You'd better be ready with a warding spell."

I looked at him wide-eyed. Ready? I had my wand. How could

he even doubt me?

I reached for the wand, and it leapt into my hand, part of me, its power filling my hand, my arm, my entire body. I was ready to take on anyone and anything. Those American witches didn't know who they were messing with.

"Warding spell? I don't need a warding spell. They're toast."

Another of them had broken off from the pack and was hurtling towards the window like a suicidal crow. I gestured with the wand and the window shattered into a thousand shards. I sent them all towards the witch and she was hidden by a cloud of glass. I didn't see what happened when it hit her, and I didn't care, but I could hear her screams fading into the distance as she fell.

Yet, even before the sound had gone, a feeling struck me. It was the same feeling of wrongness I had felt earlier, but again, I was unable to establish the reason for it. But I didn't have time for this soul-searching. I needed to defend the wand! The safety of the Parliament depended on it remaining out of the hands of the necromancers.

"So, this is the great Margaret Hammond." The new voice had a lazy Southern drawl with a nasty edge to it. One of the necromancers had landed on my windowsill without me noticing. She sounded like Blanche from the *Golden Girls,* but without the looks or the charm.

Her cat had dismounted with her and was picking its way daintily into my flat, looking for food. I knew cats. Even evil necromancers' familiars would be complete tarts for food and catnip. I forced myself to ignore it.

"And who are you?" I said to the witch.

"I am your worst nightmare, sister. Give me that wand."

"Or what? You'll cliché me to death?"

She threw a fireball at me, but I caught it on the wand, like I had speared a dumpling with a chopstick, and it dissipated in a shower of glitter.

"A glitter cloud? You learn your magic in the seventies, sister?"

I held the wand at arm's length and pointed it at the witch. Its power coursed through my body. It felt good, and I wanted more. As I aimed it at her, I knew I could kill her with just a thought.

The power was mounting, and I imagined how I could kill her. Would I burn her alive? Would I turn her inside out?

She could feel it, too. I could see the doubt appearing on her face. I glanced at Ptarmigan.

"Stop debating with her," he said. "Kill her or she'll have the wand."

I looked back at the green witch.

"Run," I told her. "I'll give you a head start."

She was on her broomstick in moments and sailing out of the window. Her cat watched her leave with disinterest.

I held out my hand for my own broomstick, and I prepared to launch myself out of the window to follow her, hot for the chase. I raised my wand, ready to deal her the killing blow.

"Miaow." The cat interrupted my thoughts and, as I reached the broken window, I stopped and looked down. I could see the block's garden below me, the body of the witch I had killed earlier spreadeagled on the grass. The bodies of the others killed by the warding box lay beside her. At that moment, the 'wrong' feeling returned with a vengeance, but this time I knew what it was. It wasn't the bitch I was chasing. It wasn't the flying coven of witches on military-grade broomsticks trying to attack my flat. It wasn't the strange cat looking expectantly up at me.

All of that was indeed wrong, but none of it was the principal source of the feeling. I knew what was causing the feeling now, and I knew how to put it right.

"Go after her," Ptarmigan said. "She's getting away."

"No."

"What do you mean? No? No, what? The great urban witch of London can't kill an underpowered necromancer?"

"This is wrong."

I looked at the witch flying away, still pointing the wand at her. The rest of her coven circled in the sky above her.

"All of this is wrong. I don't do this. I don't kill. I don't fight foreign witches. I don't kill cats. I don't have a broomstick. But, most of all," I looked at the wand in my hand, "I don't have a magic wand."

I threw the wand out of the window and the illusion collapsed. The wand vanished, the witch vanished, my window restored itself and the, admittedly rather nice, display case reverted into my mum's battered old sideboard. My crystal ball and pendulum were on the sideboard in their conventional spots and my dowsing rod was, no doubt, back in its favourite place in my toolbox.

In my hand, instead of a broomstick, I gripped my Dyson's hose. I would have died if I had thrown it out of the window and leapt after it.

My mind was my own once more and the overlay of Mags the Hero was gone. I breathed a sigh of relief.

Outside the window, the witches were nothing more than a flock of pigeons and the storm a collection of white clouds drifting lazily across the sky.

Ptarmigan was still there, wordless with shock. He was real. Sort of.

"Miaow." And so was the evil witch's familiar.

"Right," I said to Ptarmigan. "I think you have some explaining to do. Why were you trying to kill me?"

***

The sun had set, and the sky turned dark before I got any sense out of Ptarmigan. He'd collapsed after I'd thrown off his illusion. His face had been a mask of disbelief for a long time afterwards and I'd had to ply him with hot, sweet tea to calm him down. I'd also made him have a nap by drugging the tea.

The cat spent a happy half an hour wandering around inside my flat before demanding food and then settling down on my mother's chair for a nap of her own. Curiosity had certainly not killed this cat, but I worried about the other familiar I thought I'd killed along with its owner. Had they been real or illusions? And how real was this cat? Would she disappear like the witches? Why hadn't she gone already?

As soon as my guests were sound asleep, I let myself out my

front door, took the lift down to the ground floor, and ran as fast as I could to the back of the block. This was our 'garden' but was really just some leftover land that the developers had laid out to grass, and put in a few token trees, a couple of benches and some rhododendron bushes. I could see it all from my window if I pressed my head against the glass. No-one ever used it or sat on the lonely bench.

There should have been three green warty necromancer corpses down here and some dead familiars. Mercifully, however, the garden was empty. There were no dead witches, no broomsticks, and no dead cats. There wasn't a hint of blood on the grass.

The deaths, and the bodies, had all been part of the illusion. They hadn't been real.

I collapsed on the ground and threw up. I didn't care who saw me. I threw up and threw up until I had nothing left in my stomach.

Whatever had happened upstairs had left me utterly convinced that I had become a casual killer, and the thought disturbed me more than the idea that I had been about to throw myself through a sealed window with a length of hoover hose between my legs.

I sat for a while until my stomach settled, and I felt in control again. Now I needed answers from Ptarmigan.

***

I woke him with another cup of tea.

"What happened?"

"That's what I want to know. I broke your ... illusion."

"Illusion?"

"Don't pretend to not know what I mean. I stopped believing in whatever you'd done to me. The whole kit and caboodle vanished. The witches, the wand, the lot."

"Miaow."

"Apart from the cat. Now, you need to tell me what happened and why you tried to kill me."

He smiled.

"It nearly worked. You were one step from jumping."

"But your cat stopped me."

"My cat?"

"She was part of your illusion."

He shrugged. "She's not now, is she?"

"No." That was another puzzle for another day. The cat had saved my life. That was all that was important for now. The question of where she had come from would remain unanswered, for now. There remained a more immediate question.

"So, why did you try to kill me?"

"You killed my mother."

"I did what?"

"You killed my mother."

"I killed no-one. Who was your mother?"

"Dorothy."

"Dorothy Gillespie? I don't know a Dorothy Gillespie."

"Dorothy Tremarne. I was adopted."

Dorothy! The changeling. If this was her son, no wonder he could put a glamour on me so easily. I would be better prepared next time. For now, however, I had news for him.

"I didn't kill Dorothy."

"Yes, you did. I tracked her down to her house and the new owners said she'd died."

The cover story that I'd given Dave and Beth to tell others was that Dorothy was dead.

"Did they say that I'd killed her?"

"No, but when I got them to speak, they said that you'd sent her to the Kingdom. Bloody bible bashers."

***

It took me the best part of an hour to explain about the Kingdom and his mother's past. Or rather, I'd explained it in about five minutes. It took me the remaining time to make him understand.

In the end, I'd grabbed a book off my shelf, Harrison's *History of the Lands of Illusion,* and told him to read chapter eighteen, which was all about changelings. I left him alone with it and went to prepare dinner.

"This is all real?" he asked when I returned.

"Yes."

"My mother was a changeling?"

"Yes."

"That makes me half fairy?"

I frowned at his use of the term. I didn't like it. Popular mythology has fairies as cute little things, all wings, and glitter, but the Kingdom was evil. No, that wasn't right. Not evil. They just didn't see us as people. We were less than insects to them. They were as evil as a man's foot treading on an ant.

"I don't know if it works that way," I said, resisting the urge to correct him. "Magic and genetics—"

"I can weave illusions. That's not a human characteristic, is it?"

"No."

"So, I must get that from her."

"I guess so, but—"

"I need to see her."

"I can't help you there," I said. "If I opened the door again, it could be disastrous."

"Humans are such cowards," he said. He'd been as human as me, five seconds ago. "Your Witch Charter—"

"Witch's Code."

"Whatever. The Witch's Code stops you from helping me?"

It didn't. I wasn't going to help him because I was scared stiff of the Kingdom and, to be honest, I was scared stiff of him as well. I didn't want to think what could happen if he found his way to the Kingdom and I didn't want to be responsible for allowing him to get there. I certainly wasn't going to open the portal any time soon.

"Yes," I said, lying.

"I thought you would say that. I will have to find my own way there."

"No, you won't. I can't allow that to happen."

"You will let me. I know you will. Take a closer look."

That was his trigger phrase. He used it on me earlier to make me see witches when there weren't any and to convince me I had a display case in place of my mother's sideboard. I'm not sure what I was supposed to be seeing, but it wasn't working.

He looked confused.

"No, really. Take a closer look."

"It won't work."

"What won't?"

"Your illusion. Is something meant to be scaring me? Or is something going to batter down the bedroom door? Only that won't happen. Once bitten, twice shy, so to speak. I'm a witch. I can control my susceptibility to illusion if I know what to expect." That was a bit of a lie. I couldn't withstand the might of the Kingdom, but he wasn't that powerful.

"Bugger."

"And I've laced your tea with something to suppress your powers."

"What?"

"Oh yes. A few herbs and roots. Nothing dangerous, but it'll keep you from conjuring up weird stuff for a few days."

"How dare you!"

"But before it wears off, a friend will come for you. A friend who knows about people like you and who can look after you."

"I don't need—"

"You do. They'll be here before you wake up."

"Wake up? But I'm not asleep."

I clicked my fingers, and he flopped down on the pillow.

***

Later, much later, Miguel arrived. He was a Keeper and had been specially trained for people like Ptarmigan.

"I have to admit," he said, not sounding at all Spanish. "I haven't been trained for fairies."

"No-one has. The Witch's Code has a brief chapter on fairies that essentially tells us to run a mile if ever we meet one."

"That's not very encouraging."

"I'm exaggerating," I said, to reassure him, although that itself was a lie. Witches are taught to be level-headed and calm. We are trained to examine every situation carefully before choosing the appropriate solution and to execute it efficiently with the minimum of fuss. The only exception to that rule is if we encounter fairies. Various editions of the Witch's Code have been published and the advice about fairies in them ranged from *you're on your own, sister* to *run for it,* but the essential advice was to not tangle with them. I had only helped Dorothy because she had been a friend. I should not even have done that.

"He's through here," I said and opened the door to the spare bedroom. It was empty.

I'd been duped again.

***

I closed the door once I was satisfied I was no longer living in an illusion. I was as satisfied as I could be. The potion I had used to suppress Ptarmigan's abilities had only worked for a few minutes. Just long enough to convince me he was sound asleep. It would have worked for a week had he been fully human.

I would have to tell the Council about him. A fairy, even a half-fairy, loose in the world was a terrible thing.

"I'll have to tell the Witch's Council about you as well, won't I?" I said to the cat. "I mean, are you really real? Or are you a lingering illusion?"

"Miaow," said the cat and rubbed her head on my leg.

CHAPTER SEVEN

DESIRE

When people come to me, looking for help, I do sometimes have to turn them away. It's rare. I try to help everyone, but sometimes it's just beyond my abilities. Other times it's because what they want me to do is wrong or stupid.

Unfortunately, I get about three people a month turn up at my flat with some problem or other that eventually turns out with them wanting me to give them a love potion to pass on to some other poor unfortunate soul. I give them a fair hearing and try to find another solution to their problem but, in the end, I just send them away. It's all I can do.

I've told you before about love potions. Love can't and should never be forced. That is wrong, and against our code. If someone has developed an unhealthy, unrequited obsession with someone else, a good witch would help remove the obsession and not encourage a love that isn't there.

When Gary told me he wanted to get married, I thought the conversation would go in a completely different direction.

"Congratulations! What sort of service did you want? I tend to keep things simple, although I have a wedding planner friend and can—"

"No."

"No? You don't want a service? Then why are you here? Do you

TALES OF AN URBAN WITCH

need…?" I raised my eyebrows.

"I could buy Viagra in Boots if I wanted it. I don't need anything like that."

"Then I don't understand. Why are you here?"

"I need a love potion."

"I'm sorry, but I can't."

"Even though it's for me?"

He had me there. The Witch's Council had banned them to protect the innocent. Giving a potion to someone who used it on themselves broke the letter of the code, but not the spirit.

"Tell me why you need it and maybe, just maybe, I'll put in a plea for your case with the boss." We're not supposed to mention the Witch's Council to just anyone. I've told *you* already, but you're okay. Just keep it to yourself.

"I don't love her."

"Kind of guessed that. Does she love you?"

He shrugged, uncaring. "Yes. She's devoted." I doubted that was true.

"Why don't you love her? Is she ugly?"

"Yes … no… I don't know. I guess not. Not really."

"Well, that pretty much covers all bases. Why are you marrying her?"

"I have to."

"Is she pregnant? You know this isn't 1950, don't you?"

"No, she's not pregnant. At least, I don't think so."

"And if she is, it isn't yours?"

His head slumped. I didn't need an answer.

"I have to have a wife by the time I'm thirty."

"Or?"

"Or I don't get to inherit the family business when my dad dies."

"How old are you now?"

"Twenty-nine."

I must confess that money has never been my greatest motivator. If it was, then I had chosen the wrong profession. I would never work to help someone else to get rich, but I could see that this wasn't about money. Family businesses kept families alive and inheriting one was a matter of pride. Losing one would come at a great emotional cost.

"Come back to me on Wednesday. I will have something for you."

It wouldn't be a love potion, but I wasn't going to tell him that.

***

Harris and Hall had made bottles since the middle of the seventeenth century. You've used their bottles and jars every day without realising, and their factory on Helston Road was as anonymous as their products. I'd passed it practically every day of my life, but had never once wondered about what went on inside. I'd never needed to, not until today.

Although a traditional company, they had moved with the times and started regular tours of the factory for members of the public. Today that included me. I had no trouble getting myself a place at the last minute in a group with some bored tourists and a couple of excited bottle nerds. Yes, they do exist.

I don't think it was in southeast London's list of top ten attractions, however, or even the top fifty. There were only twelve of us on the tour: me, the two nerds and nine damp tourists, drying out from the rain. I enjoyed the tour, however, and the bottle-nerds were cooing at everything. We saw the furnaces that melted the glass, the moulds that shaped the bottles, the stacking area, the design shop, and a lot of other places. They had a very small plastics sections that they were phasing out. They kept us out of it to avoid killing us with the fumes. I know, right? Health and safety gone mad.

"Say what you like about glass," our guide said, several times, "but it's durable, recyclable and doesn't clog up the Pacific Ocean."

The tour ended after half an hour, and I stuck around in the gift shop until I was the last visitor. That took a while. The nerds bought *everything*.

"Excuse me," I said to the guide. "I wonder if it is possible to have a chat with someone?"

TALES OF AN URBAN WITCH

"Oh, I'm sorry. We're not hiring at the moment."

"Ah, thank you, but that wasn't what I wanted. I need to ask a few delicate questions."

"Delicate?" He laughed, and I could see this wasn't going to happen the easy way. I was going to have to cheat.

"Listen to me," I said and used the special tone of voice I don't use very often. Just call me Obi-Wan. "I need to speak to a few people. I won't steal anything. I won't damage anything. I just want to talk and to help someone. Do you see that?"

Witchcraft can work wonders on the weak-willed. This man was no dunce, but he wasn't expecting to be charmed. The tone of voice and the cadence I used worked a bit like hypnotism, but it was quicker. It was a overkill for what I needed, but I was feeling impatient. I'd wasted the best part of an hour on the tour and the gift shop.

"Yes, of course," he said with a smile. "I'll get you a visitor's pass. Come with me."

***

Harris and Hall had existed long enough to have a legal department. It was only one man, but he had his own office in a quiet part of the factory. He even had his name on the door, Trevor Pembroke. He didn't bother looking at my visitor's pass.

"What can I do for you, Miss … Mrs…?"

"Please call me Mags."

"Mags."

"Thanks. Gary Hall has come to me for help, and I thought I would talk to you for a little background."

He frowned. "Well, of course. I'll do what I can, although I fail to see what assistance I can offer."

"I was only after some information on this thing about him having to marry before he is thirty."

"Ah yes, the wedding clause. It is a bit of an odd one, I have to admit, especially in these modern times."

"My thoughts exactly. It is the twenty-first century. Why does he need to marry?"

"You have to understand that the company has been owned

by the same two families for nearly four hundred years. When the company was founded, it was felt to be imperative for it to remain in the families and to that end, the company charter was created with the proviso that the oldest sons of both families had to marry so that their children would inherit the company and perpetuate it. Do you see?"

"Ah, yes. It sounds familiar."

"Indeed. The Royal Family have utilised the same system for several centuries." He really did pronounce the capital letters.

"What if there are only girls?"

"Dear lady, it has simply never happened, but there are contingency plans for that eventuality."

"Such as?"

"The girls marry, but they retain their family name. The name is the important thing, you see."

"I see. And if there are no children at all? Or one son has children but the other one doesn't?"

"Again, it has never happened, but I believe there are arrangements with cousins."

Just like the royal family again.

"Sorry. This is my last question. What happens if a son just doesn't want to marry?"

"Then we have a problem."

***

Mr Pembroke directed me to Gary's fiancée, Sophie, a girl working in the admin section. He'd started to say, 'typing pool' but caught sight of my raised eyebrow and changed his words to 'tiny admin department.'

"Sophie?" I interrupted her while she was looking at her engagement ring.

"Yes? How can I help?" Her smile was genuine and had come quickly to her face. Her make-up was flawless, and she had obviously taken great care with it. She had, however, opted for huge fake eyelashes. They suit some women, and even some men, but Sophie wore very thick glasses, and every time she blinked, I kept thinking of spiders trapped in a jar. Large spiders.

"I'm here to help your fiancé with something. I just need a bit of a chat to get some background information."

She frowned and blinked. I shuddered.

"Is Mr Hall – I mean Jeremy – in trouble?"

"Jeremy?"

"Oh, no! I mean Gary," she said with an embarrassed laugh. "I'm still not used to using his first name."

"Is that the ring?" I said after a second or two. I glanced at her hand.

"Yes! Isn't it gorgeous?"

I made a show of looking at it. I don't wear jewellery, not even the stuff that is supposed to look 'witchy'. I wear a watch, but I don't think of that as jewellery.

"It's lovely," I said, with as much sincerity as I could manage. It was a ring. I wasn't about to do cartwheels.

"Isn't it? I feel like a princess."

Aha.

"So, how long have you and Gary been dating?"

"Oh, it's all been a bit of a whirlwind, really. I didn't think he'd even noticed me. And then, all of a sudden, he proposed. It was completely out of the blue. Said he'd been looking at me from afar and couldn't hold back anymore. Love at first sight."

"How romantic."

"He took me out for a meal and then handed me this ring." She took another look at it and sighed. "Isn't it beautiful?"

"Mmm," I said, unable to agree any more than I already had. "When is the wedding?"

"In two months. He wanted it earlier, but I put my foot down. Weddings don't organise themselves, do they?" She gestured at a collection of magazines scattered over her desk. All of them featured impossibly happy men in morning suits and radiant women in white gauzy dresses. All of them had the word 'wedding' in the title or 'bride' or 'perfect.'

"I suppose not," I said with little enthusiasm.

"I mean, there's the dress, the photographer, the seating plan…"

"Surely there are people to do that?"

"He wants me to look after it. He said it was my day, so I should have it exactly the way I want it." She beamed at me. "It will be perfect. I really will be a princess. And Mr Hall, I mean…"

"Gary."

"Yes, Gary. Gary will be my prince."

I chatted for a while longer and then made an excuse to leave. I'd noticed one of the other admin assistants glancing over during the conversation, and I thought she might have something to add. As I stood up, Sophie's gaze fell on her ring again, and she'd forgotten me already.

"She wasn't the first, you know," the other woman said in a voice that was pitched at a volume that would reach my ears and go no further. She was an Olympic-level gossip.

"Sorry?"

"Sophie. She wasn't the first one he asked."

"No? Who else?" I don't know why I asked that. I wouldn't know any of the women.

"Claire, over there." She said, with a nod to a far corner. "Becky, in accounts, and Amanda in sales."

"That's a lot. Is he a bit of a ladies' man?"

She laughed. "Hardly," she said, but didn't elaborate.

"When did he ask them?"

"All in the last couple of weeks. Princess Sophie was the only one to say yes."

"Oh dear. Gold digger?"

"Nah. She's just in love with the idea of getting married. She'd marry Adolph Hitler if she could wear a white fluffy dress. Head in the clouds, that one."

"Hitler? Is Gary violent?" I was suddenly worried he might be another satyr. I didn't think so. I knew what to look for now and he really didn't fit the bill.

She laughed again. "You don't know him very well, do you?"

***

I found Gwynneth, Gary's twin sister, in the sales department. Although she looked like Gary, she had an intensity about her that made her instantly intimidating.

"No, no, no," she said in a strident voice into the phone. "The order for Jackson's was for five-hundred green screw-top and not three-hundred brown straight-rimmed. Do you want me to come down there and show you the difference?"

I watched as she put the phone down almost hard enough to break it.

"Honestly. Packing don't know their arses from their fucking elbows."

I raised an eyebrow.

"I'm sorry. It's been a long day. Point-four here doesn't help. My back hurts like buggery."

"Point-four?"

She smiled and patted her stomach. "Two point four children."

"Ah, congratulations! I can recommend something for your back. Come and see me when you have a moment."

I handed her one of my cards.

"Witch?"

"It pays the bills." It doesn't, but it's a good thing to say. "I've helped several of my local ladies with their pregnancies."

"I've heard whispers at the antenatal classes. I will pop by. Anyway, that wasn't why you're here, is it?"

"No. I'm here to help Gary. And his marriage."

She rolled her eyes. "Such a fiasco. He really shouldn't marry that girl. What's her name?"

"Sophie."

"Oh, yes. Sophie."

"Whirlwind romance, apparently."

"Did she tell you that? Silly cow. She's worked here four years, and he barely knew she existed."

I nodded. "I got that impression. Why do you think she isn't suitable?"

"You need to ask?"

"She's not a man?"

"Bingo! Gary's as gay as a box of frogs, but he won't admit it."

ROBERT WILLIAMS

"You know, even now, some people find it hard to be open with their—"

"He's only fooling himself. The entire family knows it. Even Saint Granddad had accepted it before he died."

"Saint Granddad?"

"Granddad Hall. Gary worshipped him as a kid. They were always close. Gary idolised him. The boy was always an idiot."

"You don't get on with him?"

"Don't get me wrong. He's my brother. I love him to bits. It's just this whole 'chosen one' vibe." She did the air-quotes gesture with her fingers. "He's put himself on a pedestal and the rod up his arse won't let him climb down. He's got to do the noble thing."

"Marry and have kids?"

"Yeah."

"He could marry a man and adopt."

"That isn't what granddad would've wanted, according to Gary."

"Artificial insemination?"

"Please. Gary would have a fit if you suggested anything to do with a turkey baster."

"What would it take for Gary to accept himself as he is, do you think?"

"A miracle."

***

Michael Harris was the eldest son of the other family. He would face the same dilemma as Gary in a couple of years. Unless he already was intending to marry.

"No. No wedding bells on the horizon for me," he said, in answer to my question. He laughed, but in a way that suggested bitterness rather than humour.

"Not even a possibility?"

"I'm not really looking."

"Why is that?"

"Oh, I've just had my heart broken. I can't really look at anyone else just yet.

"This condition that you boys marry seems very old-fashioned," I said, hoping to lead him into saying more.

"Tell me about it! Most of us have talked about getting the contract changed."

"Us?"

"The two families."

"But someone stops you?"

He hesitated before speaking.

"Gary." Michael's voice cracked as he said the name.

"Gary?"

"He's a traditionalist. Has to do everything the old-fashioned way." The bitterness was back in his voice. "Couldn't let granddad down, could we?"

"He's the only objector?"

Michael nodded. "Pretty much. Even his dad doesn't care too much."

"How do you get on with Gary?"

"Why do you ask?"

"Oh, no reason. Just background."

"We were good mates. Got on really well. Well, used to." He stopped speaking, his eyes on the past. "Who are you anyway? Why does Gary want your help?"

"I'm a witch."

"A witch?" He laughed, for real this time. I kept my face humourless, and he stopped. "You're serious, aren't you?"

I nodded.

"Then why is he asking for your help?"

"He wants a love potion."

"A love potion? Is such a thing real?"

I nodded. "For himself."

"So, he really doesn't love her after all. Interesting."

I shook my head. "No, but he still wants to marry her. Her or someone else. You know that."

He sighed. "Oh yes. I know. For the good of the company and all that." He looked thoughtful for a minute. "Could you make

ROBERT WILLIAMS

me one as well?"

"Make you what?"

"A love potion. Find someone new."

"Someone new?"

"I told you I've had my heart broken. I just need to find someone, alright? That's all you need to know. It doesn't matter who."

I handed him one of my cards and told him to come and see me on Wednesday.

***

Wednesday dawned, and I spent the day preparing the flat for my visitors. I also made sure the lift was working. Easy when you know the maintenance man and he owes you a few favours.

By evening, I had arranged four makeshift cubicles separated by some old sheets held up by a washing line. Each cubicle held a chair and a small table. On each table was a glass of clear purple liquid, a blindfold, and a pair of headphones.

Gary and Sophie were the first to arrive.

"Hello again," she said with a beaming smile, the giant spiders leaping around behind her glasses. "You should have told me you were the witch."

"I don't always advertise."

"I was expecting green skin and warts."

I resisted the temptation to roll my eyes. Gary didn't but she couldn't see him.

"I'm saving up for the warts."

"Aw." Her sympathy was genuine. I wondered what reason Gary had given her to visit me. Had he told her the truth that he didn't, couldn't, love her? Would he be that cruel?

I led her to one of my cubicles and put a blindfold on her. It was necessary for my plan, but it also hid the spider-lashes. I left her listening to the Broadway cast album for *Wicked* on headphones.

"Will this take long?" Gary asked, when I had him seated in his cubicle. In the other cubicle, Sophie started singing along to *Defying Gravity*. She wasn't Idina Menzel.

96

"Not long. Just be patient. I have some more people coming."

"More?"

"Love potions are expensive to make … and illegal. I'm running a risk here. I want to get all of this out of the way as quickly as I can."

"Who's coming?"

"Ah, now, I can't tell you. Client confidentiality."

"Fair enough." He nodded.

"What did you tell her?"

"Who?"

"Who do you think? Sophie. What did you say to get her here?"

He grinned. The first time I'd seen him smile. He was a handsome man when he didn't have the weight of the company on his mind.

"I told her this was a Groupon thing. Love potion witch experience."

"That's a thing?"

"There's a witch in Lewisham who does them."

Oh her. "Why didn't you go there?"

"You get better reviews."

I patted his shoulder. "Put your headphones on."

The other two arrived separately soon after and I had them seated in short order, with no one seeing anyone else.

Then I turned to the audio system. This had, to be frank, stretched my technical abilities to the maximum. Beyond the maximum. I'd had to enlist more help from Dave to get it set up. Not only would it play extracts from *Wicked*, but it would also let me address tonight's visitors. I picked up the microphone.

"Good evening." A mumbled chorus came as a reply. Something like a school assembly, but without the enthusiasm. "Shortly, I will ask you to remove your blindfolds and drink your love potions. And then I will drop the curtain. Are you ready?"

Another mumbled chorus. I'm sure one of them said, "Yes, Miss."

"On the count of three. One … two… three! Blinds off. That's it. Drink your potion."

97

I waited until I was sure they'd taken a good, healthy swig. Well, most of them.

"Now, this next part is important. Listen carefully to my voice. I want you to close your eyes and I will count slowly down from twenty. That will give the potion time to get working. I will count with you. You will feel it working as we count. When we reach five, I want you to take off the headphones and I will continue the count. At zero, I will drop the curtains separating you from your intended lovers. Got that?"

Mumble.

"Okay then. Here we go. Close your eyes." I slipped into the special tone of voice I use for hypnosis. I call it my lullaby voice. "Twenty. You feel nicely relaxed and warm, like you're lying on the beach in the sun. Nineteen. You can hear the waves lapping at the shore."

I could see them all. Gary was fidgeting a little.

"Eighteen. You feel the sand beneath your body. It feels like warm velvet on your skin."

I wished I'd started at a lower number. I resisted the temptation to rush.

"Seventeen. You are aware of my voice, and you are paying attention to everything I say. Sixteen. You know that your intended lover is sitting opposite you. Fifteen. They will be the first person you see when the cloth falls. Fourteen. You are relaxed but eager. Thirteen. Eager to meet your future mate. Twelve. Eager to meet the love of your life."

Really, I could have started at fifteen. Or maybe ten. Next time.

"Eleven. They are your soulmate. Ten. Your beloved. Nine."

Not that I was planning to have a next time.

"You are feeling calm and relaxed. Eight. Calm and relaxed. Seven. Ready for your new adventure. Six. Your new life awaits you. Five. Just a few more breaths. Remove the headphones."

I stood up, ready to drop the curtains.

"Four," I shouted, reaching for the rope. "Three … Two. Get ready to open your eyes … One. Get ready … Now," I said as I pulled on the rope and the cloth barrier separating the chairs fell away. "Open your eyes."

Gary kept his tightly closed as if he never wanted to see anything again.

"Gary?"

Gary's eyes opened suddenly, surprised to hear a voice he recognised.

"Mike?"

The moment lasted for less than a second before the two men reacted. Gary and Michael leapt for each other, and my hastily erected cubicles collapsed. Clothes began flying across my room. Sophie shrieked, and the spider-lashes tried desperately to escape.

I guided her and Gwynneth to my kitchen for a cup of tea.

***

"I guess I'm not getting a wedding."

"Not your own. Not yet. I'm sorry. I think you'll probably be going to one."

Sophie sighed.

"Your time will come. I am sure of it."

"You've read my fortune?"

"No." I didn't need to. I'd seen women like Sophie countless times. They didn't remain single for long. She just needed to lose the lashes.

"I didn't even get to drink my love potion," she said.

"You weren't meant to," I told her. Hers was in a bottle, and I'd glued the lid shut.

"Aren't they illegal?" Gwynneth asked. I'd asked her along as emotional support. For Sophie, if my plan worked. Or for Gary, if it hadn't. Or for me, if it had really gone wrong.

"Yes."

"So...?"

"So, giving love potions to two men to make them fall in love with each other would get me thrown out of the sisterhood."

"You seem very confident that we won't report you."

"You can if you want. It doesn't matter."

"Why? Oh, I see. Very clever."

"What?" Sophie hadn't worked it out.

"They weren't love potions," Gwynneth said.

"Just Ribena," I added.

"Then…?"

"They loved each other, anyway. They were trying not to—"

"Gary was trying not to," Gwynneth interrupted.

I nodded. "Indeed, Gary was trying to live to an ideal that only he believed in. All I've done is give him a chance to be happy while having the chance to blame me."

"You're a clever one, Mags. The boys can marry each other, everyone, including Gary, will be happy, and the business will stay in the families. Very clever indeed."

"I don't get paid though."

"Don't worry about that," Gwynneth said. "The company will pay up. And you'll have a healthy bonus. Maybe you could work for us full-time?"

Become a corporate witch? The idea hung in the air between us for an uncomfortable period, while thoughts of financial security, a new flat, and holidays abroad flew around my head.

"No," I said, shaking my head, partly for emphasis and partly to dislodge the temptation. "I want to be available to anyone who needs me."

"You'd be able to see them."

"There'd be a conflict of interest."

She smiled. "I didn't think you'd accept. I like to think I'm a good judge of character."

With a nod, I turned to Sophie.

"Sorry to ruin your wedding plans," I said. Sophie sniffed, on the verge of tears.

"Never mind, girl," Gwynneth said. "Weddings are not all they're cracked up to be. I've been through two and I wish I hadn't."

Sophie made a face. "But I wanted to be a princess."

"You'll be somebody's princess someday."

"And I wanted to be a mum."

Before I could say something reassuring, Gwynneth spoke

again. "Have you got a turkey baster?"

CHAPTER EIGHT

A WALK IN THE PARK

You know how it is. You do someone a favour and then they want another. And another. And another. I'd helped Jenny with Bruce a while back. It all ended well. I was happy, Jenny was happy, and Bruce was very happy. Several times a day.

Word got round, and Keeper after Keeper came to my flat with satyrs in tow. I was happy to help, and it was easy money.

And then I got a text.

It took me a few passes to get the gist of what they were saying. I'm not the best at writing, and I am the last person to call the spelling police, but I always maintain that the words have to make sense and form a coherent message. This did nothing of the sort.

Find Alice. Go now. Find the naiad. Girl danger. Take care.

What was that supposed to mean? The naiad was missing? The naiad was called Alice? There was a girl *in* danger, or the girl *was* a danger? And define 'girl'? One witch's girl was another witch's pensioner.

They followed up with a set of coordinates. On the map, they pinpointed a pond in a local park. But that was all. The coordinates and a message with no please or thank you. Just an order expressed in the most ambiguous of ways.

Incidentally, a naiad, if you didn't know already, is a type of nymph who looks after freshwater ponds and rivers. This one, by the looks of it, had dropped off the radar, and they wanted me to find her. Maybe.

As for ending the message with the words, *take care*. That bothered me. It always does.

***

London is a surprisingly green city. Not ecologically, of course. In those terms, it's a disaster, but in terms of parks and green spaces, London is doing quite well. I read somewhere that it can be classed as a forest, but I think that's stretching things a bit.

At any rate, there are a lot of trees. And ponds. And in one of the local parks, there is an ancient pond that is being looked after by the naiad the Keepers wanted me to find. Her name, possibly, was Alice.

I hadn't been to this particular park for a long time. I'd forgotten how beautiful it was at this time of year. It was a park where the council (municipal, not … you know) had created a few token flower beds at the entrances and allowed nature to do her best in the rest with a few hundred rhododendrons a Victorian plant hunter had brought from the Far East. At the right time of year, the park is a riot of colour.

It was large enough, once I was away from the café at the entrance and the playground full of screaming children, for me to not see anyone. An illusion, of course. Winding paths and cleverly placed bushes give the impression of isolation, even when you have a dozen people nearby. You still see and hear people, just not very often.

All the paths headed down towards the ponds, a series of them, ranging in size from something barely big enough for a duck to get its feet wet to one so large that the council, in more affluent and less risk averse times, had turned it into a small boating lake for a few years.

Then there was another pond, so much older than the rest of them that it pre-dated the entire park. It was the one where the naiad lived. I didn't need to be told it was the right pond. I could feel the enchantment that lay upon it as I grew closer.

I could taste it. Again, that's not the right word, but then none of the words we use for our senses cover that particular type of magical awareness, and the word *sense* is just too cheesy. *Taste* sort of works. The enchantment, surprisingly, was intended to keep people away.

Naiads, as the hurried research in my copy of *Enchantments, Ancient, and Modern* revealed, normally wanted to lure people – men – to their ponds. Randy little minxes. After having their wicked way with the men, they would lose interest. The men, however, being simple creatures, and operating with the two little brains they kept in their trousers, hung around, with loving the naiad the only thing on their mind. To them, it was more important than anything, even eating or breathing.

The repulsion spell – again not really the right word, it was more organic than a spell – that was in place around the pond was selective. It didn't work on witches and other magical types. It was strong enough, but it had no effect on me at all, and in no time, I was standing at the edge of the pond. I stood for a few minutes just breathing it all in.

"Do you like my pond?"

I turned to see a striking young woman dressed in a white gown. Both her hair and the dress billowed like they were underwater.

"It's beautiful. So peaceful."

"I thought you'd like it."

"You must be Alice," I said, while thinking about how the Keepers were a lazy bunch. She didn't need much finding, did she?

"And you," she said, with a twinkle in her eye, "must have been sent by the Keepers."

"Yes, but I'm not one of them. I'm—"

"A witch?" She laughed. "I'm old enough to have learned the difference. I suppose they must be worried if they sent in the big guns."

"My name is Mags. They wanted me to find you."

"I could have checked in with them, I suppose." She smiled. "I was busy."

I raised an eyebrow in inquiry. What could she be doing to keep her so busy? She continued to smile.

"I met my Bob on this very spot," she said, distracted. Her words triggered the ghost of a memory in me, one that wasn't mine but almost felt like it. The memory was of a man, and of love, and of a shared life. Before I could see more, the memory dissolved.

"Was he why you were busy?" I asked.

Her face clouded, and she sighed. "In a manner of speaking, although—"

An approaching voice interrupted her, and she slid into the water, without even a ripple to show she'd been here.

***

"It's rubbish," the voice announced, when it grew loud enough for me to make out words. It was a loud voice, so I could hear it long before its owner made an appearance. She had a mobile phone clamped to her ear.

I recognised the woman. Bit of a local celebrity since she'd had a big win on the lottery. It wouldn't change her, she'd said. It hadn't. She still lived in Pine Towers, the next block along from Talltrees. She still shopped in Lidl. Still worked in the pub. Still parked her new brilliant white BMW in the street outside the block.

"No, just rubbish. There's no burger van for starters, just lots of bloody plants," she said. Her name, as I recalled, was Vicky.

Trailing behind her was a small girl. She was about seven, at a guess. Well, physically, at any rate. Her body language suggested she was a lot older. There was a world-weariness about her. Mind you, I would feel old with a mother like that.

I had a few clients in her block, but Vicky wasn't one of them. Women like her would never come to people like me with a problem, nor would they admit to having one. It was other people who had the problems. I know we shouldn't judge books by their covers, but hers was a book I'd read before.

"I don't know why I came here ... Someone said I'd like it...

How the fuck would I know? Some bloke at the pub, I expect."

The girl smiled to herself and left Vicky's side to come and stand near me beside the pond, watching a pair of coots feeding their young. She was so still, like a small girl-shaped statue.

"Do you know what these birds are called?" she asked me, after a minute or so of silence.

"Coots."

"They're funny."

"Because of their white faces?"

"No. Well, a little. I just meant because of how they feed their babies."

I looked at her with a question on my face that I didn't ask.

"Watch that one," she said, pointing. "See how it stays close to the chicks and dives down for food?"

"Yes," I answered, after I'd observed the bird diving and feeding.

"Now watch the other one."

I found the mate, swimming steadily away from the chicks until it was almost at the shore in front of us. It dived under the water for a few seconds before surfacing with something small and green in its beak. Then it swam back to one of the chicks, fed it with what it had found and then started swimming back to the shore again. The other parent had fed three of the chicks in the same time.

"Perhaps the weed under the water right here tastes better," I suggested. If I understood Coot, I might have had some idea about what was going on. I had a book on how to speak to animals and birds. Good old *Groves*. Unfortunately, I'd never read the section on waterfowl. I wish I'd had; it would have helped enormously.

The girl shrugged. Her mother was still talking loudly on her phone. I heard her say something about underwired bras. The girl rolled her eyes.

"I don't understand her, sometimes."

"No?"

"No. How can she come to a place like this and not see it? All she's done is talk to her friend all the time. She might as well be at home."

***

Memories inserted themselves into my mind.

There was the pond in a glade, and I was singing a song of such breathtaking beauty that the birds in the trees were silenced, ashamed of their own mediocre efforts. There was a man, young and filled with lust, my song dragging him through the woods to my pond. I loved him for a short time, then grew bored. He stayed and eventually died.

There was another song, and another lusty young man, who I loved. He died. There was another and another and another. And the years rolled by like days and the centuries like months. The wood shrank to a park. Men came to me, loved, and died.

And then, one day, there was a man, and he was different.

***

As reality reasserted itself, I realised only a second or two had passed since the little girl had spoken to me. The mother's conversation shifted, and she was talking about someone's loft conversion. Enough was enough.

I muttered a few words under my breath, and, out of sight of Vicky and the girl, I softly clicked the fingers on my left hand. The effect was immediate, but the woman didn't notice for at least thirty seconds.

"I went to see her new place yesterday. I said to Charice, I said, it was the dog's, you know? But it was shit. So bloody poky. Even a shortarse like you would be banging your head on the ceiling there. Too many sodding stairs as well. You know? I nearly sent for oxygen. Her kitchen was full of that vegan crap. Stinks. You know? … Hello? You there? Hello?"

The phone was dead. I had toyed with the idea of setting the phone on fire with my spell, but thought a temporary loss of signal would be better.

"What's the matter with this thing?"

She peered at the screen.

"No sodding signal! Bloody place," she said. "It's like being back in the bleeding eighties with the sodding cavemen."

I raised an eyebrow at this and looked closer at her. Her make-up and clothing had given me the impression of an older woman dressing to appear younger. Mutton dressed as lamb, so to speak. But that wasn't the case. She really was young, not even thirty, but she was trying to look older. She'd succeeded, but badly. Layers of poorly applied make-up and bad clothing made her look like an older woman desperately trying to hold on to her youth.

Goodness, I was bitchy today.

"What about you?" she asked, noticing me for the first time. "You got a signal?"

"I don't have a phone with me," I lied.

She looked at me as if I had spoken in a foreign language. She just didn't understand such a concept. No phone? How could that be? "I'm having a day off," I continued. "I want to be out of contact."

"You could just tell them to fuck off."

"That isn't good for business."

"It's what I do," she said. I wasn't surprised. "They ask me to do a shift at the pub when I'm going out, and they get the rough edge of my tongue." I wondered if it had any other edges, but didn't say anything.

***

More memories inserted themselves.

Bob was different because he wasn't a beautiful lust-filled youth, but a battle-worn man who had found himself, by chance, at my pond. My song hadn't lured him here, but he appreciated it.

"You have a beautiful voice," he said. "You have made me feel happy."

I laughed, the tinkling of a brook through a glade. "You were unhappy?"

"I have seen some horrible things," he said. "And lost many friends to the war."

I could look into his soul and could see the horrors he had witnessed. I could see he had listened to the tales about this part of the wood, and had come here to die, either from loving me or by the rope that was slung over his shoulder.

I sang for him some more.

***

Reality returned again. Those memories were disconcerting. I needed to get her to stop and just talk to me instead.

"Anyway," the woman said. "I've had enough of this place. I'm going home."

"I want to stay a bit longer," the little girl said. "I like it here."

"Your daughter and I were just chatting about the coots," I added, making conversation. I felt sorry for the little girl.

"What?" The woman looked confused.

"Coots. The black birds with the white faces," I said, but she continued to look puzzled. "Ducks," I said, with a sigh.

"Oh," she said and looked at the coots for a moment. Not seeing much to hold her attention, she turned her eyes back to me.

***

Another memory.

There was a wedding. Bob was happy, and that made me happy. I left my pond and went to live in a house. It was a different life than what I had been used to, but Bob needed me.

All the same, I missed my pond.

***

Reader, she married him. What? Naiads didn't marry, did they? I had done some quick research before I came to the park, but it hadn't mentioned marriage.

The woman continued to stare at me. "I know you, don't I?" she asked, in the same tone she would have used if she'd seen me being escorted into a police car under a blanket.

"We've never met, but I think we live on the same estate."

"Forestwood?"

I nodded. I have never liked the tautologous name, but I have lived there for long enough to get used to it and I no longer wince.

"You're that witch, innit?"

I nodded again, seeing no reason to speak.

"Load of old bunk, if you ask me."

I shrugged.

"You're a witch?" I had impressed the little girl. "Cool!"

"I mean you and your daughter no harm," I said. She looked puzzled again. What had I said? "This is my day off, remember? No witchcraft."

"It don't matter. You think you're a witch. That's enough. You're off your rocker."

"Witch is just a title. All it means is that I help people."

"I don't need no help."

"I wasn't suggesting you did."

"Do you do magic?" the girl asked me.

"When I need to," I said, answering the child. "But often I don't. Common sense is usually enough."

The woman looked confused again, and I wondered if she was drunk. She could have been. She had that glazed expression drunk people have when the world has become too confusing for them. Her daughter and I continued to ignore her.

"I bet you enjoy the magic parts more! Do you have a cat?"

I thought for a moment. The cat question was a tricky one. I was still undecided whether my cat was real, but rather than debate metaphysics with a child, albeit a bright one, I opted for simplicity.

"Yes."

"Do you take it for rides on your broomstick?"

"Sorry. I don't have a broomstick." I had taken the cat for a ride on the bus once, in a cat box, to go to the vet for her injections and to be microchipped. She didn't enjoy the experience and, on the journey back, she had a seat to herself, while I sat with the box on my lap, on the other side of the aisle. I found the microchip the vet had given her on my pillow in the morning with no sign it had ever been under the cat's skin.

"That's a shame."

***

Another memory.

There was a baby. Bob was happy to be a father, and I was happy to be a mother. I loved them both dearly, but I hated the bombs that were being dropped on London. This war with the Germans had nothing to do with me or my kind.

I missed my pond.

***

The woman turned to leave the enchanted glade.

"I don't want to go," the little girl said.

Her mother stopped and turned around.

***

The memories took a dark turn. I could feel pain and heat. There were explosions.

He tried to dig me out. My legs were buried under a pile of bricks. Buried and broken.

"Don't worry, Alice. I'll have you out of there in no time. Bloody Nazis."

Another couple of bricks fell down. They barely missed him. We both looked up.

"The rest of that wall is going to come down any minute," I told him.

"Nah! It'll hold long enough for me to dig you out."

It wouldn't. I could tell. I needed to get him away.

"Bob, you have to go."

"I'm not leaving you."

"I'll be alright. You have to look after the baby."

"No."

I sang to him then, but not the song I used to lure men to my pond. I sang a different song. It was a song to send him away.

"Stop it," he said. "I don't want to go."

He clung to me, as if trying to avoid being blown away by a strong wind. He covered his ears, but it was no use. My song didn't need to be heard.

"Alice! Stop it!"

He stood up and backed away, fighting each step.

I only stopped singing when the rest of the wall collapsed, and darkness claimed me.

She'd died? I'd been talking with a ghost? Do naiad's have ghosts? What happened to Bob? And the baby? There was more. The memories flowed faster. Snapshots of life after Alice had died…

… Bob, his life destroyed once more, thought again of ending his life, but this time, could not. There was the baby. The bomb had hurt me badly, and would have killed a human, but the water pumped from the river by the firemen restored me. Barely. I was badly hurt, but I was alive. I had to go home to heal. My real home. I would miss my husband and daughter, but I needed my pond. It would heal me.

… The little girl, the child of a naiad and a human, grew older. She would sing and charm the birds off the trees. Little boys would come running to see her. I watched from afar.

And her father would slap her.

"Don't do that," he said. "Singing is bad."

The little girl grew into womanhood, met a boy, and they had a daughter. When that little girl wanted to sing, the woman slapped her daughter, just like her father had slapped her.

"Singing is bad," she said, not knowing why.

Alice's granddaughter married, although the relationship was cheerless and sad. By some miracle, they had a daughter, although the father left soon after she was born. There was no need for little Vicky to be told not to sing. There was nothing in her heart to make her want to.

Vicky! The woman standing before me was the great-granddaughter of the naiad in the pond.

I had it now. I had worked out why she was here. Alice must need someone to look after her pond after she died. She had to be dying. It had taken eighty years, but the injuries from the bomb were killing her. She wanted the little girl. She wanted Vicky's daughter. Now I knew why the Keepers wanted me here. They wanted me to stop Alice.

I watched over baby Vicky as she slept and sang her to sleep when she woke during the night. I told her stories of the pond, and of her great-grandfather. I kept her from harm from her mother's string of drunken violent boyfriends.

I did all this knowing she wouldn't remember. Same as her mother and her grandmother. They didn't remember, but I watched over them all.

Children accept all sorts of things without question. A smiling woman smelling of pondweed wouldn't seem all that out of place. How long had Alice been planning this? There were memories of her looking in on Vicky and her mother and her grandmother. Each generation, she had been working on them. All leading to today when she would steal the child.

I prepared a spell. She had to be stopped.

***

Vicky looked at me with the same distant expression she'd used earlier, like she was looking at me but not seeing me.

"Are you okay?" I asked her.

"I … I'm good," she answered, eventually. "Why wouldn't I be?"

"You looked a bit … lost." I couldn't really describe her expression.

"You saying I'm high or something?"

She had looked it, although she was perfectly lucid now.

"No, of course not."

"I don't know what business it is of yours, anyway. If I want to be off my tits, that's up to me. I'm not doing anyone any harm."

"Other than…" I began and then stopped. I would be wasting my breath. The woman only thought for herself and had no consideration for her daughter.

***

More memories intruded. Not now! I could deal with the intransigent mother or the dangerous naiad and her memories, but not both at the same time.

… singing Vicky to sleep in her cot.

… watching Vicky being taken to school and knowing she was already forgetting.

… watching Vicky at school. Watching the rot set in. Fighting. Answering the teachers back. Detentions.

… seeing her move out and get her own place.

ROBERT WILLIAMS

... seeing her spend night after night watching Hotel Hellada.

... 'nudging' the lottery balls so that Vicky would win.

... seeing her decorate the flat.

Vicky dominated the naiad's memories. Clearly, she was obsessed with her.

***

"Other than what?" Vicky asked. She was spoiling for a fight. I could see that. I would have to be careful. I didn't want her daughter to be hurt by our exchange.

I looked at the girl, who had turned back to the pond, and something niggled at the back of my mind. A faint alarm bell. There was something not right, but I dismissed the thought. I knew if I dug at it, it would elude me. Best to leave it alone. It would come to me when the time was right.

I continued working on the spell, muttering under my breath and gesturing. Ideally, I should have a circle defined, but I hadn't brought salt, so I would have to take the risk. Some of the incantation would normally require I burn some of the spell's words, but I couldn't do that without giving my plan away.

"What are you doing?" Vicky asked. "Talking to yourself?"

I am saving your daughter's life, I thought, but didn't say out loud. Then I frowned. Why didn't I say it?

Alice chose that moment to appear. I glared at her, but she smiled at me, as if I were an old friend sharing a secret.

"Look, mummy," the little girl said. "It's the singing lady." Alice must come to her as well. Was I too late?

Why didn't I know the girl's name? The answer was obvious, but I couldn't focus on it. There was too much magic in the air and I couldn't think properly. My spell would help drain some of the magic. I gestured some more.

"I know you," said Vicky. "From a long time ago."

"I used to sing—"

"You sing to us," the girl said. Her mother ignored her, and the naiad's gaze flickered in her direction before fixing on Vicky. Alice's face clouded in that split second. Anger? She was angry with the little girl? She was angry with the girl she wanted to

TALES OF AN URBAN WITCH

take over her pond?

That didn't seem right.

I focused on the girl, while I wove some more of the spell. There was a smile on her face as she stared at the naiad, a smile of innocent joy at the woman who came to sing to her at night. Her protector. Little did she know that the woman would commandeer her life and force her to look after her pond for centuries.

"Do you remember me singing to you, Vicky?"

Hesitation. "Yes."

"I told you stories."

"Yes."

"I remember your songs," the girl said, and the naiad's face clouded again.

"Bob," Vicky said.

"That's right. I told you about Bob."

"He was scared."

Alice beamed, her face a picture of genuine joy.

I looked at the little girl's face and realised the joy I saw there was different. It was genuine enough, but it wasn't at the joy of recognising a comforting face. It was the joy of imminent triumph.

And then I saw more. The calculating depths to the eyes. Confidence that didn't come from youth. Then I remembered, or rather I saw, what Alice's memories hadn't included.

Alice was obsessed with Vicky. Vicky as a baby. Vicky as a child. Vicky as a rebellious teenager going off the rails. Vicky as a young adult buying her flat. Her one-bedroom flat that she still had, despite her win. Her one-bedroom flat she shared with a fleeting succession of men, but no-one else. No-one. Certainly not a child.

Vicky had no daughter.

I realised then that the Keepers had worded their message badly. They hadn't wanted me to find Alice. They had wanted me to find the young naiad who was trying to muscle in on Alice's pond.

115

I was ready to cast the spell. I needed one thing to fix it in place, and that was its focus. The focus would no longer be Alice.

I tapped the girl on the shoulder, and she turned to face me.

"You," I said, not knowing her name. It would be good enough for the spell.

She screamed, no longer able to fool me into thinking she was a child. Something dark and evil stood in her place, before it vanished. My spell clutched at the empty air it had left behind.

***

I texted the Keepers when I got home and tore them off a strip for sending me such an ambiguous message. Because of it, I nearly put Alice in danger and almost made her lose her pond.

She was happy I'd scared off the other naiad, however. The former girl had been too quick for my spell to do any damage. It wouldn't have killed her, anyway. I don't even know if naiads could die, but my spell would have given her something to remember for a long time. At least it gave Alice time to refine her enchantment so that she could keep her away and allow me, and Vicky, to visit.

We weren't sure if Vicky would want to come back. She'd only been there today because the other naiad had whispered suggestions in her ear. The magical world had been a closed book until then. If nothing else, I hoped today had opened her eyes.

CHAPTER NINE

AMUSEMENT

You have to be a bit creative to be an urban witch. You have to be creative to be any sort of witch, but being an urban witch demands even more creativity.

Traditional witchcraft is geared around the countryside. Harvesting herbs. Watching the stars. Working with the elements. Communing with nature. All that stuff. The cities, especially London, don't have a lot of nature to commune with. Not a nature that witching lore can use easily at any rate. City nature is a weird, twisted thing you understand if you live in one, but is strange and perverse to anyone from the outside.

So, we adapt what we're taught. And adapt it again. And again. And again. The one constant in city life is its inconstancy. The one thing that stays the same, so they say, is change. We have to be creative. Earth, air, fire, and water are the same wherever you are. Sure, you might have to look harder to find them, but they are still there. There are trees in the park, that's earth, and the wind blows through them, so that's air. The ponds in the park provide water. I might have to bring my own flame, but when I do, I have all the ingredients I need.

I just have to be inventive to combine the elements that I need for a spell. I could adapt to work with a tree and a lake in a forest, or a plant on the windowsill of my kitchen and a jam jar full of rainwater.

Sometimes, however, that creativity overflows.

When I have a slow day and there aren't any people needing my help, I get a little stressed and I need a puzzle to solve. Not just something to do, but something *creative*. That might explain why today, I found myself writing.

Normally, I'd be the first to admit that my wordcraft is not the best. My spells, although perfectly functional, would never have threatened W. Shakespeare and Sons. They worked, and they rhymed, sort of, but weren't world-class poetry. To be honest, they weren't supposed to be, but their lack of polish was a bit of a sore point to me.

Today, however, the words just flowed. I was writing a story. I'd written six thousand words already, and it was barely lunchtime. I had no idea if that was good, by the way. I have a few writer friends and they were always banging on about word counts but I rarely listened. Six thousand sounded a lot, but what did I know? Would I be classed as a slacker by people who knew what they were doing? The story sounded good as well. At least it did to me, but as my mother used to say, self-praise is no recommendation.

I was writing about a family who had become estranged. The parents had drifted apart and the siblings, all girls, had gone their separate ways. They scarcely kept in contact apart from the odd phone call and Christmas card. It was a story I'd seen repeatedly on the estate. Only last week, for instance, the family along the balcony had seen the father leave. In this case, however, it was more to do with his wandering eye than the family just drifting apart. Mike always had trouble keeping his trousers on.

The chief protagonist in my story was called Kathy, and she was one of the daughters. She had taken it on herself to bring her family back together to help one of the other sisters, who was in trouble.

I knew I must reunite us all, I had written. Kathy was my viewpoint character. *Or we will surely die. The bonds that held us together when we were younger had nourished us and strengthened us. Nothing and no-one could break us. Nothing but time.*

The sisters had been very close once. They were all creative, and each had dabbled in the arts to some degree. They were also similar in age, as close as they could be without actually being born on the same day.

Time and the pressures of the world had sent us on different paths. We were no longer a family and no longer sisters. We were just individuals and were weaker for it. Had we been stronger, still been a proper family, poor Polly wouldn't have started on her dark path.

As I read it back to myself, I was thrilled. This was fantastic. I was really engaged with what I was writing. What had happened to Polly and what was her dark path? I knew, of course, the plot stretched out in my mind as clear as the road to Croydon, but that was me as a writer. Me as a reader had no clue. The suspense was killing me.

Polly had always been the quiet one, Kathy continued. *When we were children, she was always a bit stand-offish, preferring her own company to playing with the rest of us. We would be singing and dancing while she would sit under a tree with her head in a book or, more likely, staring off into the distance, lost in her own thoughts. When she had deigned to take part in our games, she did so with an air of disapproval, and she had laid out all the rules.*

No wonder she'd taken a dark turn in her life. Whatever had she done?

Reading the story to myself, I marvelled at my use of language. It didn't even sound like me, but I had written it. It was almost as if I had been writing for someone else, someone whispering in my ear who knew how to write and had more to their creative bow than a lowly GCSE grade 6 in English Language.

"Bugger," I said under my breath, as I realised what was going on. No wonder I didn't know what had happened to Polly.

"You might as well show yourself," I said out loud. "I know who you are and what you are doing."

My fingers flew to the keyboard and started typing again.

Polly stood on the edge of the cliff, and I could see tears running down her cheeks. The eight of us stood facing her, as close as we dared without spooking her into jumping.

"Polly, please," I said. "Don't do this. We love you. We don't want you to die."

She took a step backwards. One more and she would be over the edge and gone. We needed help.

My fingers clattered on the keyboard. I watched, fascinated.

Help us, please. Help us save Polly.

"Stop," I said and took my fingers away from the keyboard. They remained tense, as if about to type more. "Show yourself."

My fingers relaxed, and seconds later, my doorbell rang.

***

Calliope sipped at her tea and sighed.

"I'm sorry," she said and sounded like she meant it.

"You could have just spoken to me."

"I know, but well, old habits die hard."

"And you couldn't resist?"

She shook her head. For a woman nearly three thousand-years old, she didn't look too bad. She had perfect olive skin, dark hair, and violet eyes, the type of looks that would have given her top billing in Hollywood had she wanted fame and fortune. But she was a goddess, so why would she?

"You were a challenge. More of a challenge than I've had in recent years."

"What?" I knew my writing talents weren't the best, but that had stung.

"Oh, I'm sorry. That sounded worse than I meant."

"You're the Muse of Epic Poetry," I said.

"And TikTok," she added. "We have to keep up with the times."

"Regardless. You knew exactly how that would sound."

She smiled in apology. "Perhaps you are right, but I really meant no insult. My domain is over people who, essentially, want to write. I take their natural inclination and give it a gentle nudge. You are…"

"… not a natural writer," I finished for her. "As well as steering me like a car, you also had to give me a bump start."

TALES OF AN URBAN WITCH

"More like a tow."

I looked at her with narrowed eyes in mock anger, and we both laughed.

"You really don't enjoy writing."

"I suppose not," I said and sighed. "You wanted my help?"

She nodded. "Most of what I'd said in the story about my family was true. My sisters and I have drifted apart in recent years. Very few people believe in us now. We do what we can here and there."

"Surely Hollywood—" I began.

"Hollywood is a fickle place. Terpsichore was popular there in the eighties, just as Clio was on Broadway. Both still wear roller-boots and legwarmers and argue about which was the more successful."

"But all the films and the shows…"

"We give a nudge here and there. We whisper a word in an author's ear when he has writer's block or do some street dance in front of a choreographer looking for some moves, but that takes up very little of our time these days. At least we have our day jobs."

"Day jobs?"

"A girl's got to eat."

"Surely—"

"It all comes down to belief and invocation in the end. And who believes in the Muses these days?"

I shrugged.

"There's a few, but they're isolated, and they are hardly enough," she said.

"What happens if no-one believes?"

"Abstraction."

"What?"

"Think about it. We are the embodiment of a set of abstract concepts. Writing, dance, art, and so on. Yes?"

I nodded.

"All that is making that embodiment happen is the belief people have in us. It doesn't take much to keep us going, but when that drops too far, we lose the bodies and return to just being concepts."

"People will still be inspired?"

"But not in the same way. It won't be directed inspiration."

I wasn't sure that was so bad. Free will and all that.

"You'll die though?"

She shrugged. Gods seemed very blasé about death.

"Yes and no. Not so much dead as potentially alive."

I looked puzzled, so she went on. "If enough people believe in us again, we come back."

"That doesn't seem to bother you."

"We're gods. We pop in and out of existence all the time. We have these human bodies, but there's more to us than that. It's complicated. We'll be fine for a while, anyway. We've had asteroids named after us."

"So, why do you need me?"

"Polly."

"Polly exists?"

"Polyhymnia, Muse of hymns, bureaucracy, and literary fiction. You know, worthy stuff. Booker Prize winners. Her statues always look po-faced."

"And she's going to throw herself off a cliff?"

"In a manner of speaking. She wants to become human. I need you to help her."

***

Polyhymnia lived in a luxury penthouse apartment in Docklands on a floor that was higher than I was comfortable visiting. I live on the sixth floor, so that will give you some idea of how high we were.

"We like high places," she said when I commented on it. "Mount Helicon, for example."

"Ah, yes. That would make sense," I said, sitting with my back firmly to the window.

"My place is even higher," said Calliope with a gleam in her eye. I wasn't sure if she was boasting or if she was enjoying making me uncomfortable.

TALES OF AN URBAN WITCH

"Sister dearest, there's no need to rub it in."

Polyhymnia dressed like a solicitor. She wore a business suit in a neutral shade and had her hair wrapped around her head in a simple coiffeur that was timeless, elegant, and dull. She'd topped the ensemble with a rather severe pair of black-framed spectacles that were obviously unnecessary. Would a goddess make herself short-sighted?

"Calliope tells me you want to become human," I said, coming straight to the point.

Polyhymnia smiled at me as if it cost her money and raised an eyebrow above her glasses.

"She is correct, although I fail to see what business it is of yours."

"I'm a witch," I said. "I can help you."

"This is the business of gods. Humans, even human witches, are of no consequence in this matter."

"You think one of your own is going to do this for you? Would Hecate let you throw away your heritage? Would Zeus?" Hecate was the goddess of witchcraft. Or the witch of the gods. One or the other. Same thing in the end.

"Zeus has not been himself recently."

"He's your father. I'm sure he—"

Both sisters looked at each other, and Calliope collapsed in laughter. Polyhymnia's lips twitched at the corners.

"You know how many children Zeus has sired?" Calliope asked.

"No," I said. Of the stories I remembered, it wasn't so much the quantity, but the series of improbable things Zeus changed into in order to get his end away without his wife finding out. There were tales of horses, bulls, showers of golden coins, among many others.

"Neither do we. And nor does he."

"I have records," Polyhymnia said.

"Our father is so fertile," Calliope said, rolling her eyes. "His penis is almost a deity in its own right."

I wasn't sure if she was being serious or making a joke. I

123

looked at Calliope in shock and she laughed at my discomfort. Polyhymnia's mouth twitched again.

"You believe you can help me?" she asked when Calliope had calmed down.

"Your sister thinks so."

"She has helped some of our satyrs, sister dear."

I could see Polyhymnia bristling. "Satyrs?" she asked, her eyebrow raising. "You equate me with those oversexed little—"

Calliope laughed. "She's worked our kind, is what I meant."

I pushed on and explained the spell I had planned for Polyhymnia. "It's a transformation spell. Easier in some ways than others. I won't have to work out what to do with any extra mass, for instance."

"She is suggesting you are overweight, sister."

"You know perfectly well that the witch means that if she changed an elephant into a mouse, that she would have an elephant-sized mouse. Don't tease the mortal."

Calliope giggled.

"That's right," I continued. "I'm transforming you from a human-sized goddess to a human-sized human. I just need to make you forget, at a fundamental level, that you are a goddess."

"I have to remember what I was. That is imperative."

I hadn't planned on that, but I wasn't going to admit to it.

"Of course. All that you will forget is *how* to be a muse. Simple."

We agreed on a price – I wasn't doing this for free – and a time for the deed to be done, and I left to go home. I had a lot to prepare.

***

Three weeks later, I'd finished my preparations, and, at two in the morning, I found myself in the centre of a circle of salt in the local park. The circle was not really part of the spell as such, but a way of making sure that external influences didn't take advantage. It would be a simple spell. Most of it was just hypnosis, planting suggestions to convince Polyhymnia that she really wasn't a muse.

Although simple, it would take a long time and require a great deal of energy. That's why I had the circle, way bigger than normal, with the four representations of the elements correspondingly huge. The west water element, for instance, was one of the park's lakes.

For reinforcement, I had all eight of Polyhymnia's sisters arranged around the outside of the circle. I would have preferred them to hold hands, but the circle was just too big and the two nearest to the lake would have to have been in it, so I just spread them out around the circle. They wanted to dance, but I vetoed that idea. Their presence was enough.

Polyhymnia stood at my side at the centre of the circle, dressed, like her sisters, in the simple robes you'd see on the more tasteful Greek sculptures.

Modern clothes were out of the question. 'Modern' was a questionable concept for them. They'd lived such long lives that bustles seemed recent. Terpsichore and Clio in their roller-disco gear were positively up to date compared to some of their sisters.

"You're sure you want to do this?" I asked Polyhymnia. "Last chance."

"I am certain."

"You can back out at any time until the switch actually happens."

"I will not, thank you. Please proceed."

Ever since Calliope had asked for my help with Polyhymnia, I had wondered why she had wanted to turn human. Neither she nor Calliope had offered me a reason, and I hadn't asked. If they wanted to keep it private, then it was not up to me to pry. All I needed to know before I started was to make sure she was completely certain this was what she wanted.

In the past few weeks, I had cross-examined her, and I could tell she was very committed in her resolve. I still didn't know why she wanted to do it, but I wasn't going to stand in her way.

I looked across at Calliope, easily seen in the bonfire's light. She nodded. All the muses outside the circle were in place. It was time to start.

ROBERT WILLIAMS

I sat cross-legged on the ground and gestured to Polyhymnia to sit in front of me.

"Look at me," I said. "I am going to talk to you and to the powers at my command. You will listen and watch and do as I say. If you change your mind, just get up and step back from me, but do not leave the safety of the circle until I say it is safe."

She nodded. "I will not change my mind. I am certain of that. I have wanted this for some time."

"You know you will die?"

"Not immediately, but yes. That is part of the attraction."

Only part? I raised an eyebrow, but she didn't expand on what she'd said.

I started the spell, calling on the powers to build up the energy around us to fuel the metamorphosis. It would stay contained within the circle, bound by the salt, the four elements and the eight Muses. It would hold. I was confident about that.

While that was happening, I started hypnotising her. I'd worked out a script that should relax her and to allow me to get her ready for the switch. It walked her through an imagined forest, then along a stream to a beach and the sea. I'd thrown in a few references to satyrs and naiads as well as Poseidon to help give her some landmarks she'd be familiar with.

As I spoke, the energy rising in the circle became a blue sphere in my mind's eye. I could feel it welling up around me and within me. My awareness expanded, and I was a trinity. I was simultaneously the sphere of blue energy, the insignificant woman within it, and a microscopic focus of concentration that was about to enter Polyhymnia's mind.

The words of the script and the words of the spell that were woven into it continued to pour out of my mouth. I was as unaware of them as I would normally be of my breathing. The words were spoken, and the mechanism of the spell moved on. I was in control of the spell, but the larger part of me was elsewhere.

Part of me was the energy filling me and the sphere. I could feel it flowing like living water, around my smaller self, around

Polyhymnia, lapping at the border of the sphere, half in the air and half under the soil. It formed eddies and swirls, transient structures of infinite beauty.

Another part was inside Polyhymnia's mind, attempting to transform the godlike into the mundane. It is difficult to describe what I was doing. It was something like one of those puzzles where you slide the tiles around until all the numbers were in the right place except that the puzzle pieces were three, four, or five-dimensional. The puzzle was made of thoughts and instincts and every movement changed the puzzle. I was untangling her mind, moving the human to one side and the non-human to another.

I moved one more piece, and the puzzle shifted. Polyhymnia was suddenly in front of me. She was on the beach, where my script had left her, admiring the setting sun. A bonfire crackled above the tidemark, and she was staring out to sea.

"You just missed Poseidon," she said.

"What did he say?"

"Nothing useful. I know that, in here, he is really me. Everything is me. The sun, the sky, the sea. Even these grains of sand under my feet are me."

I nodded. "Everything except me."

"Can I be sure of that? I can just as easily imagine you."

Another me appeared. She looked blankly at me like a stranger at a dinner party.

"How did Poseidon sound?" I asked.

"He sounded like me," Polyhymnia answered.

"That was a strange thing to ask, Margaret." This was the other me.

"Do I really sound like that?" I asked, knowing that I didn't.

Polyhymnia scowled and the other me vanished.

"Are you ready?" I asked.

"Yes."

I drew a line in the sand between us. "Cross that line," I said, "and you will leave behind everything that makes you a muse. You will be human."

Without hesitation, she stepped forward, and for a moment, there were two of her.

On the other side of the line was the Polyhymnia I knew. Forbidding, serious, ultra-controlled hair and thick-framed glasses. On my side of the line was the same person, although very different.

The hair was loose and flowing, the glasses had gone, and the clothes were infinitely less frumpy. She wasn't a middle-aged librarian about to arrange her books. She was a young girl about to go dancing. The biggest difference was the smile. Old Polyhymnia had only ever twitched her lips in amusement. The new version grinned from ear to ear.

As we watched, old Polyhymnia faded into a fog of blue energy.

"Let's go outside," I said, and clicked my fingers. My focus shifted once more. It pulled away from Polyhymnia's mind and away from the energy sphere surrounding us. My focus was once more inside my own head.

We were back in the circle. The blue glow, having already done its work, was fading.

Polyhymnia, in her classical Greek dress, sat in front of me, apparently asleep.

I called her name and her eyes opened, followed by her mouth. The grin I had seen inside her mind had followed her out.

"Thank you, Mags," she said and hugged me. She'd only ever called me Margaret before. "You don't know what you have done for me. This is amazing."

"You know you're no longer a Muse?" I asked.

"I know. I'm human, I'm frail, I no longer can influence mortals. I am going to die." The grin had faded while she said that, but it returned suddenly and was brighter than ever. "But that's an awful long time away, so in the meantime, I am going to live!"

Now I could see why she had wanted to become human. Her life, her personality, had been defined by her role. And it was a role she hadn't wanted.

"For the first time in centuries, I can be myself. Hades! I can actually find out who I am now that I'm no longer an old bitch, inspiring people to write hymns and accountancy books."

It was then I noticed that the blue glow hadn't faded entirely. It had largely gone, but it was still there. I wasn't keeping it going. It should have drained away. I looked for gaps in the circle, in case something had broken it, but it was intact. Nothing had entered the circle, and nothing had left it. So, there was no external influence in here with us. It was just the energy and us.

Nothing had left the circle. Nothing. Nothing human or animal or witch or goddess. And definitely not the abstraction of a goddess, when it had been removed from its fleshly avatar.

Do you know what happens when you have a disembodied goddess floating around in a magically charged sphere containing a newly freed former goddess and an increasingly frightened witch?

No, neither do I, but I didn't think it would be very nice.

The human that had formerly been Polyhymnia was still smiling.

"I'm going to travel," she said with resolve and absolutely no concern at my agitation. "I could go back to Greece."

"It's changed," I said, distracted. The swirls and eddies in the energy field were merging, clumping together. There were fewer of them than there had been when I pulled my consciousness back to my body.

"Not where it matters, I'm sure. I could have a holiday. First one in – ooh, let me see – two thousand years."

There was only one clump of energy now and it floated down to a spot to Polyhymnia's left.

"Just one thing to take care of," she said, noticing the energy. "And then I'll be off."

"Don't forget your passport." Old Polyhymnia said, fading into solid form out of the energy. "It's a very useful document."

"One of our better works," New Polyhymnia agreed.

"I don't understand," I said. Then, my brain suddenly catching up, I worked it out. "Of course! You believe in her."

"I used to *be* her. I have to believe in her."

Her absolute belief in the existence of Polyhymnia allowed the disembodied abstraction to manifest itself in a new body.

"You knew this all along. All of you knew it. I thought this was some sort of elaborate suicide."

"Oh no. Don't be silly. We can't die. Calliope told you that."

"Then why do this?"

"Why? It's simple. After so many centuries, my human manifestation acquired its own personality, and this was at odds with the one that Polyhymnia was supposed to have."

"Stiff and starchy, you mean?"

"Respectful of the way things are done," Old Polyhymnia said. "And should be done."

"I could see that I wanted to go in two different directions. I wanted to have fun."

"While I wanted to inspire great works."

"I wanted, needed, to live my life as a full human, but my nature wouldn't – couldn't – let me."

"And you devised this scheme to get yourself separated."

"Indeed."

I dissolved the circle, and the eight muses crowded around us. One of them started singing and all of them joined in. All but one. Polyhymnia rolled her eyes and walked off.

Polly danced with her sisters.

CHAPTER TEN

CURSES!

One of the clichés associated with witches is that we curse people. If you believe everything you read, we throw curses out left, right and centre. The only thing is, we don't. At least I don't. Curses are way too much trouble for what they're worth.

But people follow the cliché and think that's what we do. They will come to me and almost the first words out of their mouths are ones asking for a curse. Usually, they want one put on someone they dislike and it is almost always over something trivial, a slight so small that, by the time they've come to see me and described the issue, they realise that they're asking for a sledgehammer to crack a nut and the session switches from cursing to counselling.

Even on that rare occasion when the curse could be justified, I always tell them to think carefully before proceeding. *Could something else solve the problem?* I ask them. *Had they considered how the curse might cause more problems than it solves?* And often, they think again and decide to abandon the idea. Maybe take their nemesis out for a drink to bury the hatchet, or perhaps have me work on a spell to make the best of a bad situation instead.

So, despite me being asked to place curses a lot, it is very rare that my client would be so determined to still want me to cast

ROBERT WILLIAMS

one. The would-be curser has to be very determined, very stupid, or have been very badly wronged.

It was difficult to work out which of those categories the man in my kitchen fell into. His name was William Peter Fitzgibbon, and he was a solicitor. He actually introduced himself to me with his full name. That says a lot.

He didn't tell me he was a solicitor, but I'd researched him after he called me, so I'd be prepared for when he came to visit. I do that these days. It avoids a lot of surprises. You can find a lot on the internet.

Bearing this nugget of information in mind, I wasn't expecting him to be stupid. I have certain preconceptions of solicitors, but they don't include stupidity. Devious, slippery, and highly paid, but not stupid. A little googling revealed he did a lot of charity work and had a 90% success rate in all his criminal cases. A man with morals and who was used to getting his own way. What did he want with me?

"How can I help you?" I asked, once I'd got him settled in the kitchen with a cup of tea.

"I want you to put a curse on my neighbour."

"A curse? You know that's—"

"I know it will cost a lot. I don't care. I will double, no, treble your usual rate."

"Thank you. That is most welcome," I said, conflicted. I was doing okay for money at the moment, but the thing with witchcraft is that it is all freelance, so I never say no to extra cash. All the same, I felt uneasy at the prospect of potentially earning from a curse. "But I was merely going to say it's a little unusual these days."

"A colleague saw another witch only last month and had a curse placed on his ex-wife. Made her say nothing but the truth. Worked wonders in court."

"That may be the case," I said, slowly. Solicitors always made me choose my words with care. "But it is still unusual."

"If you don't want the work, I can always see the witch he saw. Some woman in Lewisham, I believe." My hackles rose. Her

132

again.

"There's no need for that. I can curse whoever you want ... if it is necessary."

"Take my word for it. It is."

I sighed. He would never have taken anyone's word as gospel in his line of work. Why should I?

"Why don't you tell me about it first? What has your neighbour done?"

"They are completely unreasonable. They—"

I could see he was getting angry recalling the memory, so I interrupted.

"Why don't you start at the beginning? Take a deep breath. Relax and try to stay calm."

To my surprise, he did as he was told. He closed his eyes, inhaled through his nose, and slowly let the air out again through his mouth. He'd done this before. When he spoke, the words came out slower and measured.

"They moved in about a year ago. Seemed nice enough at the time. Friendly, but they were new money."

"New money?"

"I'm a solicitor. So were my father and his father. My neighbours' parents worked in Tesco, but he'd made a tidy fortune on the stock market by the time he was twenty-three."

"Is that a bad thing?"

"Oh, no! Don't get me wrong. I'm no snob," In my head, I disagreed, but let him continue. "As I said, they were nice enough. Anyway, they introduced themselves to us. Took us for drinks at the local. That sort of thing."

He took another breath.

"Then one day, we caught their dog doing its business on our lawn."

"Oh dear," I said, hopefully sounding more sympathetic than I felt. Dogs were dogs. They did that sort of thing.

"We laughed it off at first. They were extremely apologetic. Told me they'd keep the dog in their garden."

"But it happened again?"

"Yes."

"You saw it?"

"Didn't need to. The evidence was there. The evidence was everywhere. On the lawn. On the patio. On the roof of the shed."

Clever dog, I thought.

"We had words with them again, but their apologies sounded less believable as time wore on. Then, one day, we came down in the morning to find one of our windows smashed and there was a … a turd on our Axminster. We raised merry hell about that, I can tell you. They denied it, but we stopped talking to them soon after."

I could tell there was more to this story, so I urged him on.

"The dog mess stopped, so we thought we'd made our point, but we still kept away from them as much as we could."

"Did they talk to you?"

"They'd occasionally say hello if we saw them outside, but we blanked them."

I nodded.

"Then one day, in the summer, the kitchen flooded."

"What happened?"

"Moira – that's my wife – came home from the shops and there was water all over the kitchen floor. The taps were full on and the plug in the sink. It was amazing there wasn't more damage."

"She hadn't left it on before she went out?"

"No. She's obsessive about all that. She goes around the house before she leaves and checks everything is turned off. Twice. She even does it before she goes to bed."

"Even so—"

"It was them. The back door was wide open, and they were in the garden. They even had the gall to wave to her."

"What happened after that?"

"We tried even harder to ignore them. Things were quiet for a while. We were even forgetting about it. They would wave to us, say hello. We began to answer them."

I nodded again. There would be an "and then". I knew it.

"And then we were outside and their dog ran over to us, tail wagging, as if it was the friendliest dog in the world. Moira even crouched down to greet it and give it a pat."

"What happened?"

"All of a sudden, it just stopped and started growling at us. It was really savage. They came over to drag it back, but it terrified Moira."

This still didn't feel enough to place a curse on the neighbours, and I could see in his eyes that there was more that he needed to tell me. It was something that had scared him and made him angry enough to seek revenge.

"Then there was the fire."

That would be it.

"A fire? Was anyone hurt?"

He took a deep breath. This was a painful memory.

"Thankfully not."

"But...?"

"But we lost a lot of old family photos. My mother's diaries. Some of Peter's toys."

"Peter?"

"Our son."

"You have a child?" That made things different. If a child was at risk, there couldn't be these stupid games.

"Had. He died when he was three years old. He would have been twenty-four now."

"Your other children weren't harmed?"

"We have no others. Moira can't have any more children."

"I'm sorry," I said. A meaningless phrase. "Was there much damage to the house?"

"Not really. It started in the garage. That's on their side of the house. Aside from the car and the contents of the spare room above it, there was little damage."

"But you lost some of Peter's things."

"Do you see now why I want a curse?"

"Yes, I do." They lost their child once. Losing precious keepsakes would have been like losing him again. "But how do you know it was your neighbour who did it?"

ROBERT WILLIAMS

"It has to be them. Who else could it be?"

Oh dear.

***

I promised to do what I could and ushered him out of the door. Despite my protestations, he was as convinced that I would lay a curse on the neighbours as I was that I wouldn't. There were always two sides to every argument, and there could easily be a third in this one. I needed to find out more.

Unfortunately, I didn't have much time for my research as it was interrupted the following morning by William Fitzgibbon arriving at my door. I could tell from the way he rang my doorbell that he wasn't happy. He gave it an insistent snippy tone, which was an achievement given that he only had the one button to press. Also, he rang it six times before I got to the door.

I could see why as soon as I opened it. He was accompanied by a worried-looking woman with a purple face.

"What's this?" he demanded, pointing at her.

"I would guess this is Mrs Fitzgibbon," I said.

His face darkened and began to resemble his wife's colouring.

"Don't get smart with me, madam. You know what I meant."

"Perhaps you had better both come in."

I sat them in my kitchen and put the kettle on. Fitzgibbon looked simultaneously annoyed and distracted.

"How long have you been like this?" I asked his wife.

"She's—"

"—capable of speaking for herself," I said, interrupting him. "Mrs Fitzgibbon? Maybe you could tell me what's happened."

She looked over at her husband, who shrugged and folded his arms, sulking like a child. He twitched.

"My name is Moira," she said, smiling but timid as a mouse. She lived in her husband's shadow and didn't see the sun very often. "It happened this morning. I just woke up, and I was purple."

"You hadn't eaten anything strange, yesterday?"

"No. I had some muesli in the morning, a sandwich for lunch, and pasta for supper with William. Just a normal day. I did

TALES OF AN URBAN WITCH

my usual things. Coffee with friends, Pilates in the afternoon, volunteering at the shop. Normal things."

"I understand. Please go on."

"I went to bed at the usual time, after saying goodnight to Peter, of course."

I must have looked puzzled as she went on. "William said he told you. I still like to say goodnight to our little boy."

I reached out to hold her hand, a brief comfort for her. Why hadn't William done that? Instead, he looked embarrassed.

"Then what happened, Moira?"

"Well, I woke up this morning and went for a shower. That's when I noticed."

"She was bloody purple! Like that girl from Willy Wonka."

"And this was before or after your shower?"

"What the bloody hell does that matter?"

"It matters a lot. Someone could have put dye in her soap, for instance."

"Then I would be purple as well."

"So it wasn't that."

"It was definitely before I showered. I got undressed, caught sight of myself in the mirror, and screamed. I was so shocked."

"I completely understand. Bear with me a minute. I think I know what this is."

I fetched my dowsing rod from my toolbox. I rushed back to Moira and gave her a few passes with the rod. It told me what I already suspected.

"Definitely a curse," I said.

"No shit, Sherlock," said Fitzgibbon. "I could have told you that. You cocked it up, didn't you?"

"No. Not me."

"How do you know?"

"I haven't cast the curse yet. These things take time, Mr Fitzgerald." Also, I still had no intention of casting one. "I would suggest, given the amount of magic involved in this situation already, that we hang back on complicating this with another curse."

137

Moira looked away. Was she embarrassed?

William stared at me for a few moments, prepared to argue, but realising he didn't have enough information. He shifted in his seat. Something else was bothering him.

"Fine. How do we nullify this curse?"

"That can be tricky. Curses – and any spells, come to that – have to be undone by the witch that cast them or if the witch dies." Fitzgibbon looked up at me when I said that, so I quickly added, "Perhaps not even then. Or if we find part of the spell, a totem, if you will, and break it."

"A totem? You mean like a bloody great pole with faces on it?"

"No. That's a different type of magic. What I'm thinking of is a small thing. A pebble, for instance, or a bit of paper," I stopped, interrupted by a thought. "No. They aren't often used in curses, so I don't think we'll find one."

There was something I needed to know, but I couldn't ask. I had to be devious.

"Would you mind if I try something?" I asked Moira. "I can do a few more quick passes with the dowsing rod. It might give me some ideas."

She nodded, he fumed, and I picked up the rod again. I made some more slow passes over her, concentrating on asking my rod some very specific questions and making chit chat while I did so. I can multi-task.

"The fire must have been awful," I said to her.

"Yes, we were lucky nothing much was damaged. Just a few photos and some of Peter's toys."

"William mentioned that. It must have been—"

"He doesn't play with them much these days, of course."

Being dead does that, I thought, but said, instead, "Of course."

"He was lucky to not have been hurt," she added.

"Now, Moira," William said, as close to tender as he could manage. "We've talked about this."

"Oh yes, sorry. Silly me. I forget sometimes."

"Easily done," I said, in a reassuring tone that didn't match what I was thinking. I carried on making passes with the rod and asking my questions.

"Ah, yes, there we are," I said eventually. "I think there might be something I can do after all."

"There is?" Moira looked hopeful. Purple but hopeful.

"You're not getting any more money, you know," William said. I ignored him.

"Yes, I'll try something later. With any luck, you'll look your normal self tomorrow morning. Leave it with me."

Smiling, she got ready to leave. They put on their coats.

"You go on ahead and call the lift, Moira," Fitzgibbon said. "I want a quick word with her."

I had seen him fidgeting, so I knew what he was going to say.

"I need your help. I have a ... problem."

"Your genitals itch?"

He looked surprised. "How did you know?"

"You haven't kept still for longer than a couple of seconds. It was obvious you had an itch down there."

"Do you think Moira noticed?"

"I think she has her own problems, don't you?"

He nodded.

"You haven't...?"

"Certainly not!"

"Then this is part of the same curse."

He opened his mouth to speak.

"Still not mine", I added. "It should go when I sort out Moira's condition."

"Thanks. I will pay you, you know. More if you get rid of this damned itching."

"I know."

***

I've never been a great lover of Lewisham. When people have asked me why – and they do – I often say it's because it doesn't give me enough of a city vibe for me to think it part of London, yet it doesn't have enough of its own identity for me to think of it as a separate town.

All lies, I'm afraid. It was because *she* lived there. *She* was

Delores, another witch. Allegedly. The craft is a vocation, but it is something you have to want to do. You are called to it, you want to do it, and it is almost second nature. The desire to help overrules everything else, but the desire has to be there in the first place.

Delores had sort of fallen into witchcraft. Her mum was a witch, as was her mum, and all the mums for generations beforehand. There was a lot of genetic inertia, and it would have been hard work for Delores to not be a witch. And if there was one thing that Delores hated, it was hard work.

She was a slovenly witch and only did enough to get by. Her spells were sloppy. The I's (not of newt) were not dotted and the T's were not crossed. Just look at the curses she'd accidentally put on the Fitzgibbons. Sloppy.

There is a particular feel to magic. I don't mean that it makes you happy or sad or anything like that. There are spells, obviously, that can make you experience a type of emotion, but that isn't what I meant. A spell can have a distinctive feel to it. Perhaps 'feel' is not the right word. Here's that sense thing again. Smell and taste and feel are almost but not quite the right words, so let's try a different tack.

If I were in a big budget American TV show, I'd say that each spell – and that includes curses – has its own signature. Yes, that works. One witch can recognise the work of another witch as easily as an art expert can identify a Van Gogh or a Renoir. I was able to recognise Delores' work as soon as I saw the Fitzgibbons earlier, but my dowsing rod confirmed it.

Her signature was distinctive. As distinctive as a fluorescent pink cross painted with a six-inch brush.

"What do you want?" she asked as soon as she opened the door. She wasted no time with pleasantries.

"I need to ask you some questions," I said.

"It'll cost you."

"I need to ask about some curses you cast. You can answer me as a matter of professional respect," I nearly choked on those words, before adding, "Or I can go through your coven leader."

TALES OF AN URBAN WITCH

Her eyes widened marginally. I'd scared her with that. She glared at me, pushed the door open, and I followed her in.

***

"What do you want?" she asked again. She hadn't even offered me a cup of tea. I didn't really want one, but it would have been nice to have been asked. Witch business is oiled with tea.

"You know the Fitzgibbons," I said. It was a fact. I didn't ask.

"Yeah?"

"You cast spells for them."

"Now and then. It isn't a crime." She was correct, but only as far as the law of the land not recognising magic, something my friend Gavin despaired over. He had to be very creative with his reports sometimes.

"No, but the Council might have a few things to say."

"Depends if someone tells them."

"Let's see if we can sort out this mess. If we can remove the effects of those curses, then I don't see we need to involve the Council."

She relaxed and smiled. Well, as close as she could manage. She was one of those people who never smile nicely. She looked like she had toothache.

And just then, there was a familiar chill in the air.

"You have a ghost?" I asked.

"Who doesn't?"

I thought of Veronica, still haunting me after all these months, and shrugged.

Delores and I were standing in her kitchen. Unwashed dishes filled the sink and most of the surfaces near it. There were two stools next to the only bit of uncluttered work surface. They looked worn and dirty, so I was glad she hadn't offered me a seat.

By the kitchen door, there was the ghost of an angry little boy. He hadn't been there earlier.

"Hello," I said to him. "Who are you? You're a lovely young man, aren't you?"

"Don't waste your breath," Delores said. "He doesn't speak. Never has."

141

He was young, but old enough to have learnt to speak. Not all spirits talk, however. Either they lacked the ability to talk after they died or didn't have the energy. I didn't think that was the case. He had energy to spare. The anger flowed off him like a river. He just didn't want to speak. It happens.

"I see you are cross with Delores," I said in my best Aunty voice. "I need to talk with her. Perhaps you could come back later?"

"That won't work either. He's an annoying little sod. Got some beef with me and won't go away."

"Have you tried finding out what his problem is?" Again, I was thinking of Veronica, who only haunted me because she thought I'd been seeing her husband. She was wrong, of course. I think she is learning.

"Nah," Delores said, and threw something out of her pocket at the ghost. He screamed and vanished.

"Ghostbane? That was harsh," I said, not attempting to hide my shock.

"Yeah, I know. Mum nags me about it. On and on."

"She's right."

"You would say that. You're her favourite."

I sighed heavily. Not this again. And, yes, Delores is my sister.

"No, I'm not. But even if I was, she'd still be unhappy for me to use ghostbane."

She sighed. "It's okay. It's diluted. Mainly salt. It just scares him off. He'll be back in a few hours. Just gets the little bastard out of my hair for a bit."

I stared at her. She'd make a lousy mother. I made a mental note to deal with this later, when I spoke to mum next. For now, we had curses to attend to.

***

The Fitzgibbon house was imposing. It was one of those houses that didn't need a sign by the door telling cold-callers and bumf-pushers to go elsewhere. Anyone, anything, with an ounce of awareness, could feel how unwelcome unannounced callers would be.

I was glad I wasn't calling there. I could see Moira, looking a lot less purple, watching me from behind the curtain. I nearly waved but contented myself with a nod and pushed the doorbell on the house next door.

The woman who came to the door greeted me with a beaming smile.

"Hello," she said. "Can I help you?"

I was expecting someone a bit more like Delores, so I was taken aback.

"Ah, yes," I said, hurriedly revising my mental script before throwing it away. "My name is Mags. I'm working for your neighbours, the Fitzgibbons."

"Oh, dear." Her face had clouded at the mention of their name. "What have we done now?"

"Nothing," I said. "At least, I don't think so. I'm just trying to help."

"Are you a private detective?"

"Good heavens, no." Candour was called for. "I'm a witch."

"Really?" Her smile came back, coloured at the surprise of her starchy neighbours resorting to using a witch. "Perhaps you should come in."

***

"We don't understand them," Paul said. "We were as nice as pie to them when we moved in. They were a bit snobby, but we seemed to get on okay."

"Then they changed overnight," Stacey continued, picking up the flow seamlessly. They were *that* sort of couple.

"And all because our dog crapped—"

"Did his business," she interrupted him.

"Yes … did his business on their lawn. The little … blighter got through the fence. He's a devil for that."

"You tried to stop him?"

"Sure, we did. Short of keeping him locked in the house. We watched him like a hawk. He only did his business on our lawn, and Paul was very careful to clear it away."

Confusion clouded his face. "I thought you…"

"I what?" she asked, equally puzzled.

"I thought you'd done it. I couldn't find any when I went to clear up."

"Could he have gone next door after all?" I asked.

"No. That's not possible. I sealed off the hole in the fence. It's as tight as a duck's—"

"Paul."

"Well, anyway, it was secure. You couldn't get an ant through that fence."

"He couldn't get over?"

"No. Small dog. Overweight. Dodgy hip. Couldn't manage it. Fat bugger."

"Paul."

"Sorry."

I scribbled a note.

"We had no idea what they were talking about when they said they had dog mess everywhere. There's no way our little Pinky could have been on their shed roof. He needs help to get on the sofa." She laughed.

"What about their flooded kitchen?"

They looked at each other.

"News to us. When was this?"

"He didn't say, but you were in the garden at the time. You waved at them. They glared at you."

"Nothing unusual there."

"Interesting." Another note. "And what about your dog? It barked at them."

"Can't think … oh, hang on!" Stacy said. "I remember that. We'd just got back from obedience classes. Pinky was being super-friendly and ran over to them."

"It was lovely," Paul said. "It looked like we could all be friends again. Pinky was happy. They were happy. Everyone was … er… happy."

"But he barked at them."

"I don't know what that was about. Something spooked him. I

could tell. His fur on the back of his neck went up. Only happens when he's scared."

"He was scared? What of?"

Paul shrugged, but Stacy frowned, looking like she was about to speak. I raised a questioning eyebrow.

"Their grandson was there," she said. "He can be a little bugger with the dog. Pinky is terrified of him."

"Grandson?"

***

The Fitzgibbons' front door, up close, was as imposing as the rest of the house had seemed from a distance. It was a grand, varnished wood affair with a large brass knocker and a pull-chain doorbell. The local kids must have loved that. I didn't get as far as ringing it before Moira, from her sentry position behind the curtains, threw the door open.

"Thank goodness you're here. We were so worried. Come in, please."

"Worried? There was no need. I can take care of myself."

"Yes, but even so…" She left her unspoken explanation hanging in the air and scurried into the house. I followed.

"Take a seat," she said, as she rushed through the sitting room, gesturing at a very plush suite. "Tea?"

"Yes, please," I answered out of reflex. I didn't need one as I'd had one next door, but it was tea, and witches never refuse tea. Unless Delores makes it.

"What did they say?" Fitzgibbon asked, suddenly appearing at the door.

"Let's wait for Moira."

"Fine," he said, and said down on another sofa. There were four. I had never seen so many in one room before. Other than in a furniture showroom, of course.

Fitzgibbon had dressed casually, but it was for show rather than for comfort. He looked as comfortable as I would be in a suit of armour.

"I see Moira is looking normal," I said. "How is the itching?"

He looked around to see if Moira was still in the room, then reddened in sullen, embarrassed anger, and said, "Fine," again.

"You're welcome," I said, beaming at the lack of gratitude. "I was able to talk to the other witch."

"They'd employed a witch as well?" Moira asked, returning to the room with a tray laden with a teapot, milk jug, cups, and saucers. All matching. There were biscuits on a plate. A matching plate, no less.

"No, they—"

"I knew it. Petty minded people," Fitzgibbon said, not listening. "They're just the type to—"

"If you'd let me finish," I said, raising my voice. "Your neighbours did not employ a witch. They are not the type to do so, and what's more, they are not petty."

The Fitzgibbons looked at me, stunned, and temporarily quiet.

"I have just spent a good deal of time talking to them," I added, taking advantage of their silence. "And I know they have had nothing to do with your recent misfortunes."

"Well, they would say that, wouldn't they?" said Fitzgibbon.

I laughed. "Yes, they would, because it's true. I'm a witch. We can tell if someone is lying." We also have several silent spells that we can invoke. I'd used one next door. Paul and Stacey hadn't lied to me. I'd put a long-lasting version of the same spell on the Fitzgibbons yesterday, with this very conversation in mind.

"They weren't responsible for what's been happening."

"Well, it wasn't their dog who threw shit through our window, or turned the taps on in the kitchen, was it?"

"No. It was … someone else," I said. I nearly said something else. Terminology is always a little hazy in this sort of arena.

"Who?" Moira asked, with a tinge of desperation in her voice. "I mean, they also set fire to our house. They could have killed little Peter."

"Moira." There was a warning in his voice.

"I'm sorry. I forget. They could have killed him … if he were still alive." The last words came with reluctance.

TALES OF AN URBAN WITCH

"Would it be possible to see his room?" I asked.

"Peter's room?" Moira smiled, almost jumping to her feet in eagerness. Her husband looked wary. He wanted to object, but had no good reason. He trailed behind as Moira led me upstairs.

"We've cleared up the fire damage," she said. She was chattering. The request to see her son's room had released a blockage. "Luckily, we'd kept the wallpaper. They don't make it anymore, but we had lots of spare rolls. Thomas the Tank Engine. It is – was – Peter's favourite."

I could feel the presence grow with each step. There was something here, and it was filled with hate.

The room was relatively small, but still large, as you'd expect a nursery to be in a house of this size. It was bigger than my kitchen, and there were toys in every nook and cranny. They hadn't just bought all this when Peter was alive. And you wouldn't have known there had been a fire.

"It's a lovely room," I said. It was something to say, while I listened and looked with other senses. My mouth has a mind of its own and is quite capable of operating independently.

"Our little Peter's oasis," Moira said.

"Why do you need to see our son's room?" Fitzgibbon asked, always the solicitor.

"I needed to check something." The presence was powerful. It was here and angry. Very angry,

"Those nasty people next door could have destroyed this," Moira said.

"Is that why you had Delores place those curses?" I asked.

Fitzgibbon jumped, but Moira didn't even flinch. To her, it had been the right thing to do.

"Of course. They could have killed our little boy."

The presence darkened, its anger deeper and familiar.

"But the curses were badly worded, weren't they?"

"I was very clear. She just isn't very good."

I could have told her that. "What did you ask for?"

"That they be cursed, obviously," she giggled.

"And how did you specify 'them' exactly?" I could see

147

something moving at my left-hand side. I ignored it. I needed to keep the pressure on Moira. "What did you say?"

"I wanted the people that were responsible for the fire to be hurt, but she got it wrong. She hurt the people who had been hurt by the fire."

If I was right, I think Delores had been spot on, for once. She hadn't got her curses wrong in the slightest. Not this time, at any rate. I had a few more questions to answer before I could be certain. I turned to my left to see what had been moving, and saw him, the ghost of the little boy I'd seen when I'd visited Delores.

"Hello," I said to him. Maybe I would get more response here. "You must be Peter."

"You can see…?" Fitzgibbon couldn't finish the question, but I nodded in answer.

"I am a witch, you know." That should be explanation enough. We can see ghosts if they are powerful enough. We can guide them to the afterlife. I mean, I don't. I can, but I don't. I generally let Agnes do that. It's her thing.

Peter was a powerful ghost. You wouldn't have known he wasn't among the living. He looked solid. He looked focussed. He looked alive.

A soft toy hitting me in the face interrupted my thoughts. It could have been a bear. Difficult to tell. Moira picked it up and cuddled it.

"Peter, don't do that," she said in that ineffectual voice that mothers used when they had read too many books on parenting. A stuffed cat hit her in the chest, but she didn't let go of the bear.

"Peter!" Fitzgibbon said, sterner. He expected to be obeyed. He wasn't. A Thomas the Tank Engine caught him on the ear. "You little bastard. Stop that." More toys rained down on him.

This felt like a scene from *Carrie*. I hoped the Fitzgibbons hadn't bought Peter any toy knives. Or a tricycle. Different film, but … you know.

There was suddenly another presence in the room. Agnes. Someone was going to the afterlife, but worryingly, she was carrying a lot more wool than she'd need to clothe a little boy. There looked enough for three adults. I tried not to wonder what she was knitting me.

The door slammed shut, and the light started flicking on and off, the switch operated by an invisible hand. Sparks flew. The connections were dodgy, obviously. How long had tiny ghostly fingers been feeling through the wall and tugging at the wires?

"I'll turn the lights off at the mains," Fitzgibbon said and tried the door. It didn't budge. Then he put his finger on the light switch, trying to stop it flicking. He slowed it down but didn't stop it. He was fighting twenty-one years of hatred.

It was time to take action.

"Moira," I said. Trying to remain calm. "You can end this." I didn't know for certain what she had done, but I could have a reasonable guess. She'd made a colossal mistake, but it was borne out of utter despair.

"End what?" she answered, smiling. Moira wasn't seeing the danger. "He's just having fun. He's only a little boy. You were a child once. Didn't you play?"

I looked at Fitzgibbon, who shook his head, still trying to stop the light switch. He pulled his finger away, replacing it with a finger on his other hand. He grimaced.

This must have been how the fire started. Loose wires and an overused switch. The Fitzgibbons – William at least – must have suspected, but it was easier to cast the blame elsewhere. Easier than accepting the truth. Moira had been, still was, in a dream. William had been in denial, but was coming out of it now.

"Moira, you need to let him go."

She ignored me.

"Moira … love," He'd hesitated. It had been a long time since he'd called her that. "Peter needs to move on. It's been twenty-one years. We need to say goodbye."

"But he's only a baby."

"No," I said. "He's a toddler. The ghost of a toddler, and he's been kept here, trapped here, for far too long."

She ignored me, but Fitzgibbons turned to face me.

"Trapped?" He looked puzzled. Obviously, he didn't know.

I glanced at Moira before answering. She was still in motherhood-la-la-land, lost in her thoughts, cuddling the bear like it was a child. We would not get any sense out of her just yet.

"The curses weren't the first time she visited Delores."

"What?"

"Shortly after your son died, she went to see her." Delores had told me some of this, the parts where she hadn't done anything dodgy. I had worked out the rest. "You'd thrown yourself into your work," I said. "Your way of coping. Only you hadn't noticed that Moira wasn't coping as well as you were."

He looked at her with remorse. Was it too late to salvage this?

"She'd heard about Delores and had gone to see her for help." This is what Delores had told me. "Without her knowing, she took little Peter with her." Ghosts of children can hang around their mothers for some time after death. The poor little things don't know they're dead and they cling to what is familiar.

"Delores no doubt gave some spiel about Peter's ghost wanting to give her a great message."

"She said he wanted to say he loved his mummy," Moira said, distracted. "I just needed to hear him say it."

"So, she let you," I said. "Only Delores messed it up. Instead of boosting his presence for a little while, for you to see him, and him to say goodbye, she bound his spirit to this world." She always was sloppy, even as a girl.

Spirit boosting takes a complicated set of spells. You have to account for a lot. She probably used an adult-sized spell and hadn't factored in the enormity of Moira's grief.

"And he's been stuck here for over twenty years. Seeing you grow older and seeing children, other people's living children, grow up.

Fitzgibbon yelped at that point and pulled his finger away from the light switch. The light pulsated ever faster. Smoke curled up from the switch. It would be long before it caught fire.

Peter's ghost smiled, on the verge of triumph. What would happen when his parents died? I wondered. Would he move on as well? Was that the point of this? Or was it just revenge?

The smoke from the light switch had been slowly thickening, and suddenly, with a theatrical whoomph, the switch burst into flame. We would not have long before the wallpaper caught.

The flames jolted Moira out of her revery.

"William!"

"Try the window," I said, then looked. "Bars? You put bars on a nursery window? What century are you people living in?"

"I could smash the window anyway and let some air in."

"You'll feed the fire. No. Keep trying the door."

I mentally reviewed my scant knowledge of binding spells. There were lots of them, but they all needed some sort of totem, a lock of hair, or a vial of blood, something of the deceased that could act as a focus for the spell. I looked around the room, but there was no conveniently obvious blood-soaked shrine.

Then I saw it. The bear. The old and well-loved bear that Moira was cuddling so hard. The one that Peter had thrown. Only he hadn't thrown it *at* me. He had been trying to give it to me.

"Moira," I said, trying to keep my voice calm. The flames were spreading up the wall. "Give me the bear."

She looked at me like I had asked to saw her own leg off.

"This is the bear he had been holding in his arms when … when…" She couldn't complete the sentence.

"When he died?"

She nodded.

"Did Delores use it?"

She didn't answer. Her eyes were unfocussed, lost in a painful memory.

Fitzgibbon stared at his wife. "Moira? Did she use the bear?"

She nodded. A minute twitch of her head.

"Moira," I said again. "We need to let him go. You have to give me the bear. It's keeping him here."

"No."

I made a grab for it, and she pulled the bear out of my reach, but brought it close to her husband. Before she knew what was happening, he grabbed the bear out of her hands.

"Give it back," she said.

"Moira, no." He put his hand on her shoulder. Not roughly. Just enough to keep her away from the bear.

The ghost stepped forward, and Agnes paused with her knitting.

"Daddy?" There was hope in the word.

"Peter?"

"Do it, Daddy."

Fitzgibbon nodded at his son's ghost, and keeping Moira at a distance, he thrust the bear into the growing flames. It started burning immediately. He held it high until the fire was well established and then dropped the bear in a metal bin.

"No!" Moira screamed. "My little boy!"

She ran to grab the bear from the fire, but Fitzgibbon held her back. She was too late anyway. The spell that had been contained in the bear was now broken.

All at once, Agnes shook her pile of knitting. What had been three adult-sized garments was now something a lot smaller. She offered it to the small ghost, who held up his arms to be dressed.

Moira continued sobbing long after he left, but Fitzgibbon held on to her and led her away, as I put the fire out. I don't think they had been as close as this for a long time. I would call in on them over the next few weeks to help them heal, but I was quietly hopeful.

Peter's garment turned out to be a cute little bear costume. Quite appropriate, really.

CHAPTER ELEVEN

A CAT'S TALE

Mrs Samson's house was spotless. Her fridge and freezer were full to bursting with meals, and her washing basket was empty. In short, there was nothing for me to do unless the old lady called down for help, but as she was sleeping peacefully, I settled down with a book.

I knew to bring one with me. I had looked after Mrs Samson before. Carol, her daughter and full-time carer, was very diligent, and I think she looked on her respite days as some sort of assessment of her caring abilities rather than as a break. I felt like she was expecting a report card when she returned. She needn't have worried. She was a credit to her mother.

Mrs Samson needed very little looking after when I covered for Carol. I think she enjoyed the break from being someone who needed to be cared for. So, I fussed over her for a bit, made her tea and chatted. I did whatever I could to make the old lady's life a little easier, but, for most of the time when I was there, all I did was read while she slept.

Today, I had brought a small collection of poetry and sincerely wished I'd brought something else. An old shopping list, perhaps, or a phone book. I tried to like poetry. I understood what it was meant to do. It's a kind of snapshot of someone's emotions, a situation, a mood, a beautiful description of a moment. If someone else reads it out loud, adding nuances and meaning that the reading voice in my head couldn't manage, then it comes alive and has more magic to it than the most powerful spells, but when I read it, it's just a collection of words.

I'd brought the book with me so that I could give myself a good run at mastering it. I was trying to get my inner voice to read a poem as if it were Richard Burton and, although the voice had his timbre and depth, he might as well have been reading the weather forecast. It is impossible for me to read something with meaning when I can't see that meaning in the first place.

It's funny. Spells are poems of a sort, and I can manage to both read and write those with no trouble at all. The meaning in a spell is obvious, however, and applies to the fundamental nature of reality. A spell is there to get a job done. I don't have to appreciate it.

Richard Burton's voice was struggling with a poem that seemed to have a rhyming structure similar to a rap song. Bored, my imagination decked him out in a tracksuit, a backwards baseball cap and a mass of bling. He didn't look happy and gave me a distinctly sour look when asked to rhyme melon with Armageddon. He held up a diamond-encrusted shoehorn meaningfully.

My imagination gets a bit carried away sometimes.

Just as I was about to make a second attempt at the poem, a commotion at the window disturbed me. I could hear frantic tweeting and branches slapping against one of Mrs Samson's windows. Glad of the distraction, I abandoned the book and walked over to the window.

The commotion had died down by the time I reached the window. A small tree or bush of some kind – I'm no expert on botany, as you can tell – was growing near to the glass, but if that was the source of the noise, there was no evidence of it. A robin hovered close by and looked me in the eye, unphased by my presence and making the same tweets I had heard just now. It was too small to have caused the rest of the commotion, however. I looked but could see nothing amiss and the bird flew away. I returned to the sofa and the dreaded book of poetry.

I'd just started on another poem. This one described the lonely existence of traffic lights. Honestly. It had just entered another cycle of red-amber-green when the commotion started up again.

This time I was quicker, but the noise stopped again just before I reached the window. The robin wasn't there and there was nothing immediately visible. I looked more carefully out of the window and at the tree outside. There was nothing wrong with the tree by the window, nor looking upwards. Looking downwards, there was also nothing – wait, there! Two small black triangles were just visible if I pushed myself right up against the glass and looked down. Ears! There was a cat at the base of the tree. No wonder the robin was upset.

I opened the window for a better look and the cat looked up at me. It was mostly black with a white bib and socks. I've always thought that an odd description for a cat. Cats don't wear clothes, least of all, bibs and socks, but if cat owners want to describe their charges like a nineteenth-century schoolgirls, who am I to argue? The cat also had a white muzzle, which was generally something schoolgirls of that era didn't wear, not even in Dickens's wilder fantasies.

I shooed it away. It gave me a look of startled innocence before it ran off onto Mrs Samson's bins and over the fence into her neighbour's garden. It wouldn't be back for a while.

I settled back onto the sofa and returned to the contemplation of the sad life of traffic lights. I couldn't read further, however. Thoughts of the cat and the bird troubled me.

Had that been Mrs Samson's cat? I didn't think so. She'd never mentioned one, and I didn't remember seeing any cat paraphernalia in the house. I checked the kitchen but there were no bowls, no litter tray and, therefore, no cat. I felt relieved and made myself a cup of tea to celebrate.

I'm still not entirely convinced my cat is real. I haven't asked anyone else if they can see her. I was worried about the answer. If the answer was no, then I had deluded myself really well. If the answer was yes, then I had a cat that had appeared out of thin air.

She ate real cat food and made use of the litter tray I'd bought her, so she had to be a real cat. Unless I was eating the cat food myself, and if that was the case, then I didn't want to think about the litter tray.

Anyway, I digress. The cat in Mrs Samson's garden was real and had been chasing the robin. I had chased it away. Job done. The robin was safe. Dismissing the thoughts, I settled back on the sofa and selected another poem. This one, ironically, was about cats. Or maybe it was about drugs. I wasn't sure, but catnip featured heavily.

***

I must have dozed off, but a third bout of commotion woke me. The tweeting, the fluttering and then the rattling of the branches in the tree. I dashed to the window once more.

The cat was in the tree, level with the window and staring at me with that wide-eyed butter-wouldn't-melt look that cats and small children have perfected. It was doing nothing wrong. What was the matter?

I tapped on the window. "Get down from there!"

It was unmoved by my shout and continued to be the picture of innocence. I could almost see a sense of amusement on its face as it looked back at me.

The robin was fluttering around again, darting at the cat and then flying away. The cat, oddly, was paying it no attention and was, instead, fully focussed on me.

"Get down!" This time I accompanied my shout with a bang on the glass, heedless of whether I would wake Mrs Samson. I didn't think to open it this time. I was still a little dozy from my nap. At least the window didn't shatter. The cat scrambled down.

I looked over to the footpath where I expected to see the cat run away and was surprised to see another one. This cat seemed younger and the innocent look it was giving me was more genuine than the one from the other cat. Its eyes were the enormous bowls of surprise that kittens had for the world. It was a little older than a kitten but had yet to gain the disdain that adult cats had for the rest of the world.

TALES OF AN URBAN WITCH

And then something at the base of the tree distracted the innocent cat, and the spell broke. The older cat came scampering out. Both cats ran away, but not before I saw the reason for the cats' interest in the tree and the robin's frantic despair.

In the older cat's mouth was something small and pink.

It all made sense. The robin had a nest in the tree and the cat had been raiding it to steal the robin's fledgling. All at once, I felt anger. Anger at myself for not realising earlier and not opening the window, anger at the robin for building its nest in such an easily accessible place, and anger at the cat for being an evil little bugger. It hadn't been just a case of cats being cats. I could swear that this had been a planned exercise. The older cat had brought the younger one along to distract me long enough for it to grab the bird.

Saddened, I turned away and went to tell Mrs Samson why I had been trying to smash her window.

***

My cat – or rather the cat that chose to live with me – leapt onto my kitchen counter as I was preparing a spell. I do all my spell preparation in the kitchen. I don't have the space for a separate spell-casting-room. I don't know anyone who has. Urban witches don't tend to have a lot of space. You try living in a large city on a witch's salary.

"You'd better get down from there, missy," I said. The cat didn't have a name. I'm sure she had her own name for herself, and I didn't dare try to foist a human name on her.

She miaowed at me.

"I know it smells good; it's meant to." It didn't to me, but then I wasn't a cat. "But it's for a spell and I don't want to cast it on you."

She miaowed and jumped off the counter in a sulk. It was odd how easily I could interpret her moods.

"This is for some very naughty cats," I called after her. "You really wouldn't like what this would do."

From the hall came something like the feline equivalent of 'whatever'.

***

A few days later, I saw the cats again. They were sitting at the front of the house next door, the older one looking bored and the younger one surprised.

I made all the pss-pss and kissy noises that cat lovers make. "Oh, you are a pretty one, aren't you?" I said in my sweetest voice. The cat responded by purring and rolling over so that I could rub his belly. If they think you are going to feed them, you are, temporarily, a cat's best friend.

The younger one dashed over and I fed both of them my specially prepared cat treats, all the while speaking to them in my cat-lover's voice. They were putty in my hands.

The little fledgling would be avenged.

***

On my next trip to Mrs Samson's house, I spent some time in her small back garden. I found a deckchair in her shed and chose a prime position to sit and read. It wasn't poetry this time. Instead, I was re-reading a book on talking to animals. Grove's *Basic Treatise on Animal Communication*. Cats were in the advanced edition. I'd glanced through that a few times. The cat language was simple, but the difficulty was in getting them to deign to understand. It's a bit like trying to speak French to Parisians, but not so difficult.

Just as I reached the end of the section on small birds in basic *Grove's*, the robin appeared and perched on the rim of a small plant pot.

"I'm sorry for your loss," I said, choosing words and emotions the robin would understand.

The bird tweeted its thanks quietly and looked at the ground.

"I have made sure that cat will not disturb you or any other bird again."

The robin looked at me and tweeted a question.

"You will see," I answered, a trifle smugly.

***

Later that day, I sat by the window and sipped at a cup of tea. I watched as the robin pecked away at some mealworms I'd put out for him on the ground. He was very focused on the food and wasn't paying attention to the rest of the garden.

It took half an hour for there to be a flicker in the shadows and the appearance of familiar black and white shapes from behind a plant pot. You thought I'd poisoned them, didn't you? Well, you were wrong.

The adult cat was intent on the bird and took great care to hide behind every piece of cover on his approach. His younger accomplice shadowed him inexpertly.

I watched them as they stalked the bird, getting closer and closer without it reacting. Eventually, they hunkered down, lying on the ground, their heads low and hidden from the robin by some plant pots. Well, the older one was hidden. Almost. If the bird had been looking, it would have spotted the cat's tail twitching above the pot and one of its eyes peering around the side. The robin didn't look up, though. Its attention was fully on the mealworms as he pecked away at them. The younger cat thought it was hidden behind a pot that would have been too small to hide the robin had the situation been reversed.

Neither cat noticed the mist gathering above their heads, their attention fully on the bird in the middle of the lawn. Nor did they see me watching from the window, a cup of tea in my hand.

The cats continued to watch the robin, each movement as he pecked at the pile of food, causing a twitch in their ears or the tips of their tail or the muscles in their legs in preparation for them to pounce. The mist above their heads grew thicker, like smoke from a small fire.

As if on cue, the robin stopped pecking at the food and stood upright. The cats, sensing the time for action was impending, tensed even more, and I realised the spell that I had put into place when feeding them my special cat treats was about to kick off.

I just needed to utter one word for the spell to be completed. One more word and…

"No!" You might guess that wasn't the word.

The clouds that had been forming above each cat had

suddenly dispersed. That should not have happened. The clouds were good to be in place for a few hours and my word would have fixed them in place.

The cats should have been followed by their own personal storm clouds, unleashing rain and lightning on them whenever they felt the need to terrorise small birds. Each time they pounced, they would be soaked. Each fledgling they stole, they would be zapped. That had been the plan. They would probably not have learnt anything from the experience, but they would have been suitably punished.

I'd debated long and hard with myself as to the suitability of my solution. Cats were difficult creatures, selfish and notoriously resistant to reason. I could have easily constructed a spell that would have killed them, but I don't kill. I have killed before, but I didn't think imaginary witches counted. There's a vast difference between that and killing a cat. Cats are cute even if they can be evil.

My spell should have worked. It would have helped local birds, even if it felt like a sticking plaster for a broken leg. It really should have worked.

What had happened? I stood up. I needed to go out to the garden to investigate, rehearsing the words for a rarely used forensic spell. I was sure I'd worded the rain spell correctly. Had I forgotten something?

Mrs Samson had an odd-shaped house. Although the living room looked out over the garden, there was no access, and so I had to go all the way to the kitchen and out the side door before I could reach the garden. It wasn't far, however. I'm not the fastest of women, but it would only take me thirty seconds, tops.

A couple of steps from the window, however, and I noticed it had become very dark. A few more steps and I heard what sounded like rain on the window. As I entered the kitchen, I could have sworn I heard thunder – and was that laughter? – but as I opened the back door, there was nothing but brilliant sunshine.

And my own cat, looking smug, and sitting in the middle of a dry circle on an otherwise soaking wet lawn.

***

"What did she say?" I asked the robin. I had tried talking to the cat, but she ignored me, pretending to not understand.

The bird tweeted a reply.

"'Who?' What do you mean 'who'? The cat, of course. I saw her come and speak to you before she left."

More tweeting.

"Yes, her. Come on, spill. What did she say?" I'm paraphrasing, of course. The Robin language is a little more formal than that.

He sang a longer answer and flew from the Christmas-card-cutesy pose on the fork handle to the arm of the deckchair and then to a nearby twig as he did so.

"The cats won't bother you again? Why? What happened to them?"

The song sounded like a little like laughter this time.

"They got wet? My spell worked all along?"

That was definitely laughter. Ever been mocked by a garden bird?

"Not my spell? Okay, so not entirely my spell? Borrowed? By whom? And what's my cat got to do with this?"

Tweet.

"Okay. Not *my* cat. I know I don't own her."

Another laughing tweet.

"She *is* a cat, right?" She had arrived in very peculiar circumstances. "She's more than a cat?"

Chirp. I wasn't going to get more out of the robin on this subject. He flew away.

***

When I got home, the cat was curled up on the sofa, fast asleep, with nothing to suggest that she'd even been outside, let alone a couple of miles away and summoning storms to scare wayward bird-scarers.

She woke when I entered the room and demanded food. I can understand enough Cat to know what she wanted. Any attempts on my part to find out what had happened resulted in stony silence.

"I will find out what you are, you know," I said to her.

"Miaow."

CHAPTER TWELVE

DREAMER

Helen had an issue with witchcraft. When she'd called to book an appointment, she told me at least three times that she'd never met a witch before and she didn't know what to expect. When the day came for her visit, I was tempted to answer my door wearing severe make-up and a black cape, but thought she wouldn't appreciate the joke, so I went for something a little more mumsy.

She lived in Spinnaker Heights, another block on my estate, so she didn't have to come far. Five minutes as the crow flies, but given that her crow would have to walk between the blocks and use the less than reliable lifts, she took twenty minutes.

We chatted in the kitchen while we drank tea. You know me well enough by now to know that's my usual ploy to get someone settled enough to speak. Helen was still tense, however, so I took a few minutes to tell her about some of the more mundane problems I'd helped people with.

It must have worked because she was a lot calmer by the time I'd finished speaking, although I think I did too good a job because, when she eventually started talking about her problem, she seemed convinced it was out of my depth.

"This is going to sound odd," she said.

"Trust me, I am a witch," I said. "Odd is my middle name." It isn't, actually. It's Jane, but that's not important right now.

"Well, if you're sure. I mean I could always go to the woman in Lewisham if it's not something you can help with. She'd dealt with ghosts and werewolves, she said."

I grimaced at her mention of Delores, and thought about introducing Helen to Veronica, the ghost of my would-be murderer, or to my cat that used to be an illusion or show her the spot in my lounge where two vampires had died, but I decided to just reassure her I would be fine and that she should go ahead when she was ready.

"I've been having some odd dreams," she said, and carried on when I nodded. "About my fiancé."

She paused, waiting for a reaction, but I just nodded again.

"They're rather erotic dreams."

"Well, that's perfectly normal."

An expression of doubt crossed her face. "We do things in those dreams that I would never even believe were possible in real life. Literally."

I wondered briefly if she meant literally in the classical way, and she really had never imagined the things she saw in her dreams. Or did she mean the modern way where literally didn't mean literally at all? Studying her concerned face, I decided on the former.

"How do you mean, not possible?"

"Parts were fitting together in my dream that I didn't even know could fit together."

"Interesting. Have you tried any of these out with your fiancé?"

Her expression changed to scandalised. "Heavens no! He would want to know where I'd learned all these things and, besides, some of them really were physically impossible."

"How so?"

"Well, as far as I know, Dennis only has the one normal-sized penis."

My eyebrows raised. "Have you talked to him about the dreams?"

"No, I can't. They would make him worry that I'd been

TALES OF AN URBAN WITCH

messing about with another bloke while he's away."

"He's away?"

"Yes, he works on an oil rig. He's been away for nearly six months. He's due back next week."

"And you've not…?"

"No. I couldn't. I'm just not that sort of girl."

I could see she was telling me the truth. At least, the truth as she believed it. I worded a question in my mind, but before I could open my mouth, she spoke again.

"And I know you're thinking I'm getting these dreams out of frustration, but I'm not. Sex isn't as big a thing for me – for us – as it is for most other people. I know it sounds corny, but when we're together, we make love. For us, it's quality rather than quantity that's important."

I could see that she meant it and the words she spoke weren't just words. Whether her fiancé shared that view was another matter. Call me cynical.

"Okay, fine. So, you're here to get me to interpret the dreams?"

"No! I don't need to know what they mean."

"Stop them, then?"

She nodded. "Yes, please. They are rather disturbing. And …"

And. This was a word ripe with possibilities. The one Helen had uttered was followed by a hesitation and that meant that something else was coming. Something big. It was probably bigger than she had talked about before. I wasn't wrong.

"There's something else?"

"I'm pregnant."

***

I'm a great advocate for taking one problem at a time. Often the solution for one would lend itself nicely to solving the next. I wasn't sure how that would happen in this case, but I thought I would start with the dreams. If nothing else, it would give time to think about the baby.

"Well, the dreams started out fairly innocent, really. I'd be with Dennis somewhere. At the theatre or out for a meal. Those were lovely. I felt more in love with him in those dreams than I have done since he left for the rig."

I made notes of this. There's usually a heavy element of symbolism in dreams and I would have to analyse every element later. *Dating dreams. Love. Dennis. Falling out of love?* She may have seen me.

"Oh, don't get me wrong. I definitely still love him and want to marry him, but you know the saying 'absence makes the heart grow fonder'? Well, it doesn't. It can't. Not with me, at any rate. I had to get on with my life without bursting into tears every five minutes. I needed to keep control."

I nodded, but made another note. *Absence makes the heart grow meh.*

"Then what happened?"

"Well, those early dreams just ended pretty much there. We'd go out on a date. I'd feel all loved up, and that was it."

I nodded to indicate that she carry on.

"After that, the dreams would get a little fruitier. We'd go home, and he'd start trying it on. I'd resist and the dream would end, but in the next dream he would get further with me."

"So, there was continuity?"

She looked puzzled.

"Each dream built on the last?" I asked.

"Sort of. It was like Dennis was able to learn from the last dream."

I wrote, *lucid dreaming?* Then I thought for a moment and wrote, *External control?*

"You were aware of your dreams?"

"I usually am. Normally, they involved me going to work or driving to Lidl. Nothing exciting."

"So, presumably your dreams progressed to where Dennis would take you to bed and then you'd make love?"

"Again, sort of. Although it was Dennis, it didn't feel like Dennis. You know? It didn't feel like making love. It just felt like sex with a stranger. Not that I'd know what that was like, but me and Dennis know each other. We know what we like."

"He knows what turns you on."

TALES OF AN URBAN WITCH

"We know what we like," she said firmly.

The dreams take her out of her comfort zone, I wrote. I thought that maybe a dream-master or even another satyr was involved in some way.

"But somehow, Dennis in the dream was able to make this odd sex seem normal so that I'd start off not wanting what he was doing but ended up begging him for it.

Another note, *Manipulation.*

"Was that when it went odd?"

She nodded. "More or less."

"And how odd? You mentioned a second penis."

"That was one time, yes. That time was like there were two men in bed with me." She hesitated, and I reassured her I couldn't be shocked. "It was as if there was him Dennis in front and another Dennis behind me, but there was just him. In any case, I was lying on my back on the bed so no-one could have been behind me. And while he was doing it, I felt down there, and he definitely had two."

"What else?"

"Well, these are going to sound either sordid or silly. Are you sure you are going to want to hear them?"

"Until you tell me, I won't know. I've a feeling these dreams are going to be the most important."

She shrugged. "There was one time when he suddenly became my neighbour's rottweiler. Or maybe a werewolf. There were lots of big teeth and I remember thinking that I should feel terrified, but I wasn't."

She talked through a few other times where Dennis had become something else. The list had included a dinosaur, a unicorn, a really old man, an enormous pile of twenty-pound notes, fire, and a gorilla. I noted down each of the apparitions in her dreams.

"Thanks for that," I said. "I will go away and do a little research."

I didn't think I would uncover much symbolism.

"And you say you felt okay?"

167

"Yes, I was enjoying all of it," she continued, "and even though I was thinking how I should be scared or repulsed or revolted, I was having the time of my life."

I underlined the word *manipulation*.

"What shall I do about the baby?" she asked, without warning.

"Nothing just yet. I'll see you in a few days. At that time, you need to think and decide what you want to do. I might have some information for you that will help you decide. You have three options, of course: adoption, keeping the child, or termination."

There was a noise. It sounded like a gasp, but it wasn't Helen.

"I can't perform the termination. I'm not allowed to do it." Pro-life Witch's Code Amendment 392. Too many back street abortionists had labelled themselves as witches. "But I will, if you want, go with you to the clinic."

"What will I tell Dennis?"

"Nothing for now. We will cross that bridge if – and when – we get to it. Have you told anyone else yet?"

"My sister knows that something is up. She keeps asking me, but I won't tell her anything."

"Keep it that way. Understand?"

We picked a date and time to meet a few days later and she left, looking a bit more confident than when she'd arrived. As soon as the door closed, I picked up my phone and scrolled a short way down my contacts before making a call.

"Calliope? It's Mags. I think your father might be up to his old tricks again."

***

Just after one o'clock the following morning, my phone rang. I'm not at my best in the middle of the night. It takes me a while to get focused on the real world. I spent a good few seconds trying to turn my alarm off before I realised the noise was coming from my phone and then more seconds staring at it stupidly.

"Hello?" At least that's what I wanted to say. It probably sounded more like "Ugh?"

"Mags? It's Helen."

"Hmm."

TALES OF AN URBAN WITCH

"The dreams have got worse." She sounded tearful, if not actually crying. "I don't know what to do. I'm scared to go to sleep. Can I come over?"

I wanted to say no. I wanted to say go back to sleep. Do you know what the time is? None of those words escaped my lips as anything other than a sigh.

"You do sound in a bad way," I said. "Yes, come over. You can sleep in my spare room. My entire flat is safe. You should be able to sleep okay here." Not only did it have every sort of magical protection I could think of, but I had stripped all the wallpaper and lined every surface with aluminium foil some months ago. Nothing would be capable of disturbing her sleep.

She must have been dressed and had a bag ready because she was here in under half an hour. I sat her down and gave her a hot chocolate as an encouragement to sleep as soon as she could.

"What happened in the dream?" I asked.

"Which one? There were two."

"Start with the first one."

"Well, it was more a group of dreams, really. They were all the same. Babies, happy, jolly laughing babies, but they were dying. All dying. And, as each one died, I knew it was my fault. I could save them if I made the right decision."

This was Zeus's hand. My conversation with Calliope had confirmed my conclusions. He had made Helen pregnant. He had been with her as one or all the monstrous creatures in her bed, from the two-dicked version of Helen's absent fiancé, to the werewolf and the dinosaur. My money was on the old man she mentioned as the one that had actually knocked her up, but there was no telling.

Of course, Zeus wanted the child. He adored fathering children and wouldn't have been happy to have Helen even consider having a termination.

The original dreams themselves had been Zeus's way into Helen's life. Get past her defences with some comforting dreams about Dennis, slip in a few odd ones and then hit her with a bedful of strange and very randy creatures. All Zeus. She

169

wouldn't have known the dreams from reality. It was likely she had been wide awake but still thinking she was dreaming.

Calliope and I also concluded that Zeus had another god helping him by spying on Helen. We weren't sure which yet, although we had a shortlist.

"Tell me about the other group of dreams," I said to Helen, urging her to continue.

"Well, there was only one, really. It was about Dennis. Except he was his normal self, even though he looked different. He had a beard. I've never seen him with a beard before."

Could this be Zeus again?

"What happened?"

"I was in a hotel corridor. One of those endless corridors with numbers on the doors and tinny music playing. I couldn't make out what it was. You never can, can you?" She gave a self-effacing giggle which was on the verge of turning into tears, so I grabbed her hand until she was able to carry on.

"I knocked on a door and Dennis answered. He was wearing a towel like he'd just been in the shower."

She stopped again.

"He was smiling. He has the loveliest smile. It looked even better with the beard, somehow, and I don't generally like beards, but it kind of framed his mouth nicely."

I patted her hand again to reassure her. I could tell this dream was about to get worse.

"Anyway, as soon as he answered the door and saw me, the smile went away. He was confused, scared even, and he asked me what I was doing there. And then … and then… then I pushed him back into the room and I stabbed him. I stabbed and stabbed and stabbed. Over and over again. And that's when I woke up. I've been crying ever since."

She burst into tears again and I put my arms around her. As she sobbed her heart out, I wondered what Zeus was up to.

***

The following morning, Gavin was surprised to hear from me. As the local police's unofficial-yet-secretly-official witch liaison officer, he usually contacted me if there was a magic-related crime. I never called him. Not until now.

I quickly explained about Helen dreaming about Dennis's murder and I could hear him making notes. I included Dennis's full name and that he was working on an oil rig.

"There's not much for me to go on," he said. "There hasn't actually been a crime committed, but what I can do is check his whereabouts and confirm he is okay."

"That would be great," I said. "Helen is at her wit's end here. She thinks she has really killed him."

"Leave it with me. I'll call you back in an hour."

Forty-seven minutes went by, and my doorbell rang. It was Gavin. He'd come to arrest Helen.

"Dennis left the rig two weeks ago," he told her.

"What? I don't understand. He said he'd be back next week."

"He'd been working his way slowly down the country ever since he arrived on shore. Blackpool, Manchester, Birmingham, Bristol, Swansea, and probably a few others. He stayed in a hotel in each town. He ended up in Croydon and had been there three days."

"What was he doing in all those places?" she asked, barely holding back more tears. She hadn't noticed that Gavin had said 'had'.

"We have yet to confirm that," he said in a flat voice, but looked me in the eye and shook his head when Helen wasn't looking.

"And why Croydon? That's so close. He might as well have come home."

"We don't know yet." Gavin told me later that Dennis had been visited by a string of women in each hotel. I'd already guessed from the look he'd given me.

"So where is he now? Is he coming home?"

Gavin looked at me, a question in his eyes. It was a pointless question, but I nodded in response, anyway. He had to tell her the truth.

"Helen, I'm sorry to have to tell you, but Dennis is dead. They found his body late last night."

"No! My dream. It's true. It's all true." She collapsed in tears again. "I stabbed him."

"Can you tell me where you were between ten o'clock and midnight last night, Helen?"

"I was trying to sleep. But the dreams…"

"So, you were alone?"

"Until I called Mags and came over to see her."

"That was when?"

"About one o'clock," I said. "Helen arrived here about half past. She stayed in my spare room until about eight and I called you at nine."

"I must have killed him," Helen said, on the verge of tears.

"How? You drove over to Croydon in your sleep?" I knew she was innocent.

"I must have. How could I have seen myself killing him? He was stabbed, wasn't he?"

Gavin stuttered something non-committal.

"Wasn't he?" she asked again.

He nodded, but looked doubtful.

"Let's see," she said. "Just inside the doorway, wearing a towel, stabbed at least four times in the chest. Right so far?"

"That matches what we found," he said with reluctance.

"Did he have a beard?"

"Yes."

"When he'd left, he was clean-shaven. How would I know about the beard if I hadn't seen him? He never mentioned it in any of our calls, and he didn't have a good enough connection to use Zoom."

"Helen, you didn't kill him." I still believed that, but I didn't see how I could.

"How do I know all this if I didn't do it? Put the cuffs on."

"We won't need handcuffs, but you are right. I will have to arrest you."

As Gavin led her away, I began planning out how to help Helen. It didn't take me long. I had no idea what I could do.

***

I called Calliope and asked her if this could have been something that Zeus would have done.

"Unless this Dennis had done something exceptionally bad to him, no. He can be quite vengeful, but there has to be something that needs avenging."

"This wouldn't have been a warning to Helen about the possibility of her having a termination?"

"Not his style. My father is reactive rather than pro-active and not without warning. 'If you do this, I will turn you into a cat and take you to a dog's home' is his sort of thing. Killing a fiancé isn't."

"So, the dream Helen had that showed her Dennis's murder wasn't down to Zeus or his tame dream-caster?"

For the tiniest of seconds, I heard another voice speak. It was quiet and fast, but I definitely heard a male voice say, "Bitch!"

Calliope heard nothing, or at least gave no indication of having heard the voice. I guessed it was Zeus's spying henchgod. He was here with me. Invisible or something close to it.

"What can happen is that human minds get a little broadened when exposed to Olympian meddling. I guess she was able to pick up on the trauma of Dennis's death and see it happen."

"That sort of makes sense," I said, but deep down, I remained unconvinced.

***

Gavin phoned me in the morning. "Helen is definitely innocent," he said.

"Why have you decided that?"

"There's been another death. A woman this time. Same murder weapon. The depths of the knife strokes were the same. Helen, however, has been here all the time."

"Have you told her?"

"Yes, but she already knew."

"Another dream?"

"Yes."

Now, that confused me. If she saw Dennis's murder because

of a connection with him, then why was she seeing a different murder? Could there be some transfer of the connection to the weapon or the killer? That was not something I'd heard of before, but then again, I was dealing with gods, so I was a little out of my depth.

Helen was waiting for me at the police station.

"Oh Mags," she said. "It was horrible. That poor girl."

"Was it the same?"

"Sort of. Lots of stabbing and lots of blood."

"Tell me from the beginning."

"Well, in the dream, I was walking towards a house. I knocked, and a woman came to the door. Her name was Brenda Michaels. Then I asked her if she knew Dennis and she said … she said …"

"Take your time," I said, wondering what the woman could have said that would have upset Helen more than seeing her stabbed.

"She said that he was her fiancé."

"Oh no," I said and covered her hand with my own.

"Then that's when the knife came out and…" Helen burst into tears again.

"We're going to take her to a safe house," Gavin said. "We know she's not responsible for the murders, but she could be in danger. We'll track down those other women as well. We don't have his little black book, but we can go through his phone records."

"Keep them all safe," I told him.

***

Over the next week, there were more murders. Some of them were fiancées, but most were just girlfriends.

"Are you okay?" I asked Helen, when I visited her in the safe house.

She nodded, distracted.

"My sister has been popping in to see me. She's been a great help over the past couple of days. So have you and Gavin. You staying here in the evenings has been such a comfort. I can't thank you both enough." She smiled and her face lit up for a few

TALES OF AN URBAN WITCH

seconds, but then the haunted look returned. "The murders are awful, though. I keep seeing them even when I'm not dreaming. There's always so much blood."

"And each time you learn more about Dennis's secret life."

She sighed, and then she surprised me by saying, "The lying little shit."

The last murder didn't fit the pattern as the victim was a middle-aged man.

"Sorry to ask this," Gavin said with some hesitation.

"Don't worry about offending me. Nothing you could ask me now would do that. I can guess what you want to ask, though. Could Dennis have swung both ways?"

Gavin nodded.

"I don't think he did," she said. "But, after all I've seen and heard these past few days, goodness knows. I recognised the victim though. A mate of his from the *Dog and Dragon*. On the darts team. If Dennis was shagging him, he has – had – crap taste in men."

"There was nothing in the dreams to suggest why he was killed?"

"No. Not a thing. He didn't have a chance to say anything. The murderer stabbed him from behind without warning."

That was when I noticed that she'd stopped referring to the murderer in the dream as herself. Progress, of sorts. I wondered why the murderer had killed the man. There had to be a reason. And I didn't think it was because Dennis was having sex with him.

"Was Dennis's friend also a friend of yours?" I asked.

"No. I mean, I talked with his friends, but they were definitely just Dennis's mates. All men together, you know? Drinking and joking and laughing. Typical blokey blokes."

Gavin rolled his eyes at this.

"Were you friends with the man's wife?"

"Yes, I was. Poor girl."

Her sympathy was misplaced, I thought. At least the widow hadn't seen her husband murdered first-hand.

175

ROBERT WILLIAMS

***

I asked Gavin if I could come along with him when he interviewed the wife. You can imagine what he said. He wasn't supposed to. Police procedure. Civilians. Blah blah. I convinced him it might be useful though, so he grudgingly agreed to me sitting in on Mandy's interview.

"Who would kill my Phil?" she asked. "Who?"

"The world is a savage place," I said, in my best caring voice. "There are a lot of nasty people out there."

"Did Phil have any enemies?" Gavin asked.

"Only my mother," Mandy said. "They hated each other's guts. He was never good enough for me in her eyes."

"Could she have killed him?"

Mandy laughed.

"I doubt it. She's been dead three years." Gavin glanced at me, and I made a note. We both knew what was possible.

"But no one living you can think of?"

"No. My Phil was friends with everyone. Life and soul, he was. Life and soul. Why would anyone want to kill him?" She descended into tears.

"How did he get on with Dennis?" Gavin asked, when the sobs had subsided.

"They were mates. Got on like a house on fire. Drinking buddies. You know?"

"Could there have been more there? Nothing sexual?"

"You saying my Phil was a bender?"

"I have to ask," Gavin said. "It's a normal question we ask in this sort of case."

"Well, in that case, no, he wasn't. Any bloke who tried it on with him would get a smack in the teeth. He hated poofs."

Gavin made notes but didn't comment. He remained outwardly calm, but he was raging inside. I knew the signs.

"How well do you know Helen?" I asked, changing the subject.

"We're friends, but we're not that close. We'd talk at the pub when the boys were talking about football or playing darts, you know? That sort of thing. Helen's not part of the gang yet. Not

TALES OF AN URBAN WITCH

properly. She didn't have Dennis under her thumb."

"They were engaged."

"They might as well have been single. Dennis was a lad. Played the field."

"You knew about the other women?"

"Oh yes. Dennis used to brag about them to the boys. The boys just laughed themselves silly."

"And none of you thought to tell Helen?"

If she had any shame at not speaking up, she hid it well.

"No, of course not. Boys will be boys. They all settle down once we have them married."

I disagreed with her but didn't say anything.

"And who would Dennis marry?" I asked. "He had a few fiancées on the go."

"I dunno. What has this got to do with my Phil, anyway? That's what I want to know. Why would anyone want to kill him?"

What did it have to do with Phil's murder? That would remain to be seen.

***

I decided to try something. It would be dangerous and so, in case Gavin wanted to stop me, I kept it quiet. My plan involved telling two people two separate things, and both required magic. Sort of.

The safe house had a large room that would suit my purposes well. It was just big enough for me to create a circle and put in a few tokens of the elements at the cardinal points. Helen was with me as I made my preparations.

"You are clear about what you need to do?" I asked her.

"You want me to fall asleep and dream? I'm not sure if I can."

"Don't worry about that. I'll help."

"And that's it?"

"That's it."

I'm good at hypnosis. I can usually get anyone under in a few minutes. Helen was so tired, poor girl, she almost went under too quickly. Luckily, there was just enough time to talk her

ROBERT WILLIAMS

through what I needed her to do. Then I did what I needed to do. Neither took long.

When I'd finished, I started clearing up. I left Helen to sleep naturally for a while, but I started dismantling the circle. I hadn't actually used magic while I was hypnotising Helen. Hypnosis isn't magic. Zeus's henchgod was listening. The circle offered me some privacy while I worked on Plan A. Plan B needed something else.

A circle has to be dismantled carefully as it exposes the unwary witch to all sorts of malign influences. Anything could enter as soon as there was the tiniest break in the circle.

I wasn't being unwary, but there was a specific malign influence I needed.

I broke the circle and felt what I expected: the smallest of puffs of wind. It, or rather he, was in the circle with me. With one movement, I closed the circle again and cast another spell under my breath.

It was a tricky spell to cast. In many spells, we call on influences. Sometimes these are nature spirits and sometimes spirits of people who have passed away, although I avoided those types of spells. Certain branches of magic called on the energy created by people in the act of dying. I certainly didn't meddle with that. That was necromancy and just wasn't nice. I would have avoided that even if it wasn't forbidden by the Witch's Council.

Other types of magic had us invoking the old gods. For instance, for something creative, I could call on Calliope or one of her sisters. And for something about love, I might call on Aphrodite.

My spell was difficult because the god I was invoking was the god I wanted to catch. I hoped he wasn't listening, either in person or by using whatever sense gods used to listen to spells and prayers. To play safe, I'd written most of what I wanted to say in the spell on some rice paper and cast it into the fire that formed part of my circle. That completed, I picked up the large bag of salt I used to create my circle and whirled it around my

TALES OF AN URBAN WITCH

head and body in a complex path, and then I struck.

"Oof!" said Hermes and collapsed on the floor, clutching at his testicles. He hadn't been invisible, but he had been racing around the inside of my circle so fast that he might as well have been. "That hurt! Why did you do that?"

"Oh, good," I said. "I'm glad I've got your attention. I need you to take a message to Zeus."

***

Later, at night, I was at home. Helen was at the safe house, protected by all that I could give her, as well as by Gavin's colleagues. I had nothing to protect me other than a few tricks up my sleeve. I hadn't even put on my latch-chain and everyone who knew me also knew that I never locked my door when I was home. Anyone could walk in. Absolutely anyone.

My front door has a creak that lets me know whenever it opened. It is a creak with nuances. When I return home, carrying a heavy bag of shopping, and I fling the door open, it squeals to me in welcome but, when a friend comes to visit, the door announces them as clearly as if they had called out their name. Calliope's flamboyant screech was completely different to Gavin's cautious creak, for instance.

The creak that I could hear announced somebody I didn't know. It was somebody trying to be careful. Somebody trying not to be heard. Somebody expecting me to be in bed and not sitting on my sofa about to turn on the lights as soon as they entered the room. They were surprised when I did so.

"Hello there," I said, as if I'd bumped into her at Lidl. "You must be Helen's sister. I'm Mags. I'm afraid I don't know your name."

"Fran. I know who you are, and I know what you know," she said.

"You know what I told Helen to dream?" The dreams worked both ways. Helen saw the murders, while Fran here heard what I'd said to Helen.

"What did you know?" she asked, with a sneer.

"Nothing. I know a lot more now. Why did you do it?"

She said nothing, but glared at me.

"Was it because you love your sister and couldn't stand Dennis betraying her?"

Still nothing.

"Was it because of his bragging to his mates of the women he'd had behind Helen's back?" She'd had access to the same group of friends and heard the same whispers and the same laughter.

She didn't speak, but her body shifted ever so slightly. She was getting ready to pounce. I made myself ready as well, but not in such an obvious way.

"A man like that would never be able to resist the challenge of two sisters, of course," I said. "Did he try it on with you?"

Another shift.

"Ah! Not only did he try, but he succeeded."

"He said he loved me."

"Like he loved all those other women. Like he loved Helen?"

"I was different. I was better. He was going to dump Helen."

"But he didn't, did he? In fact, he made the situation worse and proposed to her and the others."

"There are more. They've got it coming to them as well. As soon as I've finished with you and dealt with his stupid mates."

She jumped at me then, but she was clumsy with hatred and it's harder than you think to attack someone with a knife while they're on a sofa and you're standing. I expect the army and the SAS have special classes for that sort of thing, but not everyone gets to go to those. I rolled off the sofa onto the floor. She missed me completely and stabbed one of my cushions.

"And what about Helen?"

"I'm saving her for last. Traitorous bitch. I'll kill her and her little bastard."

"You would kill my child?" Zeus's voice was as impressive as it was sudden. He had received my message. His voice filled the room, as you would expect, but it came from nowhere. He sounded like he was standing in front of me and behind me and above and below all at once.

I heard my front door open. The creak told me it was Gavin.

"Really? Is that the best you can do? That sounds nothing like Dennis.

My living room door opened a crack. Gavin was watching.

"Please, Fran, believe me," I said. "That's Zeus, and he really is the father of Helen's baby. Don't laugh at him."

She laughed. "Honestly. Helen said you were good, but this is just sad. You're still going to have to die."

At that moment, three things happened at once. She dived across the sofa at me. Gavin pushed open the living room door and jumped towards me and a great wind blew across my living room towards my window. That last was Zeus, I guess.

The window flew open in a shower of flakes of ancient paint. Gavin connected with me, and we both fell to the floor as the wind took Fran and flung her out of the window. We didn't even hear her scream.

***

I went to see Helen, once all the fuss had died down, and she had settled back into her old flat.

"I'm sorry," I said. "About your sister, I mean."

"Thank you, but don't be. Fran was always a spiteful cow. I thought it was funny at the time that she was being so nice to me. And all the while, she was the one who killed Dennis and all those other people."

"How much did you see?"

"All of it. The dream was very detailed, but I woke up before she hit the ground."

"I'm glad of that. I don't know what would have happened if she'd died while you were still connected to her."

"Something woke me up. It felt like someone shaking me, but when I woke up, there was no-one there."

That was probably Hermes. Zeus wouldn't want his child harmed by its mother dying in a dream. I didn't say anything. I thought she'd had enough to handle without knowing there was a Greek god spying on her.

"Good that you woke though," I said instead.

She nodded, then was thoughtful for a few seconds. "Am I really carrying Zeus's baby?"

"Yes."

"Will it be human?"

"Yes, it'll be human. I asked." I'd asked Hermes that very question.

"Not half-human?" Helen asked.

"No. It will be fully human."

"I've done some reading, you see. I know how some of Zeus's children turned out. Half human and half something else. A monster."

I knew how some of those children turned out as well. That's why I'd asked Hermes.

"Zeus only fathers human children with human mothers these days," I said, repeating what Hermes had said to me word for word.

"Why's that?" Helen asked, and I shrugged in answer. I'd wanted to ask why, but Hermes had run off before I'd even opened my mouth.

The gods don't like questions. I had hundreds more.

CHAPTER THIRTEEN

HORSEMAN

I don't like séances as a rule. I prefer to leave the dead to their own devices. They deserve their rest, and so my usual reaction to being asked to contact Aunty Mabel on the other side – just to make sure she's okay – is to say no. Mabel's probably doing well on her own, thank you very much, and if she never told you where she hid the money then that's her business.

Occasionally, however, I find myself in my darkened sitting room, clasping the sweaty palms of comparative strangers and asking myself how I'd been talked into it yet again. I'm a sucker for a sob story, I guess. I bump into someone at the laundrette who's missing their husband/wife/best friend's dog and before I know it, I'm asking if there's anybody there.

Mrs Harris was in a state of embarrassed shock. She'd had a surprise visit from Mr Harris, who told her he knew about her and the man from the fish counter in Waitrose. This threw her off kilter, as she had planned to talk with her mother to keep her up to date with *Hotel Hellada*.

She'd come with a friend, Mrs Benson, who had initially watched with stony-faced disbelief, having accompanied Mrs Harris to see me purely for moral support. She'd declared she didn't believe in 'this claptrap', although she'd nodded sagely during the Waitrose announcement and had carried the tiniest smile on her face ever since.

The other members of the group were two young men. They were here, I think, on a dare. They'd come for a laugh, but young Johnny Spiers had received a visit from the spirit of his granny, who told him he'd always been her favourite and that she kept an eye on him. I think granny had meant that in a kindly way, and he had seemed pleased as punch that she'd said it, but, afterwards, he'd sat wide-eyed and distracted, no doubt wondering what exactly his grandmother had seen. Occasionally, he blushed.

The other young man, Mike, was a friend of Johnny's and very much a Jack-the-lad. He'd come for a laugh, I think, and the only spirits he'd been interested in were in my drinks cabinet. He'd tried helping himself to my special fortified brandy before we started, but I'd caught him just in time. I wouldn't have minded if he'd drunk some, had it just been brandy, but most of it was sleeping potion. And, by most of it, I meant that the brandy was only there to add flavour. Truth be told, I really just wanted the bottle as a convenient container.

"Is there anybody there?" I'd asked. That doesn't actually do anything, you know. They were just ritual words that the punters expect to hear. The spirits come regardless, working on their own agenda. I hadn't expected an answer and had been surprised when we were joined by a spirit, then disappointed when it had turned out to be Veronica.

***

"Bad man!" she said.

I ignored her and asked again, "Is there anybody there?" I hoped she'd get the message.

"Bad man!"

Veronica's vocabulary was rather limited. Even now, she was like a faulty computer from the eighties. She couldn't hold her husband's name in her memory, so instead of Jake, she would call him 'bad man'. I'd grown to learn that she could mean a variety of things by the term, and I had to listen to the emotional inflections in her voice to tell the difference.

Today she sounded agitated, a step backward to the days when she believed he'd cheated on her. He hadn't. He had been devoted to her in life and hadn't even looked at anyone else since she'd died.

I sighed and prepared myself for an argument, but then something unusual happened.

"Mags," Veronica said. "Please."

That's when I knew that something was wrong. She never used my name. Never. So, I called a halt to the séance, and ushered the group out.

"Veronica. What's the matter?" I asked as soon as they had gone.

"Bad man. No. Bad man. No. Not bad man. Ba ... ba... Good man. Good. Jake."

"Take it slow. Concentrate on the words. What's the matter?"

She never used his name. She never used my name. She just didn't do names. She barely did words.

"Jake bad. Bad man. Bad ... bad... not man." She was struggling for a word.

"Jake is not a bad man?" I asked.

She nodded, but then frowned and shook her head.

"Jake ... bad. No. Jake ... Jake... Jake hurt."

"Jake's hurt?"

"Yes."

"Where is he?"

"Come."

She vanished and reappeared by my front door, eager to go. I grabbed my coat and ran to follow.

***

She led me to the garage under the block, where Jake was lying on the ground in a pool of blood. It looked like he'd been trampled by a herd of cows and shot at by arrows. There was one in his shoulder and another in his chest. It was a miracle he was still alive. Although, looking around me at dozens of other arrows strewn across the floor, whole and trampled, I realised it was probably more miraculous that any of them had hit Jake at all.

I did what I could for him and called for an ambulance. Veronica stood nearby.

"Jake bad?"

"He'll live," I said, although I wasn't all that sure if he would. I couldn't see why he wasn't already dead. His injuries were severe, but Veronica was a fragile soul, so I couldn't tell her that. I know she was dead herself, but this was no time for logic.

"Don't worry," I said. "You did well, Veronica."

There had been a lot of blood, but I had stopped most of the bleeding. I left the arrows in him, as there would have been a lot more blood loss if I pulled them out. There might also still be internal injuries. He needed to be seen by a doctor.

Where was that ambulance?

I studied his injuries, trying to picture what had happened. Who had done this to him? As well as the arrows, he had hoofprints on his head and chest. I was no expert, but they looked like horses had made them. Why would anyone ride through a south London underground garage on a horse shooting at someone with arrows? Just as importantly, who would do such a thing? Who even had a horse around here?

I called the police, or rather I called Gavin, then went back to waiting for the ambulance.

***

I wanted to go with Jake in the ambulance but, in the end, I sent Veronica. The garage was a crime scene of sorts, and I needed to make sure it wasn't disturbed until Gavin and his people arrived. It gave me an opportunity to poke around as well. Gavin wouldn't mind. Well, he probably would, but he wasn't here to say no.

I gave the paramedics Jake's details before they left. Veronica couldn't help with that, even if anyone in the hospital could see or hear her. In her distressed state, she was less than useless, her vocabulary almost non-existent.

I'd asked her about the men on the horses and she gave me nothing useful. Nothing about the riders.

"Bad men. Bad horses. Bad men. Bad," was all she said, which

TALES OF AN URBAN WITCH

didn't help.

I counted forty-eight arrows on or around the garage. Out of fifty arrows, only two had made contact with Jake. Seven were embedded in the concrete walls. Deeply embedded. These guys were powerful but bad shots.

The arrows were fancy. Their heads were razor sharp, metal – bronze, I thought – and hand-finished with carved writing and figures. I couldn't make any of it out in the gloom of the car park. As I looked at one, touching it gingerly, I had a feeling, a tingle that went from my fingertips to the back of my head. That bothered me.

I could also tell they were old, just by looking at them. And by old, I don't mean like your nan had found them at the back of a cupboard. I mean, really old. Museum old. These were ancient and obviously worth a fortune, but someone had just left them here like they didn't matter.

I picked a few up carefully, using my scarf, and popped them in my bag. I knew I was technically tampering with evidence, but four or five wouldn't make a difference. I needed them for a few tests of my own, and the police had plenty of others to look at for fingerprints.

Gavin arrived soon after that and I briefed him on what I knew. I didn't tell him about the contents of my bag, and I felt vaguely guilty.

"Did he have any enemies?" he asked me, once he'd set his men looking for evidence.

"Not that I know of," I said. I liked Jake and knew the rest of the block liked him, too. He was that type of man.

"You think there's a supernatural element here? His wife's ghost aside. She would be just as concerned if he had just been mugged."

I nodded. "Of course, but just look at these arrows."

"The arrows? Are they magic?"

"I don't know. There's something about them that bothers me. Maybe magic. Maybe something else."

"Take a few with you. Check them out."

187

ROBERT WILLIAMS

"Umm … I already have."

I was expecting a lecture about evidence and scenes of crime, but he just smiled at me and nodded. I think he was pleased with my initiative.

"Let me know if you sense anything," he said. "And I'll let you know what we find. In the meantime, get yourself off to the hospital."

***

I found Jake eventually. A&E reception had no record of Jake Hopkins being admitted and they had to search through the ambulance admissions just in case he had been admitted under the wrong name. Just in case. Ten minutes later, we found that John Hopgood was currently in theatre, and the receptionist directed me to a waiting room.

Two familiar faces greeted me. Veronica was pacing fretfully around the empty waiting room and Agnes had taken up residence on one of the corner chairs. Predictably, she was knitting. She looked up when I entered and acknowledged me with a smile and a nod.

Her presence worried me. She was a dear friend, and I'd known her for many years, but she specialised in escorting people to whatever afterlife they believed in. She was dead, herself, but even when she was alive, she'd had a talent for not being noticed, which she still had. Veronica wasn't paying her any attention at any rate, but given her state of agitation, I don't think she would have noticed if Queen Victoria had drifted past on roller skates playing an accordion.

If Agnes was there, someone nearby was going to die. Yes, it was a hospital and people die there all the time, but I was concerned for Jake. It didn't look good.

"Mags. Bad man. Bad man bad." Veronica really was worried, the poor thing.

"How is he?" I asked her.

"Bad."

"Have you been in to see him?" I asked and then nodded towards the operating theatre. Veronica looked at the theatre

188

door and then at me. She shook her head.

"Door," she said. I stared at her until she gave me a brief nod and glided through it. She sometimes forgets she is a ghost.

She returned quickly, looking pale and sick.

"Knives. Blood. Jake. Bad."

I said something reassuring. Possibly. I don't remember. She went back to pacing, and I chose a chair near to Agnes.

"Hello Agnes," I said.

She nodded a greeting, but her needles didn't stop and, as usual, I had no idea what she was knitting.

"You're here to collect someone."

She nodded.

"Care to tell me who?"

She shook her head and concentrated on her knitting. I hadn't heard her speak since the day she died.

An hour or so passed. I think you wait so long you sort of hypnotise yourself and, although you're not quite asleep, you're also not quite awake as well, and time passes without you noticing. Anyway, it only seemed like a few minutes and the door burst open and a busy-looking surgeon came over to me.

"Mrs Hopgood?"

"Hopkins," I said. Correcting him. "But I'm not his wife. Just a friend, but I found him."

He looked at me with a face filled with uncertainty.

"I really should be talking to his wife," the surgeon said.

"He's widowed, I'm afraid." I didn't add that he would still be talking to his wife, who was currently staring at him. "I am a friend."

"Oh, I see. Okay. *Friend.* Yes. Of course." There was a world of assumptions in the way he said the word and I thought about correcting him, but decided it would take too long. It didn't matter. "Anyway, he's stable for now."

"For now?"

"Yes. He's out of immediate danger, but he really is in a bad way. He lost a lot of blood and there were a number of internal injuries, including a bleed to the brain."

"Will he be okay?" It was a stupid question, but it's one of those things you ask in this sort of situation.

"We will know in the next twenty-four hours or so. He will either wake up or…" He left the sentence hanging. We both knew the alternative to Jake waking up. The doctor's expression wasn't encouraging. I glanced at Agnes, but she was giving me no hints. She hadn't even looked up from her knitting.

"Will Jake die?" This was the most coherent question I'd ever heard from Veronica, dead or alive.

"We just have to wait," I said to Veronica while looking at the doctor. I made sound like a question to him and a statement to her. Try it. It's kind of tricky.

"Yes," he said. "Wait. We've done all we can for now."

"Can we – I mean, can I – see him?"

"Of course. Let us clean him up a bit, and I'll send someone out to bring you in."

***

I could barely recognise Jake. His face was one big bruise and his head looked like a rejected potato. I held his hand for a while and listened to his vitals. The doctor's assessment was correct. He was in a very bad way. I still didn't see how he was alive, but at least he was stable.

I could do nothing here, but I could try to find out who had done this. I needed to go home. There were arrows to be looked at.

I left Veronica and Agnes with him and gave Veronica strict instructions to come and get me if anything changed. My phone beeped on the way back. A message from Gavin. He had some information for me. I changed buses and made my way to the police station.

"I can tell you what we found," he said, when I got there. "It isn't much at the moment, but it is puzzling."

"Go on."

"That garage isn't used very often, is it?"

"No. Not many of the residents have cars to park there and those that do park them in the street where they can keep an eye on them."

"What about criminals? Drug dealers and the like."

"I keep them away. We have a few rough sleepers make use of the space."

"That might explain the large number of empty bottles of cheap cider we found."

"Cider? Not my lot. They're clean. I keep them sober."

"We found twenty bottles. They had some party down there while they were waiting for Jake."

"Any idea of how many people were there?"

"They had walked their horses through a large puddle at some point, which was helpful. We found four sets of hoofprints. No footprints, though. That would have been more helpful."

"No CCTV?"

"No, not there."

"Anything else?"

He hesitated, about to say something but not making up his mind.

"What?" I asked.

"This is going to sound daft. The hoofprints were not very steady. It's like the horses were drunk."

"It takes a lot to make a horse drunk."

"Would five litres of cider be enough?"

"That should do it."

"But that's just stupid. How could they give the cider to the horses?"

"'Why would they?' would be a better question."

***

I pondered what Gavin had told me on the way up to my flat and felt I was missing something obvious. At least four archers on horseback had attacked Jake. They had been drinking heavily enough to affect their aim and the control of their horses. Or perhaps the horses really were drunk as well. But that was crazy.

Had the horsemen really intended to kill Jake? Had they been waiting for him, or had he just stumbled on their gathering? And why was Jake in the garage, anyway? It was pretty much out of his way. He didn't have a car.

I hoped that my analysis of the arrows would help answer these questions, or at least give some sort of clue as to what we were dealing with. I had picked up a tingle from the arrows earlier and I thought I should be able to get more from them under the right conditions.

I had five arrows in my bag. The one I'd handled was loose and was, in psychic terms, contaminated. The others I'd picked up with my scarf and it was those I laid on my kitchen table.

My psychometry is weak. Some of my more talented colleagues could pick up a pen and tell you the name of the person it belonged to, where they lived, and their shoe size. I could tell you if they were male or female and their general state of health, and that was about it. Not generally useful, but there were ways of enhancing it. I thought I would try with my crystal ball.

I put a small circle in place. I felt I needed its safety and luckily, my kitchen was just about big enough for a very small circle. It's okay if I don't stand up. The circle defines a sphere. Whoever lived in the flat below me had a very well protected ceiling.

I gave the ball a wipe and laid it on the black velvet cloth on the floor in front of me. Then I took one of the arrows from my scarf, held it in both hands and gazed into the ball. I didn't look for images, but concentrated on the tingle from the arrow, focusing all of my attention on it.

The tingle intensified and spread to both my hands. Something was there, but I couldn't get it to resolve into anything I could understand. It was just the tingle. Psychic static. Blurred, unfocused, it was like trying to read a book when there's not enough light. You know something's there, but all you can see are a load of blurry shapes that won't resolve into words. The tingle was suggesting something, but nothing I could understand, and a wave of frustration built up in me. I was angry. I was trying to save the life of a friend by finding out who had attacked him and this ... this... this *thing* was not cooperating.

"Oh, come on! Bloody stupid arrow!" I gripped the shaft a little too tightly, and it snapped under my fingers like an autumn twig. I flung the pieces to the floor in disgust, and to my surprise, the anger dissipated.

I reached out to the pieces of the arrow on my floor. Not with my hand, but with my other senses. I felt the anger again, but I realised it wasn't mine. The rage was in the arrow. Its owner had been furious about something.

I took a deep breath and looked at the three remaining arrows wrapped in my scarf. I knew taking one would make me angry, but to employ a well-worn cliché, forewarned is forearmed. Knowing what would happen would let me deal with it. I had to get myself in the right frame of mind before touching them.

I stared at the crystal ball for a few minutes, losing myself in the cloudy patches of white within it and let my consciousness drift. I needed to find a balance point. If I took the arrow too soon, I'd only see rage and, if I waited too long, I would be sucked into looking at whatever appeared in the ball. It might be useful, but would likely have nothing to do with the arrow.

It was like trying to pinpoint those few seconds between being awake and falling asleep, but when I felt I had the right frame of mind, I reached out a hand and grabbed an arrow. I was aware of the tingle immediately, but it was like it was in someone else's hand and so my focus remained on the ball.

There was the rage, but I knew it wasn't mine, and rode it out. The ball responded almost immediately. The cloudy white deposits in the ball started to shift and swirl. The mist cleared and I could see grass speeding past below me, daisies and buttercups dotted amongst the green stalks. Hoofbeats and voices filled the air, and I could feel the powerful muscles in my legs as I surged along. Racing along like this felt joyous. It felt right.

This was an exceptionally powerful impression. I don't normally hear or feel anything. I had to be picking up on the horse's thoughts and feelings somehow. I needed to concentrate on the rage of the rider. Ignore the joy of the horse, galloping through the grass. Feel the rage.

I focussed again on the arrow in my hands, the tingle against my skin and, there, the rage it kindled in my mind. The images in the ball still showed grass, however, so I stayed with it. I had no alternative for the moment. All I could do was hope it would lead somewhere useful.

The shouts I could hear over the noise of the hoofbeats intensified, and I could make out the odd word here and there. Emotionally, the joy of the gallop was overlaid with darker tones. Bloodlust, hatred, anger, and the rage I had picked up from the arrow. I was confused. Was this still the horse or the rider? Or some weird amalgam of both?

"Death to the sons of Heracles! Death to the traitor!"

I dropped the arrow in surprise. Heracles? The ancient Greek hero?

Was this the Greeks *again*?

***

The session with the crystal ball and the arrow had left me drained and unsettled. I wanted a cup of tea and a sit down, but I was suddenly aware of the time. I needed to go back to the hospital to see how Jake was doing.

Was he connected to the sons of Heracles? Who were the sons of Heracles, anyway? Was Jake the traitor?

The age of the arrow suggested I needed another chat with Calliope. Or maybe Hermes? That chat, with whoever it would be, would have to wait until later, however.

Veronica looked different when I arrived at the hospital. She was smiling.

I need to back-pedal a bit here. Veronica smiles occasionally, but rarely. She wasn't that happy a woman when she was alive and was still pretty dour as a ghost. The only times I've seen her smile were when she thought she'd got something over on me. This smile was different because she actually looked like she was happy.

Her normal expression was worried. The world, since she died, had been a confusing place with lots she didn't understand

TALES OF AN URBAN WITCH

and plenty that scared her. She worried about all of it.

Yet, here she was, sitting on Jake's bed, gazing at his face, and smiling.

"Hello Mags," she said, when she saw me. Agnes hadn't moved from the corner, and Veronica was still ignoring her. She nodded.

"Veronica," I answered. It was like she was a stranger. "How is he?"

"Stable." Stable? This from a woman who could barely say her husband's name this morning. I would have expected "good" at best.

"Doctor said stable. No better. No worse. No worse good."

"He spoke to you? The doctor actually spoke to you? He saw you?" She'd undergone such a change over the last few hours, I would have believed her had she said so.

"No." She laughed. She actually laughed. "Doctor spoke to nurse."

Jake looked worse to me, to be honest, and I hoped the doctor had known what he was talking about. Veronica seemed happy enough to cling to the little bit of hope that the doctor's words held, and I guessed happiness made her more vocal.

Perhaps now she would be able to tell me more about what happened to Jake.

"You were there when Jake was hurt, weren't you?"

Her face clouded, and I worried she wouldn't be able to speak. "Yes."

"Can you tell me what happened?"

"Running."

"Jake was running?"

"Yes. Chased."

"He was being chased? By who?"

"Horses. Bad horses."

"Where was this?"

"Park."

She meant the local recreation ground across the road from the estate. All the locals called it the park, but it was only just a bit of grass. This park didn't even have a pond.

"How many were there?"

"Two."

"And they chased him into the garage?"

She nodded.

"How many more horses were waiting in there?"

"Two," she said again. "Bad horses. Bad men."

That filled out a little of the story. Jake had been chased into the garage by two men on horseback and then was ambushed by two other horsemen. The question remained, however, as to why they were shooting at him.

Maybe Gavin would have some answers.

***

As luck would have it, he called me on my way home from the hospital. The phone rang as the bus entered my estate. The bus was nearly empty at this time of night, so the phone sounded very loud, and everyone looked at me.

"I heard from my expert," he said. "Those arrows are old."

I knew that from my psychometry experiment earlier, but it was nice to get it confirmed. Although that meant I was involved with the ancient Greeks again. If they were involved, then trouble would follow.

"In fact, he used the word 'ancient'. Ancient Greek. Well, Cypriot to be exact. He would like to have the arrows in the museum. He mentioned money."

"How much?" I know I sounded mercenary at this point, but as I've mentioned before, I'm freelance.

"Well, I wouldn't say life-changing, but you wouldn't have to worry about paying the rent for a few years."

"Sounds life-changing enough to me. What else did he say?"

"You saw the markings on its head?"

"I did, but I haven't examined them in detail." The bus pulled up outside my block and I stepped out onto the pavement, into a pool of light from a streetlamp. Gavin kept up his end of the conversation.

"You should. They mention an old friend of yours."

"Who?" I asked, already guessing the answer.

"Zeus."

I groaned. How had my life became entwined with the old gods so heavily? Counting Muses among my friends probably had something to do with it. As had defusing a few live satyrs before that.

"There are more markings, but that one stood out. I thought you'd want to know."

"Cheers."

I was looking for my keys in my bag, the phone held between my ear and my shoulder. My attention wasn't on the outside world and so I nearly missed it. Hoofbeats. I could hear hoofbeats, and they were getting louder. And were there voices as well?

"Gavin," I said. "I think I can hear a horse."

"Get inside, quickly," he answered.

I ran for the stairs and called for the lift when I reached the first floor. Horses or no horses, there was no way I could run up all those stairs. Hopefully, they hadn't seen me duck inside. I listened for hoofbeats while I waited for the lift, but heard nothing. By the time the lift had taken its usual slow time to reach my floor, I had partly convinced myself that the hoofbeats I'd heard were all in my imagination.

I said as much to Gavin, who had waited on the line while I ran up the first flight of stairs and then panted heavily at him in the lift.

"I expect you're right," he said. "Do you need me to pop round to make sure you're safe?"

I said I was okay and rang off, suddenly embarrassed at being scared. As I put the key in the lock of my front door, I listened to the noises of the city carried on the night air. No hoofbeats. No voices. Nothing. It had been in my imagination, after all. I smiled as I stepped into my flat, but stopped as I heard another noise.

Swish.

What was that?

Swish. Swish.

ROBERT WILLIAMS

The noises could have been birds, disturbed by something, or even bats. We do get them in town. Or could have been arrows, launched carelessly by a drunken archer.

"Nah," I said and closed the front door. That was enough imagination for one night.

***

More psychometry. I still had some arrows and a bit more information to work with. Perhaps I would be able to find out something useful this time.

I laid an arrow down in front of the crystal ball without touching it and studied the markings on the head. They were worn, but still clear. There was indeed a symbol for Zeus. How did I miss it before?

Remembering the shapes, thinking about Jake, keeping the rage as an abstract concept, and feeling for the balance point of concentration, I stared into the ball looking for images, before reaching for the arrow.

I'm making it sound easy. It wasn't. Imagine trying to juggle a bowling ball, a plate, and a chainsaw all at once while doing a cryptic crossword. It was a bit like that.

Somehow, I didn't lose concentration, or get so annoyed that I broke another arrow. Images started to form.

I could see Jake ahead of me and, in the distance, the dark forbidding entrance to the garage. All of this was accompanied by the sound of hooves on concrete and voices calling for a traitor's death. There were the strange mixed-up feelings of rage and power, and drunkenness and purpose. Were these coming from the man or the horse? It didn't matter, I couldn't waste time trying to separate the impressions. I had to go with what I was seeing.

"Death to the traitor!"

"Death to the sons of Heracles!"

The voice came from my left but, unhelpfully, my viewpoint, whether the horse's or its rider, was firmly fixed on Jake.

"Head him off," the rider shouted. The words were mushy, slurred. The rider was drunk. "Make sure he heads down to the others."

"It shall be so," the voice to my left said. "He will see his former brothers one last time."

Both riders laughed and, for the briefest of moments, my viewpoint moved so that I caught a glimpse of the other horseman. With that glimpse, I lost concentration, and I dropped the figurative chainsaw, along with everything else.

The other voice, and presumably my viewpoint's voice as well, belonged to a centaur.

"So now you know who we are."

Was I still in the vision? The crystal ball was just a globe of polished quartz. My shock at seeing a centaur had broken the connection. How could I still be hearing his voice?

"You know who we are, and you know the traitor. You must die, witch."

The voice came from behind me and I turned to see a centaur. There was a centaur in my flat. A centaur. An impossible creature that was half man and half horse. In my flat. Yes, I know I am repeating myself, but that was because there was a centaur in my flat. A centaur with horns. In my flat.

I knew they existed. The Keepers had mentioned them, but they were rare, apparently. I'd never seen one before. You wouldn't expect one in London and definitely not in my kitchen.

"How are you even here?" I asked. He was the size of a horse with a rider on top. He should not have been able to fit through the doors. He was having to lean over just to fit in under the ceiling. His being in my kitchen was impossible. His horns were in danger of getting tangled in the light fitting.

I mean, how had he even fit in the lift?

He was, however, just outside my circle, which showed that it was working at keeping him out. I wasn't too sure I could say the same for the arrow that he had pointed vaguely in my direction. Although he was magical, and the arrow imbued with his magic by long association with him, it still obeyed the laws of physics, and it would sail through the protection of my circle like it was nothing.

He shrugged an answer to my question, and the motion made him totter uncertainly on his hooves. He was drunk.

"Why are you here?" I asked him, spacing out the words so that he would understand.

"I am here to kill you," he said and hiccupped. He tried to take aim with the arrow once more, but it slipped and he had to reposition it. "One moment, please."

"Why?"

"You know the gods, you know us, and you know him, the traitor."

"You mean Jake? The man you were shooting at. Why is he a traitor?"

"Ha! Enough questions," he said. "Die." The arrow missed by a wide margin and embedded itself in my kitchen wall. The second one smashed into my plate cupboard. I didn't stick around for the third and dived out of the other kitchen door. That he could miss me at such a small distance spoke volumes about how drunk he was. Going on the hit-rate with Jake, I had a one in twenty-five chance of being hit. Good odds, until you remember Jake was in hospital.

I know a little about centaurs. I read up on them after I encountered Bruce the satyr and his keeper a while back. Centaurs were the lager louts of the Greek mythological menagerie, famed for crashing parties and holding grudges. Think Oliver Reed with hooves.

You don't know Oliver Reed? How about Colin Farrell? Paul Gascoigne? No? I give up. Think of someone who is often drunk – Reg from accounts at the office party, if you must – and stick hooves on them.

There were different tribes of centaurs. One group formed because someone had sex with a cloud, and the result of that union got jiggy with some horses. Honestly, those ancient Greeks would have sex with *anything*.

Another group formed because someone else refused to have sex with Zeus – probably the only living creature in Ancient Greece – and, frustrated, Zeus … um… 'spilled his seed' on the

TALES OF AN URBAN WITCH

ground and centaurs sprang up from that. That group came from Cyprus and had horns, just like my four-legged-friend in the kitchen.

Anyway, that's enough of a history lesson. My visitor was still chasing me.

Now, as far as flats go, mine isn't huge. The hall gives access to the kitchen, bathroom, both bedrooms, and the lounge. The kitchen and lounge have a connecting door and that's about it. The flat doesn't offer much scope for a chase. I was surviving because the centaur was so tall. He had to stoop everywhere, and he was as drunk as a lord.

He let off a few arrows, but they went nowhere near me. There just wasn't the room and he couldn't aim properly. All he was able to do was keep me in the flat. At every point in our chase, despite me keeping ahead of him, he blocked the hall. I couldn't get past him to the front door and to safety.

I'd ran into my lounge for the eighth time when I had an idea. I stopped running and took the centaur by surprise when he followed me into the room a second later.

"Please," I said, in my best breathless voice. I wouldn't make the Oscars, but I was convincing enough. "You have me. Please let me have something to drink before you shoot me."

"Drink? You have drink?"

"Sure. In the cabinet beside you. Pass me a bottle and—"

"Drinking to numb the pain of death is a waste. I will drink it instead."

He eyed the bottles speculatively. There weren't that many. He grabbed one at random. It was a sweet and rather disappointing sherry given to me by one of my regulars. He downed it in a few gulps.

"That is not a warrior's drink."

"I'm not a warrior."

"What is this one?"

"Whisky." Another gift. I don't like whisky, but I keep it in case I have guests. It's a twelve-year-old single malt. Apparently, that's a good thing. The man who gave it to me assured me it was. He would have winced at the way the centaur drank it.

I made a move towards the hall. An arrow in my sofa stopped that idea.

"Nice try," he said with a leer. "I haven't finished drinking. That last one was worthy. I want more."

I sighed. "I don't have any more of that one."

He bristled at me. "What about this?"

"Oh, that's brandy," I said. "That's pretty similar." I have no idea, really. I don't drink brandy either and so I don't know how it compares to whisky. I know they're both pretty strong.

"Brandy! A warrior's drink." He picked up the bottle and swallowed the contents in an instant.

Let me just repeat what he had drunk. He had downed an entire bottle of brandy. It was not any old brandy, however. It was my special fortified brandy. Remember that from earlier? 99% sleeping potion? Yes, that one.

"That tasted funny," he said and picked up another bottle to wash it away.

"Not my Pinot Noir!"

He laughed. It was a cruel laugh, intended to hurt.

"It does not matter. You will die soon."

"I was saving that." It was probably one of the few bottles in my cabinet that I actually wanted to drink.

"What else ... what... what else have you... do you have?"

The potion was taking effect. He swayed more than usual, and his eyelids drooped.

"Try the gin," I said.

"Gih ... gih..."

He collapsed, as best he could, on my sofa, his horse body on the cushions and his human body draped over the back. His legs seemed to have multiplied and took up the rest of the room. No sooner was he there than his eyes closed, and he produced the loudest snores I have ever heard.

He had drunk enough to drop an elephant, so I didn't think he would wake for another couple of hours. I tried to make him comfortable with a blanket. Yes, I know he'd just tried to kill me,

TALES OF AN URBAN WITCH

but making people comfortable is woven into my DNA. It's what I do, even if the people in question were homicidal centaurs.

***

Back at the hospital, there was no change with Jake. Veronica continued to see his stability as a good sign. Agnes was still knitting, so no change there, either. I wondered, idly, if she was waiting for Jake, or had someone else she was going to escort to the afterlife.

I sent Veronica away for a foolish errand. Obviously, the old 'fetch a cup of tea' excuse would not work, so I got her to spy on the doctors to see if they were saying anything useful.

"Jake. Jake. Can you hear me?" I said as soon as she was out of earshot. There was no response, but I hadn't expected one. "I know about the centaurs, Jake. I know why they were chasing you. You're Chiron, aren't you?"

I worked it out on the way over. The centaur in the vision had said Jake was a traitor, but he also said that he would see his brothers one last time. Chiron was the only centaur who stood apart from the others and was therefore, somehow, a traitor. It didn't help that he wasn't related to either the centaurs that were the grandsons of Nephele, the cloud, or the ones with horns that came from Zeus having some 'me time' in Cyprus.

What happened next was both expected and unexpected in equal measure. What happened itself was expected: Jake turned into a centaur. I just didn't expect the way it happened.

I was expecting some sort of stretching and groaning and screaming as the centaur shape grew out of the man shape, in the way of many a Hollywood werewolf. That didn't happen. This transformation was so subtle that it made me question the nature of reality. It was a bit like being in a dream.

Before the transformation, Jake was Jake and had always looked like Jake. Two arms, two legs, one head. The usual. After the transformation, Jake was Chiron and, again, *had always looked like Chiron*. Two arms, *four legs*, one head, no horns. And *that* was the usual as well. Jake had somehow always been half a horse, and it was inconceivable that he could ever have been

203

ROBERT WILLIAMS

anything else, even though I knew he had two legs normally.

He was also fully conscious.

"Hello Mags," he said as if we were old friends. We were. Sort of.

"Nice to see you awake. Do I call you Jake or Chiron?"

"Jake will do for now. Keeps this normal."

"Normal? You're a centaur."

"I always was. You just never noticed."

I shrugged. "And you're a traitor?"

"Oh, you know centaurs. Talk to anyone outside the tribe and it's World War Three. And they hold grudges like you wouldn't believe."

"I would."

"Anyway, the traitor stuff is old news. They're only in a paddy because they found out I'd faked my death and was in hiding."

"And chased you all over South London."

"They sent word they wanted to talk, and, like a fool, I went along. I'm way too trusting."

"It was an ambush."

"Yes. I would have got away had I not run into Veronica."

"Veronica? You can see her?"

"When I'm like this, yes, but not when I only have the two legs."

"But you were shot as a human."

"Exactly. I have to change when I'm near a human."

"Present company excepted?"

"You know now. That's different."

Oh! I am so stupid. "Veronica described the other centaurs as bad horses and bad men. Horse, pause, man. Horse, man."

"Makes sense. You've got it now."

"I guess. The police were checking out backstreet riding schools."

Jake laughed. "She never was the best at description."

"She's got worse," I said, and laughed with him. "Anyway, who are the sons of Heracles?"

"You."

TALES OF AN URBAN WITCH

"Me?"

"Well, not you *per se*, but humans. People."

"Eh?"

"Centaurs hold grudges for millennia. You expect sense?"

"I guess not."

"Anyway, I was galloping back to the flat when I felt her nearby, and so I had to change."

"Then they shot you. Badly."

"They're always drunk."

"They didn't feel the need to change?"

"Not in front of ghosts."

My friend, Calliope, the Muse, exists as two interdependent entities. There's the goddess that I invoke in some of my spells, and there's also the human personification of the goddess. Unless she's concentrating, or is nearby, the human Calliope doesn't know about the invocations or any of the upper-level goddess stuff.

It's apparently the same, with variations, for all the Ancient Greek deities, major, and minor as well as the supporting cast, such as the centaurs. I do sometimes invoke Chiron in the occasional healing spell. I know, for a fact, that I've invoked him when trying to heal Jake. That vaguely embarrassed me. I'd been asking him to heal himself.

How did it work for the other centaurs? Did they have a spiritual essence as well? I was about to ask, but it turned out that was a question for another time.

"Veronica is," Chiron began, suddenly, but finished as Jake. "Coming back."

"The doctor was worried," she said as she returned to the room. Agnes looked up, her knitting suddenly finished.

"Hello Veronica," Jake said, as if this was the most natural meeting in the world, and his wife wasn't a ghost, and he hadn't just been a centaur, or been in a coma before that.

"Jake! You're better. Wait – you can see me. How?"

Her vocabulary was almost normal.

"He was nearly dead, Veronica," I said, supplying a plausible excuse. "Perhaps that's given him a bit of extra sight."

She seemed to accept that, thankfully. I didn't think we had time for the whole your-husband-is-secretly-a-centaur scenario. She went to hug him, realised she couldn't, but tried anyway.

"Oh, Jake, I'm so sorry," she said.

"Sorry? Why?"

"I was such a cow. I thought you were having an affair with Mags. I nearly killed you and ended up dying on my way to kill her."

"But you didn't, did you? It takes a lot to kill me."

Probably a lot more than she could have managed, anyway. Bashing him over the head with a frying pan didn't even come close.

"I was so angry. I shouldn't have been. I know I was wrong."

"It's okay, love."

"And then I died on the way to kill Mags. I tripped over a bloody cat, of all things."

Cat? I opened my mouth to ask a question, but she carried on talking, and I lost my opportunity.

"But I was still a cow and I'm sorry. It's taken me a long time to realise that. Can you forgive me?"

"I already have."

Time isn't so much a healer as people think. You don't forget how someone hurt you, but time gives perspective, and those painful events just cease to matter so much. I guess that's what was behind Jake's forgiveness. It was either that or some other perspective that being an immortal centaur gives you. Whatever. He forgave her and he meant it.

Agnes walked up to Veronica and handed her the product of her knitting. This time, it was a simple robe.

"You'd better put it on, Veronica," I said. "It's your time to go."

"Oh Jake, there is so much I want to say. I just don't know where to—"

"I love you too," he said.

"You're a good man, Jake."

He smiled at her with tears in his eyes.

TALES OF AN URBAN WITCH

Agnes took hold of Veronica's elbow and led her towards the door, which opened out onto something my eyes weren't allowed to see and certainly was not the corridor that should have been there. I closed my eyes in reflex, and I heard the door close. When I opened them again, both women had gone.

"Mags?" Jake said. "What happened? Am I in hospital?"

***

I gave Jake an explanation of sorts as to why he was there. I told him he'd been mugged. I didn't mention the arrows or the hoofprints. All evidence of both had gone, as had his memories of being a centaur and of seeing Veronica.

The doctor seemed quite happy to go along with the fictional mugging explanation. There was no way he could prove anything about the injuries, and he seemed to think I had something to do with them disappearing. He received Jake's thanks for helping him recover from the mugging and gave me a sly wink as we were leaving.

I took Jake back to his flat. He was fine and protested that he didn't need looking after, but I went with him, anyway.

"Do you think about Veronica much?" I asked him.

"I feel like she's still around sometimes. Does that sound weird?"

"No. Not at all."

He thought for a minute before speaking. "It's probably time to move on, though. Don't you think?"

"I think she would be okay with that."

"No, she wouldn't," he said with a laugh. "But she's not here now."

We laughed, and I said my goodbyes. I was going to miss Veronica. She annoyed me to distraction, but she'd grown on me.

***

I remembered the centaur on my sofa as soon as I entered my flat and smelt a combination of cider fumes and hay. He wasn't there. Not as a centaur, anyway. I found a man groaning loudly and clutching his head.

I had the oddest feeling I had seen him before. He wasn't a

207

ROBERT WILLIAMS

friend, obviously, and I didn't recognise him as a client. Perhaps he lived on the estate. No, that didn't feel right. Where—?

"What was I drinking?" he asked, interrupting my train of thought. Not that the train had been going anywhere useful.

"Cider. Lots and lots of cider. And whisky, wine, brandy..." I left out the sleeping potion.

His eyes opened wide at the sound of my voice. I don't know if he was expecting someone else or not expecting anyone at all.

"Where am I? Who are you?"

"I'm Mags. You're in my flat."

He looked desperately under the blanket I'd thrown over him before I'd left. As a centaur, he was naked, but as a man, he was wearing jeans and a fleece. How did that work? I shrugged mentally.

"Did I...?" he asked. "I mean, did we...?"

"No. Nothing like that happened."

He breathed a sigh of relief and I looked at him with narrowed eyes, insulted.

"Let me get you something for that hangover," I said. Strychnine, maybe.

He groaned again and collapsed back onto the cushions, and I went to the kitchen. My hangover cures are very popular on the estate, so I keep a stock of them ready-made in the cupboard under the sink. I mixed a hefty dose of it with some hot water and took it through.

"Thanks," he said when I handed it to him. "What is it?"

"A traditional remedy for hangovers. Don't ask what's in it. Just drink it."

He shrugged and sat quietly, sipping at the hot drink.

"I'm sorry," he said, between sips. "I really have no idea how I got here."

He was telling the truth. It wasn't just a hangover cure. He really didn't remember why he was here.

"You were very drunk. I took pity on you and offered you somewhere to sleep."

"Thanks," he said, then yawned. This combination of

TALES OF AN URBAN WITCH

hangover cure and truth potion creates an overpowering need to sleep. I'd used it a few times. On the positive side, he'd feel amazing when he woke up. "I'm sorry. I didn't think I was so tired."

"Have a nap if you want one."

"I really need to get back to the st ... office. I need to get back to work."

"You work on a Sunday?"

"No rest for the wicked," he said, yawning.

"You'd be better off sleeping."

He didn't need telling again.

I rang Jenny as soon as his eyes were closed and asked her to send an emergency Keeper round. They looked after centaurs, amongst other things. There must be one missing.

After that, I needed to talk to someone else, but I didn't have his number. There was only one way to do this, and it wouldn't make me popular. I burnt a slip of paper on my stove and muttered a handful of words.

I picked up an empty bottle cast aside by the centaur earlier and swung it carefully. Yes, it would do.

I threw the bottle at my armchair, but it hit something else before it got there. Hermes was doubled up on the floor, clutching his testicles.

"You bitch! You did it again. What do you want now?"

"I need to get another message to Zeus. He's got problems."

CHAPTER FOURTEEN

A MURDER ON THE CARDS

Witches don't always work in isolation. A lot of us urban witches keep in regular contact with each other and exchange words every few weeks or so. People think we communicate through crystal balls much like the wicked witch in The Wizard of Oz when she wanted to spy on Dorothy. They think there's some sort of magical network of communication lines linking crystal balls all over the world. In reality, we use mobile phones. They are much more convenient and usually much more reliable, depending on the network.

The thing about witches is that we're practical. We like to use the right tool for the job. If mobile phones were not available, we might try a crystal ball, but we'd see if there were any other routes we could try first. A carrier pigeon, perhaps, or a messenger boy. We stopped using crystal balls when the postal service started. Later we had telephones and then we had texting and WhatsApp. Lol.

All of which leads nicely into me telling you that my phone was ringing. It was my friend Emily. She's a rural witch, but I don't hold that against her. I do actually know, and like, several rural witches. Don't tell everyone. I make a big thing about not liking rural witches, but that's just talk. It's like people in Bromley pretending not to like people in Croydon.

"Hello Mags, dear. Something awful is going to happen," she

TALES OF AN URBAN WITCH

said. Her voice was strained.

"What's the matter?"

"I'm going to be murdered."

Emily can be a bit of a drama queen sometimes, but this was extreme even for her.

"Murdered? Are you sure?"

"Of course, I'm sure, dear. I've checked the cards, the tea leaves, and even the entrails. Every scrying method I know. All the same. I can see so far, but after that nothing. I have no future."

Scrying was Emily's speciality. She could read almost anything to get an impression of the future. You name it and I've seen her use it. She was always so accurate. If she told you it would happen, then it would happen. If she said she would die, then it was extremely likely she would die.

"I'm so sorry," I said, temporarily lost for anything useful to say. "How…?"

"I don't know, dear, but I know who does it. It's the witch who's working for Harris and Hall. She is there in all the readings I make of the future. It's her. I know it."

"You've seen her do it?" Accusing a witch of murdering another witch was obviously a serious allegation. About as bad as you could get.

She hesitated before replying. There was doubt in her voice when she spoke. "No, I don't see her kill me, but she's near me just before the end, and I know she's shouting at me. I can feel the aggression."

The problem with scrying was that it would only give you signs. The skill of the scryer lay in interpreting those signs. Emily was exceedingly skilled, but all she had told me so far didn't mean that the other witch would kill her. Not for certain. I knew that, and she knew it too. It would take me a while to get her to admit it, however. I decided to try a new line of questions.

"But why? Why would she … why would they want to kill you?"

"They're planning on building a new bottle factory in the

211

village. I'm organising the resistance. I have fifteen signatures on my petition already."

"And you think that's a good enough reason for them to want to kill you?"

"Yes."

"Are you sure? This is the twenty-first century. They could sue you into the middle of next week if they wanted and bribe someone to go ahead with the planning approval. Why go to the bother of killing you and risk getting caught?"

"Then why do I die?"

There could be any number of reasons, but she was convinced it was because of Harris and Hall. I told her to come to stay with me for a few days so we could talk it over and work out what to do. She was already on her way.

***

Once she was sitting on my sofa with a cup of tea in her hand, she was remarkably calm talking about her own death.

"Why can't you see it?" I asked her. Witches, by and large, are not squeamish about death, even their own. We've seen enough of it, and we see souls after they have left their bodies. We know it isn't the end. To a witch, the thought of her own death isn't as big an issue as it is for other people.

Emily sighed before answering. "I really don't know," she said. "There's something blocking my vision. That's never happened before."

Emily is a very good scryer and her interpretations are very accurate, but they are not direct sight. Some witches can get clear visions of the future in a crystal ball, like they're watching TV, but they aren't scryers.

She took a reflective sip of her tea before speaking again. "I know there's a house, Mags. Harris and Hall's witch is there. We're both outside and she shouts at me. I don't know why, and I can't work out what she's saying. Then we go in and it all cuts off. I can see nothing after stepping through that door."

"Where am I?"

"I don't know, but you are nearby. Perhaps you are on the

other side of the door."

"When does all this happen?"

"Tonight."

I all but spat out my tea and glared at her, tempted to kill her myself.

"That doesn't give us much time," I said. Mags Hammond, Mistress of Understatement, at your service.

"Sorry," she said. "I wasn't sure exactly when it would be until this morning."

"And you don't know where it's going to happen?"

"I figured it was somewhere near here, as I knew I had to come to you. I tried dowsing for where it would happen, but I couldn't find it."

Emily's dowsing skills for finding places are as good as mine for reading the future. In other words, next to useless.

I thought of possible ways I could use to find out the identity of Harris and Hall's corporate witch. It wouldn't be on their website. Companies were secretive about things like that and, if they employed a witch, she would be squirrelled away in an obscure HR department. I thought about calling someone at H&H. My best contact, Gwynneth, however, was busy with her new baby. And although I'd helped him, her brother was not my number one fan. He still refuses to drink Ribena.

In the end, I decided I should go a different route and get someone to look for the witch while I looked into where Emily's murder would take place. Emily was as much use as a chocolate teapot with anything other than scrying. I called Gavin.

"Hello Mags," he said. "This is becoming a bit of a habit. You know there's another number to call for help. Nine – nine – something. I forget the rest."

"Goodness me, you're funny. Ever thought of doing standup? Listen, I need your help. One of my friends is going to be murdered."

"Have they been threatened?"

"No. It's a premonition."

"I was scrying," Emily said in an annoyed whisper. I gave her a look that tried to show I was talking to someone who wouldn't know the difference, but I don't think she got it. She was laying out Tarot cards. It was a habit that was almost an instinct with her.

"You know I can't help until there's actually been a crime," Gavin said.

"Maybe you can. There's something about a witch working for Harris and Hall. Can you find out who that is?"

"I don't know—"

"Please. It's important. It might save a life."

There was a loud sigh at the other end of the line and Gavin promised to call back.

"He will find her," Emily said, as I hung up. "The cards say so."

"Good. Now, shall we try to find out where this will happen?"

I decided the best option was a pendulum on a local map. It was more precise than the dowsing rod and, although my crystal ball would give me images of where we were looking for, the images it gave were something only I could look at. I needed Emily to be looking to see if what I found rang any bells. Also, her presence would influence the pendulum. Hopefully.

I had Emily hold my large-scale *A-to-Z* open on my page and we both hoped it would contain the house she was looking for. Just in case, I stuck a post-it on the edge of the page with the word *No* written on it in marker pen. If the pendulum drifted over it, then I would know to use a map that covered a larger area and then another page in the *A-to-Z*. Given Emily's foresight, I had a strong suspicion that I wouldn't need to do that.

I cleared my mind, which is harder than it sounds. Try it. You'll wonder if your mind is clear yet. I held the pendulum over the map with my right hand and gave Emily my left hand to hold.

"Emily," I said. "Tell me about where Harris and Hall's witch shouts at you."

"Well, dear," she said, addressing the pendulum and not me. She actually raised her voice as well. No wonder she couldn't use one. "It is somewhere near here. The street is full of houses.

TALES OF AN URBAN WITCH

They're all crammed next to each other. There are no gaps between the houses. And there are a lot of cars."

She must have cast the cards dozens of times to get so much detail. Even so, this sounded like any street in southeast London, but luckily, the pendulum didn't work on mere words. As she spoke, Emily thought of the street, and those thoughts were shaping, through me, the path of the pendulum. It twitched and dragged my hand towards a different part of the page. It swung back and forth, but at the end of each swing, it was a little further north and west.

"Tell me about the argument you have with the other witch."

"I don't know what she says. I know she's angry. She points at the house. She shouts at me and then she drags me into the house."

The pendulum was responding. I could feel it moving with more certainty, creeping slowly across the page. North and west. Then north and west again, until its motion across the page halted. It was circling an area covering half a dozen streets.

"It's here," I said.

"There? But look at all of those little streets crammed in together. Saltash Street, Marazion Mews, Helston Road. It'll take days to look at them properly and we don't have that long. Can't you narrow it down?"

I didn't have to. I knew these streets. They were the Cornish Cluster, and although they now boasted internal toilets and central heating, the houses on the streets looked very much the same as they did when the Victorians built them. Right in the centre of the circle defined by my pendulum was Bodmin Street, where my former friend Dorothy used to live. You remember her? Dorothy, the changeling? The Dorothy that had gone back to live with her father in the Kingdom and her son had tried to kill me with a psychotic illusion? Yes, that Dorothy.

The house where she used to live was where Emily thought she would die. I would bet my crystal ball on it.

"I know the house."

"You do?"

ROBERT WILLIAMS

"Yes. You stay here. I'm going to check it out."

If the house was involved, then something was going on. The portal to the Kingdom may have reopened again and it could be that it was something from the other side of the portal that kills Emily. I had to investigate, and there was no way she could be there with me while I did so.

"I won't be long. Take a message from Gavin when he calls back. And if he gives you the address, don't go to see the other witch on your own. You got that?"

"Yes, dear," she said, distracted, already dealing another Tarot layout. As I left, I hoped I could believe her, but I worried I couldn't.

***

In most crime-thrillers on television, when all the clues have stacked up and the identity of the killer or thief or arsonist is known, the mismatched police duo or hard-bitten private detective and his apparently gormless but actually highly intelligent assistant will leap into a car and zoom off to stop the killer or prevent another murder. This was exactly the same, except that I was on the bus. I really had to buy a car. Or maybe find out how to use Uber.

There's nothing wrong with using the bus. It gets me from near point A to near point B fairly quickly and gives me time to think. Plenty of time.

Gwynneth Hall had offered me the chance to be Harris and Hall's corporate witch but I turned her down. She hadn't really expected me to accept, but she'd felt it was right to offer. She still kept in touch, and I helped her with her baby. Her brother and his husband were doing well, the last I heard. The boys were happily married, there was a baby on the way, and the business of making bottles was going well. It must have been, if they were setting up another plant on Emily's doorstep.

No-one mentioned the corporate witch, however. I guess they felt that was a little delicate.

Why would their corporate witch want to kill Emily? And why do it at the site of a known portal to the Kingdom? Had she turned against her sisters? Was she going to sacrifice Emily to the fairies? What would she gain from that?

My phone interrupted my thoughts with a buzz. Gavin was calling me.

"Did you get my message? I spoke to your friend. She sounded a bit..."

"Dizzy?"

"Distracted."

"Emily. She's the one who's going to be murdered. What was the message?"

"The corporate witch is called Hammond, Delores Hammond. She a relative?"

"She's my sister."

Delores had got herself a job with Harris and Hall as their corporate witch? How did that happen? I would have thought they'd have had more sense.

"I guess you don't need her address, in that case."

"Tell me you didn't give it to Emily."

He didn't answer.

"You did, didn't you?"

"Shouldn't I have?"

"It wasn't your best idea."

"Care to tell me why?"

I looked around me. At this time of night, the bus contained a mix of exhausted workers on their way home and young people heading into town for fun and frolics. Unlikely to be listening, but I still didn't want to say that I feared for Emily's life out loud.

"Not here. Let's just say they won't get along."

I told him where I was going and that he had to keep Emily away. I ended the call and saw I'd had a couple of texts. The first was from Emily.

Found out who the H&H witch is. On my way to see her.

Bugger! Why was Emily so stupid? If she thought Delores was going to kill her, why go and see her?

The other text was from Delores herself.

Who this mad bitch? Why U send her here?

I tried to think how to answer both of them but couldn't think of anything. Whatever I said would not help. I knew nothing would happen at Delores's flat, however. The action would happen in Bodmin Street. I had a little time, but I needed to get there faster, so I cast a silent spell to make the bus driver miss a few stops on the way and the passengers to doze in their seats. I made sure the driver stuck to the speed limit, however, and did not miss any red lights.

***

Bodmin Street was dark and quiet when I arrived. I'd left the bus in something of a state of chaos. The other passengers woke to find they had all missed their stops and started shouting at the poor bus driver when I allowed him to pay attention to his route again.

Dorothy's old house looked as well kept as it had the last time I was there. Of course, that was summer, and it was now winter and dark to boot, but there was enough light from the streetlights to show plenty of plants and a clean, leaf-free path.

"Mags! Come on in." Dave was his usual cheerful self. He was holding baby Dorothy in his arms as he opened the door. "We haven't seen Aunty Mags in ages, have we?" he said to her.

Dorothy wouldn't remember me. Depending on how you measured her age, she was either coming up for her first birthday or was a hundred and thirty. She had been swapped for a fairy when she was a young baby, well over a century ago, but hadn't aged a day. Time was funny in the Kingdom.

"Has the portal done anything recently?" I asked.

"Not that I could tell. I check every day."

"You don't go inside, do you?"

He laughed. "Do I look daft? I don't go any closer than the attic steps."

"Mind if I look?" I asked, and in answer, he pointed me towards the loft. As I stepped up the stairs, I couldn't feel anything untoward from the portal, but we had hidden it away in a spell-warded Faraday cage. There was no way I should feel anything.

Up against the door, however, it was a different story. I could hear a voice, not distinctly enough to make out the words, but I could tell it was male and demanding. It sounded like Dorothy's father, the King.

"Take Beth and Dorothy somewhere safe," I said. "I have to go in and this could turn ugly."

He nodded and left, knowing better than to argue.

I studied the barrier spell I had left on my last visit. The semi-circle on the wall was untouched, but the one on the floor was a little scuffed, so I carefully refreshed it with a bag of salt I had brought along.

Then I took a large brass key from a hook on the wall and unlocked the door.

**

The room was exactly as I had left it. There wasn't anything that could change. There was literally nothing in the room. Nothing, that is, apart from the aluminium foil lining the walls, floor, ceiling, and the door, and the portal hanging in the air in the centre of the room. It was no longer the rugby-ball-sized volume of glowing air I'd left here, however, and, instead, filled the room from floor to ceiling.

The portal was just a patch of glowing air for the moment. I couldn't see through it. I could hear, however. The fairy choir was there. Perhaps they needed to be there to keep the portal open from their side, sounding as beautiful and ethereal as ever. They were very much in the background, however. Over the chorus, one male voice kept up a tirade.

"I want the witch. Bring her to me! Bring her now."

I said nothing. If there was a chance I could find out what was going on without the Kingdom knowing I was here, the safer I would be.

"Ah! I know you're there, witch." So much for that. "I can smell you."

More likely he felt the surge in radio waves when I opened the door but, you know, any chance to put the boot in.

"What do you want?"

"I want you."

"Nice to know I've still got it. Why do you want me so urgently?"

"We are ready to take back your world. My daughter says you can make it easy for us."

Oh, no you don't, sunshine.

"I'm sorry, but I won't help you."

"Why not? It will happen one way or another. You know this as truth."

"How? This is the only—"

He ignored me.

"You will just make it happen sooner rather than later."

The voices, the beautiful fairy voices had changed without me noticing. Their song was now full of joy and laughter, beguiling, and it was working its magic on me. Digging itself under my skin. It was a song I wanted to join, and I needed to be part of the choir to sing it. My left foot, all on its own, took a step forward.

"Come to me, witch. Come and serve me. Help me lead my fairy army to reclaim your world.

My right foot moved closer to the portal. The voices grew louder and more enticing.

"That's it. You will serve me and I shall reward you."

Reward? I couldn't think of anything better than being in the Kingdom. My left leg moved again. Why was my progress so slow? Why wasn't I running into the portal?

"A part of you is scared," he said, as if answering my thoughts. "Don't be afraid. You will help us, or you will die."

Both options sounded amazing. My right foot stepped forward and I could suddenly feel the outer edge of the portal caress my face. I gasped.

"Come to us. Serve us. Die for us."

One more step and I would be there. I would see fairyland. I would be part of it. The anticipation was almost overpowering, and I could feel my movements in infinite slowness. My left leg moved, the foot lifting off the ground a millimetre. My foot edged forward. I could feel my weight shifting and I started slipping further into the portal. The choir's voices were the most beautiful thing I had ever heard. They were so clear this close to the portal. They were calling my name! They loved me. They —

Something cold wrapped itself around me and I was dragged backwards.

"Come on now, Mags! You don't want to go there, do you? Silly mare."

I wailed wordlessly, my longing for fairyland inarticulate, an emptiness in my soul. The cold thing wrapped around me was a chain, an iron chain, that held me back from the portal.

"This won't hold me. I belong there."

"Bring her back!" My lord was commanding them to return me. Why weren't they obeying? Didn't they feel his words echo in their blood, like they echoed in mine?

"No, you don't, Mags. Stay here." That was Delores. I recognised her voice. Why was she here? I fought against my bonds, but they weren't shifting. "Ignore him."

"This might work," said another voice behind me. Emily! I knew I couldn't trust Delores, but Emily? I could trust no-one. Neither of them took any notice of my lord.

"Do it," Delores said.

"Whatever you do," said a man's voice. It sounded like Gavin. Another traitor. "Do it quickly. I won't be able to hold her for long."

"This might hurt, dear," Emily said … and then it felt like a red-hot poker had been slammed into my arm and I screamed. The voice on the other side of the portal screamed as well, but then was silent.

My thoughts were my own.

"Thank you," I said, once the pain had subsided. "Steel needle?"

"Yes. Did it work?"

I nodded, feeling too drained to speak.

"Let her go," Delores said. "She's okay now."

"Are you sure, dear?"

"She's not struggling, so that's a good sign," Gavin said, and relaxed his grip on the chain. I slipped myself out of the loop and faced the three of them.

"I was so close to going through. You stopped me. Thank you." I still wasn't sure if I meant it.

"What were you doing here?" Delores asked.

"Emily's prediction is centred on here. She said you were going to be shouting at her outside—"

"I was! She dragged me here because she said you were in danger, and then dithered around in the street like an old woman."

"But ... but I am an old woman, dear."

"You know what I meant."

"Thanks for coming," I said.

"S'okay."

"All the same, you should have kept her away from here," I turned to Gavin. "Both of you."

"And you were definitely in danger, dear. I checked the cards again."

"So why did you come in, Mags?" Delores asked. "We weren't here yet. You could have waited outside."

"I came in to check on the portal and then there was a lot of shouting from the Kingdom," I said. "I could hear through the door."

"Yes. What did he want, dear?"

"He needs me to help him invade."

On cue, or perhaps he was listening, the voice started again. "Come to me, witch."

"Never," I said, shouting at the portal. "We need to do something about this," I said to the others.

"Couldn't you just close this thing?" Gavin asked.

I nodded. "I have all I need to close it and keep it closed."

For a second, I worried about the portals that used to exist. The ones from long ago, when the Kingdom had access to our world. The Council had closed them, but how weakened had the barrier between our worlds become? Had they all been closed properly?

I shook my head.

That was a problem for another time. We needed to deal with this portal right now.

"Well, what can we do then?"

"I don't know. Last time I left the portal partially open, but obviously they pried it open from the other side. We need to close it this time."

"Wait a minute," Emily said and sat on the floor, facing the portal. She started shuffling her Tarot deck.

"Emily," I said. "We don't have time for this."

"Shh, dear, I'm concentrating."

She took one card from the pack and lay it face down in front of her.

"This will tell us what to do," she said and turned the card over.

Death. Upside down.

"That isn't encouraging," Gavin said.

"It means change is coming," Delores said, obviously having done her homework for once. "Not necessarily death, although that is a change of sorts."

"That was stupid of me," Emily said. "I wasn't thinking of the question clearly enough."

"We *really* don't have time for this, Emily."

"I have to know what to do, Mags. Do we close the portal? How do we close it? How do we make sure it stays closed? I have to know. *We* have to know."

She shuffled and picked out another card. It was death reversed again.

"I don't understand."

"You were wondering if we close the portal," I said. "Perhaps we do. It would be the death of the portal."

"Yes, I was distracted. But how should the answer be this? What change can we embrace to help?"

"You are a scryer." the voice said. "That is useful. You will help us."

Emily stood up and started moving towards the portal.

"No!" I said. "He's got her now. Quickly, Gavin, grab the chain."

Emily stopped and turned to face me.

"Stop panicking, dear. He doesn't have me. Not even close. I just want to be closer to the portal to get a clearer answer."

"Emily, no. It's too dangerous. You know what they're like. Get away from it."

"Yeah, come away from there, you silly cow. It's not safe. Even I know that." A bit of refreshing honesty from Delores there.

Emily hesitated then and started moving away from the portal. None of us saw it until it was too late. As she took another hesitant step towards me, an arm snaked out from the portal and grabbed her, pulling her into the Kingdom. She didn't even have time to scream.

The fairy choir cut off, and the portal began to shrink.

"If that thing closes, we'll never get her out of there!"

"I know that! What can we do to stop it closing?"

I couldn't answer Delores. The spell I had used to open it originally needed elements that I just didn't have with me. I had brought everything I needed to close it, but nothing to open it.

There was a metallic ringing noise, and something flew past me into the portal.

"Get that out of here!" The voice on the other side screamed at us in rage while the portal continued to shrink. It shrank so far but was stopped from closing by the chain that Gavin was holding in his hands.

"I'll call mum," Delores said, reaching for her phone. "She'll know what to do."

Despite the situation, I found myself insulted by the suggestion. The Hammond sisters couldn't get themselves out of their own mess and had to call their mother. After a second of reflection, however, I realised that we needed all the help we could get. I nodded to Delores in agreement, then stopped.

I'd had an idea.

I pulled out my own phone and scrolled through my contacts until I reached E. Then I picked a number and hit 'call'.

"I hope this works," I said, opening the room's door to allow

TALES OF AN URBAN WITCH

the signal to get past the foil barrier.

"What?" asked Gavin and Delores. At the same time, a phone started ringing in the distance, small and tinny. It was the Imperial March from *Star Wars*. Cheeky cow.

Soon after that, the screaming started. The ethereal choir and the King all sounded in sudden and powerful pain.

"Hello, Mags," Emily answered the phone as if this were a regular occurrence.

"Hi Emily, it's Mags." I said. I know it was stupid. It wasn't a normal call. It's a habit. Sue me. "What's going on?"

"The King and all of his people are rolling around on the floor, dear. You must be able to hear them."

"Yes, quite clearly."

"I don't think they like my mobile phone, dear. Shall I turn it off?"

"No! Get away from them. Can you jump through the portal?"

"Yes, I think so, dear."

"Then what are you waiting for?"

Emily landed heavily on the floor.

***

The screaming stopped as soon as Emily left the Kingdom, so I wasted no time in putting my plan into action of closing the portal. It didn't need much encouragement, as it had been trying to close by itself, our chains stopping it. I had Gavin pull them out, while I enlisted the help of Delores and Emily to speed up the portal's closure.

Then we had a pot of tea in Dave's kitchen, and I gave him a call. I told him what had happened, and that I needed someone to watch out for the portal re-opening, in case the Kingdom had any other ideas about making a visit. It was *probably* safe, I added, but couldn't make any greater assurances than that. It was a weak spot, and they would test it continually.

I would give Dave and his family some of the charms that the three of us would use to protect ourselves from the Kingdom.

He had no qualms about returning to the house with his family, however, saying my 'probably' carried more weight with

him than someone else's sure thing.
I wish I had his confidence.

CHAPTER FIFTEEN

REBELLION

L ondon is a great cultural mixing pot. People from all over the world come here to live. Their ways become our ways and ours become theirs. Often, there are little cultural communities dotted around here and there, where people live alongside friends and family from their homelands. These areas all add colour to the city, and the people living in them, most of the time, become Londoners eventually.

In my part of London, my estate, and the group of streets in the Cornish Cluster, we have Greektown and Little Rome. Not their official names, of course, but the people that live in them seemed proud of the labels and so they stuck. They'd had those names for as long as I could remember.

Each area has its own businesses and shops, all of which miraculously thrive despite competition from each other, from large chains, and from the Internet. They are two islands of commercial success.

For reasons that escape me, however, given the usual accord between Italy and Greece, the inhabitants of Greektown and Little Rome hated each other with barely controlled passion.

It was unfortunate that they faced each other across the same stretch of Tintagel Road. The road was a mirror, the Greek side reflecting the Italian and the Italian reflecting the Greek.

Bax, the rather trendy Italian artisan bar, has been accused of writing false bad TripAdvisor reviews about the rather more basic, but equally popular, Greek taverna that faced it. The Greek nail bar and the Italian tanning salon often had ridiculous price wars with extreme discounts and special offers to attract customers from their rivals across the road.

The two taxi firms got on well enough and made a token show of hostility. I think there was more than enough business for both of them. Uber had no impact on their clientele at all, and they were always busy. They complained about stealing each other's customers, but I would often see their drivers drinking together in the *Werewolf and Tin Mine*, three streets away in Warleggan Avenue.

Incidentally, the *Werewolf's* landlord really was a Cornish werewolf. He'd had all his shots, however, and his Keeper had taken him to obedience classes, so I felt safe enough leaving him to his own devices.

The crowning glories of the two communities were the restaurants that faced each other like fortresses. The establishments had remained civil to each other as far as I knew, although I had heard Greek-accented rumours that the pizzeria had been serving chicken-topped pizza, a gross insult of the highest order.

They were only rumours, however, and attempts to link them to *Olympus*, the Greek restaurant opposite, quickly foundered. *Olympus* was a family business, nominally run by a man called Diomidis, the patriarch of Greektown.

Most of the time, his involvement with the restaurant seemed to extend no further than sitting with the customers, eating, drinking, and chatting, as if the restaurant were an extension of his home, and he'd invited all his friends round. I was a regular at the restaurant. I loved the food, and I'd chatted with Diomidis many times. When his wife wasn't in sight, he was the most dreadful flirt.

"Ah, Miss Mags!" His greetings whenever I entered his restaurant were always enthusiastic. "How wonderful to see you. Come in, come in. Sit. Sit."

TALES OF AN URBAN WITCH

"Hello, Diomidis. You're busy." It was ten in the morning and the restaurant was already full of people. It always was.

"People like it here. They come early and stay late. Can I offer you some wine?"

"It's a little early for me."

He shrugged. "Coffee then?"

I nodded. "Coffee would be lovely." Greek coffee is very strong, so I take the variety that's made with sugar. Diomidis gestured to one of his waiters, who brought me a steaming cup.

"Aren't you going to join me for a coffee?" I asked, knowing he would have to. It was rude of the host not to share.

"Of course."

And while the waiter distracted him, I made my move. I threw a small slip of rice paper into the flame of the candle on the table. It flared and disappeared before anyone noticed. The long and complicated spell I had written on it hung invisibly in the air, awaiting direction.

"Enjoy your coffee, Diomidis," I said, emphasising his name, and gesturing under the table. The spell would know what to do, and I felt it drift over to him. We chatted about inconsequentialities, before I said, "Actually, can I have a word with you in private?"

He stood and gestured me into his office. Just as he was closing the door, I uttered a few words to activate the spell.

"May my words be heard as truth."

Out of context of the rest of the spell, that sounded like I wanted to practise some deceit. Actually, the opposite was the case. I needed to tell Diomidis something, and I wanted him to know that I was telling the truth without having to waste time convincing him.

"Did you say something, Miss Mags?"

"I know you are Zeus," I said.

Diomidis paused, hunched over, with his hand on the doorknob as if deep in thought, and then suddenly straightened up. He stood taller and prouder than he had been a few seconds ago.

229

ROBERT WILLIAMS

"Very well played, Mags," Zeus said in a voice that could have doubled for James Mason. "What can I do for you?"

***

This entire business of the Greek gods is confusing, so let me explain it again. The gods exist in two separate, yet connected, forms. There's the godlike essence, the part that performs miracles and to which their followers pray. Then there's the god's human avatar, their bodily presence, which is just as happy performing miracles but doesn't have to listen to prayers and whatnot.

The two aren't well connected. The essence handles most of the day-to-day god stuff, while the avatar gets on with life and fills out the tax returns. I think of the earthly presence as the actual god, while the essence is like an autonomous answering machine. I could be completely wrong about that, of course.

Hermes had let me know where Zeus was hiding out. I have no idea why he had chosen to slum it here, or why he was running a restaurant, but as far as gods are concerned, I've learned there's no way to understand their logic. They move in mysterious ways, after all.

"We have a problem," I said.

"We?"

"You and I."

"And what is *our* problem?"

"Do you know where your satyrs are? And your centaurs?" Especially the centaurs.

"Of course! They are all living and working here."

"Are you sure about that?"

"I am Zeus. I am omnipotent and omniscient. I know everything."

I smiled at his confidence.

"Why not take a look?"

"I don't need to. I know where they all are. Remember, I know everything."

"Indulge me."

"You are testing my patience, witch." Always it's 'witch'. Can't

TALES OF AN URBAN WITCH

even Zeus think of a better insult?

I glared at him. "I've got better things to do than this, you know. Just have a chat with your essence."

"My what?"

"You know. The other you. You upstairs. Disembodied you."

"Ah, *me*. I don't chat with me, you know. That isn't the way it works."

"I don't care what you do. He, you, he … er… knows what I am talking about.

"Very well," he said, then closed his eyes, reopening them an instant later. They blazed and his hair crackled around him, full of static. His beard had grown out, and he wore flowing robes in place of jacket and jeans. He looked like you'd expect Zeus to look when wardrobe and the special effects department had a decent budget.

"Where are they? Where are my centaurs?"

I shrugged. "I can tell you where some of them are and how to find others but, as for the rest…"

"They should be here."

"What should keep them here?"

"Obedience to me, their father, their god." Goodness me, he had an ego problem and no mistake. "Hera! Hermes! Attend me."

A puff of wind announced the arrival of Hermes. A shriek and a crash from the main dining room was followed by Diomidis's wife hurrying in, wiping her hands on her apron and looking dazed. She took one look at special-effects Zeus, realised the restaurant owner's wife act was not needed and assumed a more regal pose.

"My apologies, great Zeus," she said. "I was serving table nine their starters."

She turned and noticed me for the first time. The room turned suddenly chilly.

"And who is this … woman?" She made the word sound like 'slut'.

"Hello," I said, standing up and smiling. "My name is Mags. It's a—" I would have continued, but she cut me off.

ROBERT WILLIAMS

"Zeus?"

Zeus's aura dimmed, so he looked again like Diomidis but standing straighter and with a big bushy beard.

"Calm down, Hera. Mags has brought a problem to our attention."

"And what is that?" She stared at me as if afraid that I would seduce Zeus while she blinked. She was definitely the jealous type.

"The centaurs are gone," Zeus said.

"The centaurs?"

"And the satyrs," I added.

Anger crossed her face. Sluts weren't allowed to speak, apparently.

"They're gone? What do you mean?"

"They aren't here," Zeus said. "I can only feel one or two satyrs and there are no centaurs at all."

"Are they dead? Satyrs cannot die." Ah! I'd wondered about that.

"No, they are just not here."

"But they should all be here. The waiters are still in the restaurant."

"They are not satyrs. Ask one."

She nodded, and a waiter appeared in the middle of the room. He looked at us and started screaming. I nearly joined him. I've seen many odd things as an urban witch, especially since I started spending time with not-so-ancient Greek gods, but people appearing out of thin air was alarming.

The waiter's screams were silenced by a gesture from Hera, and he looked at the four of us placidly, as if waiting to take our order.

"Hello Yiannis," she said to him.

He nodded at her, casually. Teleportation was now nothing to worry about in his world.

"Tell Zeus who you are."

"Zeus?" He looked surprised.

Hera frowned. "Yes, Zeus," pointing at her husband with her

TALES OF AN URBAN WITCH

chin.

Yiannis raised his eyebrows and smirked. "Zeus?"

"He sees Diomidis," I said in a whisper to Hera. "And now he thinks 'Zeus' is your pet name for him."

"Thank you, whore. I can see that for myself." Whore? Well, I suppose it was made a change from 'witch'.

"Remember your true self," she said to the waiter, giving it one last try, even though she knew she was wasting her time.

He laughed openly at her. "Hey Dio! Your missus has been hitting the *ouzo* a little early today, eh?"

Hera's face became thunderous, and, with a gesture, she made the waiter sleep and then vanish.

"They're all like that," Hermes said with forced patience. "Human."

"You don't sound surprised," Zeus said.

Hermes shrugged. "It's been happening for years."

"Years?" The special effects halo reasserted itself. "Why was I not told?"

"We thought you knew. What with you being omniscient and all-powerful and all."

"Enough with the insolence, messenger. Who else knows about this?"

"Everyone."

"Even Hera?"

Hera bristled. "I can assure you I did not know about this."

"Everyone except Hera," Hermes said, and I could see why none of the other gods had mentioned it. Both Hera and Zeus were prickly.

"Excuse me," I said. "But who knew and who didn't tell you doesn't matter at this stage. You need to sort out your missing people." Especially the centaurs and most especially the ones who had been shooting at me.

Hera looked at me as if I were a talking turd, and Zeus's aura flamed.

"Forgive me, noble father," Hermes said. "But she is right. We were wrong in not informing you and we should be punished,

233

but first we need to deal with the escaped satyrs, centaurs, and who knows what else is missing."

Both Zeus and his wife had flaming auras at this point.

"You dare to tell us what we need to do?" they said, speaking as one. Neat trick.

"How much damage do you think just one escaped centaur can do in twenty-first century London?" I asked, thinking of the arrows I had had to pull from my walls and my sofa, thankful that the centaur had been too drunk to aim straight.

Zeus shrugged, not caring.

"Alright then. Let's assume that one centaur could do quite a bit of damage." They can. "Now, there's definitely more than one missing. I don't know exactly how—"

There was a puff of air as Hermes left and re-entered the room. He whispered a number in my ear.

"How much damage could thirty-eight do?" I asked Zeus and Hera.

"To the human world? Does it matter?" Hera said.

"But what signal does it give your people?"

The auras dimmed but were still flaming. I pressed on.

"Who's next? Who's going to say, 'old Zeus can't keep the horses in the stable anymore, let's go' or worse? Who's going to think they'd do a better job?"

The auras died.

"You make a good point," Zeus said. "What do we do?"

***

There was a lot of talking. I told him about the Keepers and how their members dedicated their lives to keeping the rest of the world safe by keeping satyrs, centaurs, and everything else bonded to them. I told him about Bruce, the satyr, and his Keeper. I told him about the drunken centaur chasing me round my flat. I told him of Chiron, who I knew as my friend Jake. The gods nodded and mumbled something that might have been an apology or might have been a murmured curse.

Hermes, Zeus, and Hera then reviewed the inhabitants of Greektown. Cyclops, gorgons, dryads, nymphs. Many of them

TALES OF AN URBAN WITCH

were missing. Worryingly, however, there was a problem.

"Now, I'm no accountant," I said, "but things don't add up."

I had been comparing the numbers of missing creatures with the numbers that the Keepers told me they had been looking after.

"Perhaps some have evaded the Keepers," Zeus said. "There must be a few who were wily enough to keep their heads down. You said there was at least one herd of centaurs on the loose."

"Oh, I agree, but that doesn't explain why the Keepers are looking after fifty-four satyrs when you only have twenty-nine missing."

"What? How? Oh." In the course of those three words, Zeus's expression had changed from smug satisfaction at explaining why the Keepers had too few satyrs, to puzzlement at them having too many and, finally, to a strange mix of embarrassment and sullen anger.

"Oh?"

"Zeus, my lord. It might not be them," Hera said quickly. "You know how stupid humans can be. Perhaps the Keepers of whom the witch speaks are unable to count."

"No," he said, with resignation heavy in his voice. "It's *them*. I can feel it."

"Who are *they*?" I asked, but Hera and Zeus ignored me.

"*Them*. You know. The *Romans*," Hermes said the word in a hissed whisper, but Zeus still heard it and groaned.

"The Romans?" I repeated, not understanding.

The three of them looked at each other.

"Jupiter," said Zeus.

"Mercury," said Hermes.

"I will not sully my lips with that harlot's name," said Hera.

"Juno?" I asked, and Zeus nodded slowly. Hera fumed.

"But I thought…"

"Yes?" Zeus asked in a way that made me hold my tongue. Hermes, standing behind Zeus, was making very clear 'shut up' style gestures at me. I was going to say that I thought that Jupiter, Juno, and Mercury were just the names the Romans had

235

ROBERT WILLIAMS

given to Zeus, Hera, and Hermes. Clearly, I was wrong.

"I thought," I started again, "that the Roman gods were over in Italy."

My improvisation was lame. They all knew exactly what I had been about to say. Zeus's eyes blazed, but he reined in his aura. Hermes gave me a cautious thumbs-up, and Hera hated me. She already did, so at least I hadn't made matters worse.

"No, they are not there. They had to migrate when we did."

The penny dropped.

"Oh, my G —" I stopped myself again from making another faux pas. "They're in Little Rome. They live across the road."

***

You'd think, when my life started to include Greek gods, that I would have worked out there was a more than reasonable chance that I would be able to meet their Roman equivalents. It hadn't even occurred to me they had independent lives to the Greeks.

A little history is appropriate here. You can surf the web as well as I can, but I can tell you're lazy. The Romans, when they met a new civilisation, would incorporate elements of that culture into their own, with a few little tweaks here and there. They were particularly fond of doing it with gods, and including the Greek pantheon into theirs was wildly successful. Zeus, Hera, and the others became the Romans' primary gods, but renamed. Mostly.

What I hadn't realised until today was that in doing so, the Romans had created new gods, and not just created new legends and new statues, but called into being new actual gods. Zeus was still Zeus, but Jupiter was a Johnny-cum-lately.

***

If I hadn't seen the connection before, then having Zeus and Jupiter, Hera, and Juno, and Hermes and Mercury in the same room at the same time, made it obvious. Zeus and Jupiter could have been identical twins whose mother had dressed them in different outfits. Zeus, as I'd mentioned, looked exactly like the hundreds of statues and paintings of him. Robes, flowing white

236

TALES OF AN URBAN WITCH

hair and beard. He sounded more British than a BBC presenter from the fifties. Jupiter, on the other hand, had a shaven scalp and designer stubble. He wore a snazzy suit and dark glasses that looked more expensive than most cars. He had a pronounced, but obviously affected, Italian accent that wouldn't have been out of place in a sixties sitcom, when people thought of Italy as a faraway place that was as out of their reach as the moon. He looked like Zeus, but with an *Inspector Montalbano* makeover.

Considering that these were gods and could choose every aspect of their physical avatars, the way they looked and sounded said a lot about them. Exactly what it said is left as an exercise for the reader, but I have to say that both gods looked uncomfortable with the other's chosen appearance. Embarrassed, even.

Hera and Juno were another story. Both women wore outfits that complemented their husbands' choices of clothing and yet somehow matched each other. Hera's simple robe could have been modelled from one of her statues and Juno's elegant dress could have jumped off a catwalk in Milan. Both outfits, however, looked almost identical. Like their husbands, they could have been twins.

Regardless of their similarities, however, there was no way they would call each other sister. They obviously hated each other. If Hera's dislike of me could be rated as an eight on a scale of one to ten, then Juno would have scored twenty-nine. Were they cats, they would have been circling each other with their claws out. Soon, one of them would screech and leap at the other.

The boys, Hermes and Mercury, were different again. Both looked identical, even down to the same winged helmets. They also wore tight, briefer-than-brief loincloths that left nothing to the imagination. I really had seen thicker belts. No, that's untrue. I had seen thicker shoelaces. They paid lip service to the idea that they were supposed to hate each other. The words were there, but they were accompanied by million-volt glances that made me feel like I'd wandered into a gay porn movie. Had this been the seventies, they would have had moustaches and be dressed

237

as plumbers.

We were in neutral ground, a squash court in the local leisure centre. The overweight middle-aged salesmen originally intending to give each other heart attacks here had come down with simultaneous tummy bugs and had to cancel. Nothing to do with me. Honest.

Hermes had issued the invitation, and the meeting was arranged within minutes. The gods could move quickly when it suited them. Hermes and Mercury always moved quickly, of course, but that wasn't what I meant.

"Eh, Zeus! What's up, man?" Jupiter asked.

Zeus ran through the issue that I'd outlined earlier, and the three Romans went through the same stage of disbelief before checking.

"Our male centaurs have all vanished," Mercury reported. "Some of the females remain. We have most of our fauns—"

"Fauns?" Zeus asked, not understanding.

"Faun is the Roman name for satyr," I replied, trying to be helpful.

"And you have female centaurs?" Hera asked. "We don't have those. Thankfully."

She raised a questioning eyebrow at Juno, who looked at Jupiter in disgust and nodded. Both women tutted.

I had Mercury give me the total number of missing creatures and I added them to the totals Hermes had given me earlier.

"Well, the good news is that the numbers of fauns, satyrs, and centaurs are all above the totals given to me by the keepers."

"And what is the bad news?" Zeus asked.

"There's different types of bad news."

"Eh, just spit it out, signora."

I shrugged. "There are still a lot of things missing. The Keepers only look after three centaurs, for instance. And they are all male."

"Shit," said Hermes.

"There's more, isn't there?" Zeus said, and I nodded.

"Neither of you have trolls, do you?" They gave me a blank

look. "I suppose they're more Norse than anything else. You got Odin's phone number somewhere?"

I laughed at my own weak joke but stopped when Jupiter extracted a very expensive-looking phone from a pocket in his jacket.

"I follow him on Twitter."

***

We repeated the exercise with Odin and Amun-Ra and a few other gods I hadn't heard of. Each added to the totals that I was running and mopping up the odd monster and demigod that the Keepers were looking after.

All the patriarchs looked different, but all shared some element of Zeus-ness, for want of a better word. In a movie, they'd all be played by the same talented actor. The most imposing was Zeus, the most aloof was Amun-Ra, and the best dressed was Jupiter. Dagda, the Celtic patriarch, was trying to be everyone's friend, although my favourite was Odin, but that was because he'd turned up with his wolves.

"Careful! They're vicious," he'd said, as they'd both rolled onto their backs so I could tickle their tummies.

The increase in numbers – the patriarchs had all brought a catalogue of other gods with them – meant we had to move from the squash court to the main hall, evicting four sets of people due to play badminton. More tummy bugs. We could have moved to the park, but that felt too public.

We accounted for all the creatures that the Keepers looked after, apart from a few latter-day monsters like vampires and werewolves, that the Keepers knew about that the gods didn't. That didn't go the other way, however. There were still centaurs, fauns, satyrs, naiads, gorgons, and trolls missing from the pantheons' 'stables' that the Keepers hadn't even seen.

"So, where are they?" I asked the assembled gods again. I was tired of asking. "The Keepers don't know where they are and there have been no reports of suspicious activity from the police." Thank you, Gavin.

The gods looked at each other, embarrassed, like a class full of children who hadn't been listening properly and still didn't know which side was the hypotenuse.

Dagda shrugged and popped open a tin of lager.

"I know you said earlier that satyrs didn't die, but what about the rest of them? Could they be dead?" I asked. I knew the newer creatures could die. Vampires definitely could.

"No," Zeus said, with a sigh. "They can't. At least, not permanently. That means they must be hiding somewhere."

"Eh, Miss Mags," Jupiter said, "Can we not just talk to one of the centaurs? Or a faun? The Keepers must be able to have one of them to talk to us."

"You think I haven't asked the Keepers? All I get is a load of flannel. They know nothing. Or so they tell me."

"The centaurs could tell us," Zeus said.

"I can be very persuasive," said Jupiter, sounding like Robert De Niro.

I shrugged. "I know a satyr and a centaur. Maybe Hermes could—"

There was a draught. "Found them," he said. "I looked them up in your phone. Maybe Mercury could give me a hand to bring them here?"

He winked at his counterpart, who winked back, and they vanished in a blur. Those boys were not subtle.

While we waited for the messengers to return with Jake, I mean Chiron, and Bruce, I made small talk with the gods. I had a million questions, but the one burning itself onto my tongue was this: why were they here? London, I mean. I wasn't questioning their existence. I wasn't sure I needed the answer to anything existential. But why London?

None of the gods had had to come far for this gathering. The Greeks and the Romans lived around the corner. The Norse lived in Rotherhithe, the Egyptians near Heathrow, the Babylonians near King's Cross. The Celts in Kilburn. Why? Why had they left their homes? What was so special about London to have attracted them here.

"You want to know about Judaism and Christianity?" Zeus

asked, before I could ask a thing. A smile played on his lips.

I looked around to see if Jesus had turned up and helped himself to one of Dagda's beers.

Zeus and a few other gods laughed.

"Relax. They're not coming."

"Why not?"

"Too busy. They've got people praying in their ears every second of every day. The admin alone is a nightmare. We're retired and have just enough followers to keep us ticking over."

"That makes sense," I said and nodded as a sort of mental full stop. I still hadn't asked them about London.

***

I made more uncomfortable small talk with the gods, somehow unable to bring up the subject of London with them. Eventually, we could hear hooves in the corridor outside the hall, and we all breathed a silent sigh of relief. Hermes and Mercury sauntered in, looking smug. Chiron followed them, with Bruce on his back. Trailing in reluctantly was another centaur, the one that had cornered me in my flat. I had never learned his name.

"I found this one watching Chiron," Hermes announced. I had wondered.

"Great Father Zeus," Chiron said, swooping into an impressive bow. Bruce leapt off Chiron's back mid-bow and dived into a bow of his own.

The other centaur made a grudging nod, but didn't address Zeus by name, or even call him 'father'. Zeus bristled at the implied insult, and his aura flickered into being for a moment, but he bit his tongue. I was proud of him. He was learning.

"The witch, Mags, tells us that your brothers are running loose in the world of men." Witch, again! At least he used my name this time. "Is this true?"

He knew it was true already, so I guessed this was some Olympian management technique.

"It is true, great Father." Chiron was brown-nosing. "Most of us are looked after by a member of the Sisterhood of Keepers, however." They weren't all sisters these days.

"Looked after," the other centaur said in a mumble, shaking his head.

"Do you wish to say something, centaur?"

I still had no idea what his name was, centaur or human. He'd looked like a Bob or a Dave. Something blokey. After he'd passed out drunk on my sofa, and was briefly a human, he seemed quite personable. Unlike his four-legged incarnation.

I thought he was going to defer to Zeus. He'd looked at his hooves, embarrassed, but then he straightened up and looked Zeus in the eye.

"Yes, Zeus, I do. This is no life for us, being 'looked after' by humans. We are not children. We are not enfeebled. We do not need to be looked after."

"You cannot roam freely in this world. Not now."

"Why?"

"Because," Zeus flared, "I say you cannot."

"We should take this world as our own. And you—" he said, pointing. He actually pointed at Zeus. I couldn't imagine that going down well. The beginnings of an aura flickered in Zeus's hair. The centaur couldn't have missed it, but he kept talking. "—you are living in secret, running a restaurant. Serving the humans. What life is that for a god? They should worship you. You should—"

Zeus's aura was now blazing.

"Silence!"

The other gods were also staring at the centaur, their auras fully ablaze.

"You know why we are here." My ears metaphorically twitched. Was Zeus about to say why they lived in London?

"But we don't—"

"We do as I say."

"Only because he—"

"Be quiet, brother!" Chiron interrupted, in a voice that was struggling to be calm.

"Quiet? You have spent your entire existence being quiet … brother." He delayed the word, making it an insult.

242

TALES OF AN URBAN WITCH

"Yes, but—"

"You spend your life pretending to be human. Unaware. Forgetting your nature. And you, cousin, are worse."

"I enjoy it," Bruce said.

"You think wanking in the bathroom mirror is being alive? You are under a spell. You are an immortal. You should be roaming the forests, seducing maidens."

"But, dude, it's fun. I'm hot."

"You should—"

"Again, enough," Zeus said. "You use the word 'should' a lot. It is not your choice how others live their lives."

"Perhaps not, but it is my choice how I live my life."

"You live your life according to *my rules*!"

The centaur didn't answer, but bowed his head. Zeus dimmed his halo, thinking he'd won the point, but then the centaur raised his head with insolent slowness, and smiled. It was the smile that a card player would have if they held five aces.

"I'm afraid not, my lord."

He switched then to his human form and smiled at me. That's when I recognised him. He'd looked familiar when I saw him on my sofa, but I couldn't place him then. But now I knew him. Context is key. That smile was all-important.

"You dare to challenge me?" Zeus flared brighter than ever. To state the obvious, trouble was brewing.

The man who had been a centaur shrugged. "If you choose to interpret it that way, sure. Whatever rocks your boat."

You see someone out of context, you often don't recognise them. You see, for instance, the woman from the flat next door while you're in the supermarket, and you don't notice her. She's not in her proper setting, so you don't see her as someone to be recognised until she says hello, and you have to walk around Sainsbury's with her.

"I am Zeus, your lord, and father."

"Yes, well, that doesn't mean much these days."

"What?"

"Face it, old man, your time is—"

ROBERT WILLIAMS

Zeus blazed brighter than I'd seen him before and lightning filled the space between him and the centaur. It was as if his anger had taken form. The centaur glowed, and Zeus bellowed a cry of rage. The man screamed as well, although I could barely hear him over Zeus and the thunder reverberating around the hall. The other gods stepped back, afraid, although trying heroically not to show it.

The lightning flowed for a full minute at least, before it stopped, and for a few seconds, nothing could be seen except the overwhelming glow of what was left of the man. He had to be nothing but bones and ash by now. And then the shouting stopped, and the thunder stopped, and as the glow reduced, we could hear the screams.

The gods looked at each other in disbelief. How could he still be alive?

As that surprise sunk in, another came to the fore. It wasn't screaming we could hear, but laughter. Sure enough, when the glow faded, the centaur in human form remained in the same spot, unscathed, the same knowing smile on his face.

"You live. How is this possible?" Zeus asked.

The centaur looked at me then. "You know why," he said. "I see it on your face. You tell him."

He turned and started walking out of the hall, but then stopped to speak to me again. "Do not worry, witch. We're not trying to kill you anymore. We have what we want from you." While I was puzzling about what he meant, he added, "I'm done here. Don't let them follow me."

They didn't attempt to. At least Zeus didn't attempt to, and the others watched him. If he'd made a move against the centaur, they might have followed. Or might not. Fifty-fifty, I thought.

"Can you explain, Margaret?" Zeus asked. Margaret? Was that out of anger or respect?

I took a deep breath.

"You know how your power comes from people's belief in you?"

"Yes."

TALES OF AN URBAN WITCH

"Well, we mainly believe in each other these days," Hermes added, and Hera scowled at him. Zeus rolled his eyes.

"That's a very good point," I said, nodding. "People these days don't believe in gods too much."

Several of the gods tutted and shook their heads. I heard mutterings about what the world was coming to, and I wondered if I should buy them a *Daily Mail*.

"Many people, at least round here, seem to be more interested in celebrities."

"Movie stars," said one of the muses, with a wistful note in her voice. She was part of the problem, but she didn't know it yet. She wasn't a muse I'd spoken to before, nor one of the ones in leg warmers, so I didn't know her name.

"Yes, and TV stars, footballers, models, pop stars, and people who seem to be famous just for being famous. Get your face on a magazine cover and you're set for life."

"That's all very well," said Hera, "but why was that centaur able to resist Zeus's all-powerful lightning?"

"Easy," I said. "What do you think would be the effect of all of that celebrity hero worship, if that centaur – in human form, admittedly – was on the cover of a magazine?"

Someone gasped. Zeus buried his face in his hands.

I'd only recognised him when he changed just now. He wasn't hungover this time or wrapped in one of my old blankets. As I said, I'm not good at recognising people out of context, so a bedraggled man on my sofa won't make me think of a waiter I saw on my TV screen three times a week. This time, however, he had smiled his trademark smile and the 20:20 vision of context fell into place.

The centaur was Kostas Filo, the star of *Hotel Hellada*. Millions of people watch it. Women all over the world – and quite a few men too – would give anything for a night with his character, Lucas. Thousands worshipped him. Tens of thousands. Probably more. And that gave him tens of thousands more worshippers than any of the gods in the hall in front of me.

The gods understood now. They knew their creatures had

ROBERT WILLIAMS

gone and had the nagging doubt that they were in trouble.

CHAPTER SIXTEEN

HOTEL HELLADA

There's often a correlation between how much someone likes something with how good they are at it. It's not a hard-and-fast rule, obviously. People can love what they do, but be totally rubbish at it, or they can be experts in a field they really hate. On the whole, however, if they're good at something, they like it more. It becomes a passion and defines them.

Witches are no different. There are elements of the craft that we take to better than others. I enjoy finding things, and my friend Emily lives to interpret the future and is renowned as a scryer. Agnes, when she was alive, loved to lead the dead to the afterlife.

It is one of the traditional roles of witches, but it has fallen into decline, to be honest, and few of us do it these days. Agnes really took to this aspect of the job, however, and would actively seek out the newly deceased, leading them to their rest, whether they wanted to go or not. She enjoyed it so much that, when she died, she put off going to her own version of the afterlife just so she could carry on leading people to theirs. She also knitted them a suitable garment in the process.

Today, she was taking me to Hades. I'm not dead. I just thought I should point that out. I know. Spoilers. Sue me.

At least, I didn't think I was dead. I was dressed in jeans and a hoodie. Neither of which looked like they had been knitted, so that pointed to me being alive. But, on the other hand, I was sitting in Charon's ferry.

"Agnes," I said. "Just tell me. I'm not dead, am I?"

She rolled her eyes and shook her head.

"That's the fifth time you've asked her," Charon said. I expected him to have a hollow voice with Shakespearian intonations, but he sounded rather blokey. He could have driven a black cab in London. He had that sort of voice.

"I've told you before," he continued. "Death is confusing enough for the dead. It's a thousand times worse when you're still alive."

I tried to remember where I was going, but my thinking wasn't clear. I knew my ultimate destination wasn't Hades. Agnes was taking me somewhere else. Hades wasn't even on the way. I knew that much. I wanted somewhere else.

I closed my eyes and tried harder to remember. Faces, words, images flittered in and out of focus in my mind. Emily. Vicky. Alice. Gavin. Simon. Gavin again. Agnes. Gavin.

Gavin was important. Why?

Oh. I was going to the Kingdom.

***

My reasoning had been simple. Everywhere has an afterlife. Everyone dies. Everyone mortal, that is. Gods, demigods, and so-called mythical creatures aside, everyone dies, and regardless of what they believed waited for them, Agnes, or someone like her, came along and took them to the afterlife. Their afterlife.

What if all these afterlives were actually the same place? They just looked different. Same afterlife, different wallpaper.

I asked Agnes some careful questions, ones that could be answered with nods and headshakes. She confirmed my theory and then answered another important question: does the Kingdom have an afterlife?

***

I could remember that part, but I couldn't remember why I was going. Not exactly. I knew Gavin had something to do with it.

Why couldn't I remember?

I looked around me and noticed I was on a boat, on a river, in the dark. And Agnes was sitting with me.

"Agnes? What are you doing here? What am I doing here? Oh, no ... am I dead?"

From behind me, a bored cabbie's voice drifted through the darkness. "Twenty-eight."

***

I remembered Gavin had called me, asking for help. This was Gavin, however, so he left a voicemail asking for help without actually asking for help. Typical. It was a long, rambling message. I can't remember the details, but it had something to do with Simon. At least I think so. I'm sure it was Simon.

***

Another memory. Even hazier. It might have been a dream.

Help us. Please. Help us.

***

"Miaow."

I looked down, confused. My mind was drifting between the present, the past, and possibly the future, although that was doubtful. You know what I'm like with the future.

So, it was likely to be now, which meant that I'd brought my cat with me on the Hades ferry. Why? Why did I decide to bring my cat on the ferryboat?

"Hello you," I said. I had never managed to name her. She seemed happy enough with whatever name she gave herself. A human name would have been irrelevant. "What are you doing here?"

"Miaow."

She stared at me. Was she trying to tell me something? Not for the first time since she'd arrived in my life, I wished I'd read that chapter on talking with cats. Not that it would have helped. She was definitely not just a cat.

I stared her in the eye. I've said before that eyes are not really windows into the soul but, if you're a trained witch, you can see a lot more than just eye. I could see something familiar in my cat's eyes. Familiar and unexpected.

I looked up and immediately forgot what I had seen.

***

The normal route for the ferryboat is from the land of the living to the land of the dead. At least that is the route for most passengers. A few notable exceptions made the return journey, and a tiny number, such as Agnes, were on the ferry so often they had a season ticket. Not that there were any tickets, but you get my drift.

Even fewer passengers, as far as I knew, had gone from one living side to another living side. I was missing out on Hades proper to get to the Kingdom. That was a shame, as I would have liked to have met Cerberus. I love dogs.

I could see us approaching lights on the shore. The management, whoever they were, had gone for a definite theme. The jetty on the shore I had left was dark and illuminated only by a couple of flaming torches. And, *quelle surprise*, the Kingdom jetty was also dark and illuminated by a couple of flaming torches. Darkness was part of the deal. Saved on electricity, I guess.

As we got closer, I again felt the urge to ask Agnes if I was dead, but it was weak, and I held it back. I was beginning to remember. The proximity of the shore, even though it was the Kingdom, brought with it some of my memory, which I found encouraging.

"We will shortly be arriving at the Kingdom," Charon announced. "Would passengers restore their seats and tray-tables to the upright position, and kindly make sure they have all their belongings with them when leaving the ferry. Thank you for travelling with Hades Express."

Everyone's a joker.

The torches grew brighter, and I felt a bump as the boat brushed against the jetty. The cat jumped ashore as soon as she could. She didn't enjoy being on the water.

Some dark shapes shuffled forward; the dead of the Kingdom, eager to make the journey to whatever afterlife lay ahead for them.

"Oi! You lot! Wait!" Charon shouted. "Let the lady off first. There's plenty of time. You've got all eternity. No need to hurry."

They ignored him and surged forward. I nodded goodbye to Agnes, who busied herself with her knitting, and I waded through the crowd, not paying attention to the shades all around me, until I reached the shore proper.

There I found Agnes. How had she done that?

"Oh, you're here. I thought you were going back," I said. She shrugged and started walking up the slope away from the river.

***

I was expecting the Kingdom to be weird. It was, after all, another plane of existence. I knew the people were all beautiful, and time did funny things. Yet, the weirdest thing about it was how familiar it felt.

After we'd crested the riverbank, instead of dark fields or a city or a fairy-tale castle shrouded in glittering rainbows, I found myself at a door that had opened to reveal a corridor, and a feeling that it was a corridor I recognised.

I asked Agnes if she knew it, and she nodded. Stupid question, I suppose. She couldn't elaborate. Instead of more questions, I paid more attention to my surroundings. I could see that the corridor had doors, and every door had a number.

"This is a hotel," I said, and Agnes tutted. My, she was tetchy. How many times had I asked her if I was dead? I must have really irritated her.

Why would they have a hotel in the Kingdom? And why was it so familiar to me? I had been on holiday enough times to recognise that it was a hotel corridor, but I'd never stayed in one long enough that I felt I could find my way around blind-folded, which is exactly how familiar this felt.

I knew that if I walked down this corridor, for instance, with a few twists and turns, would eventually lead to Reception. If I turned right, I would find the outdoor bar and the swimming pool and the laundry room where Andreas had so heartlessly—

Wait! Reception? Pool? *Andreas*? My conscious brain suddenly realised what my subconscious had been telling it since we arrived.

"This is Hotel Hellada."

Agnes stopped and turned to look at me, her expression telling me a lot. The slow hand clap was completely unnecessary.

"Yes, thank you for that. I know I'm being a bit stupid. It's been a tough day."

And this was the Kingdom, after all. I might be thinking clearer than I had been on the ferry, but this place was notorious for fogging the mind. I was so befuddled. If you'd given me a mirror and asked me to identify who I saw in it, I probably would have struggled.

"The Kingdom have created an illusion of *Hotel Hellada*. Why have they done this? Do they know I am here?"

Agnes rolled her eyes again, then carried on along the corridor. She obviously knew where she was going and was eager to get there. I had to hurry to keep up.

I wanted to ask her why we were here. Both in the sense of why we were in a copy of a Greek Crossroads, and, returning to my earlier confusion on the river, why were we in the Kingdom at all. I hadn't regained all of my pre-Hades memories yet. I knew it was something to do with Gavin, but that was about it.

Agnes led me into another corridor and then another and another. Each one seemed to be smaller and tighter, and each turn reflected the way I was thinking. I felt pressure building up like the mother of all migraines.

And then, all of a sudden, we turned a corner, and there was light and air, and I could breathe again. It took me a moment to realise we were in reception.

There were people here, just like there would be in an episode of *Hotel Hellada*. Extras mainly, of course. Or rather, the illusion of extras. And the illusions of cameras and illusions of film crew. I had to remind myself that none of this was real.

The extras were dotted around reception in that way that extras were in soap operas. They talked without making a noise and pointed at lunch menus without looking at the text. Agnes

TALES OF AN URBAN WITCH

glided past them, and the cameras, as if they weren't there.

And in the corner, looking dazed, was Gavin. I ran over to him.

"Mags!"

As soon as I saw him, I remembered why he was here and why I had followed. I knew the reason.

He had been an idiot.

Of course, he wasn't. Not really. The police don't recruit idiots and they certainly don't make idiots into liaison officers, not even supernatural liaison officers. I'd worked with him a lot. I knew he wasn't stupid. The trouble was, men don't always think with their brains, not even good men like Gavin.

To be fair, women don't always think with their brains either, but keep that to yourself. You didn't hear that from me. I don't want to be drummed out of the Sisterhood.

A few months ago, Simon, Gavin's boyfriend, had been seduced by a vampire and died. He came back as a vampire himself, and died again, but this time saving Gavin's life. He'd saved mine as well, for that matter, but the point was, Gavin had lost Simon twice. It messed with his head, but Gavin, being British and male, he kept his upper lip stiff and didn't let on just how messed up he was.

And then the Kingdom had interfered.

"It was Simon. He called to me."

I frowned.

"I went back to check on the portal," Gavin explained. "I know you said it had gone, but I needed to check."

That was our Gavin. Thorough.

"I listened at the door, but I couldn't hear anything, so I went home. Then later…"

His voice trailed off, but I could work out the rest. Later, at home in the darkness, when he'd been trying to sleep, the whispers had started. I wondered how long he'd lasted before the temptation had grown too strong and he found his way into the Kingdom. A day? Two? A week?

I cursed myself. The Kingdom preyed on the unprotected. We, Delores, Emily, and me, we knew how to protect ourselves. We all had charms. Witches carry them as a matter of course. I didn't give Gavin a charm. I didn't think he'd need one. I thought we'd closed the only door between the Kingdom and our world.

Obviously, I'd been wrong. On every count. There must have been a tiny opening. Too small for me to feel, but large enough for *them* to call out to him, to do their tricks. Or maybe there was another door somewhere.

"He wasn't really here," I said in my professional voice.

"I know. I knew that as soon as I got here. I knew it before, really, but—"

"The voice in your head told you otherwise."

He nodded. "It was his voice. Simon's voice. It was like he was back. And now you're here as well."

"I couldn't leave you here, could I?"

"That's not what I meant," he said. "Are you really you?"

"I am, but then I would say that."

"I could tell with Simon. He faded away as soon as I got here."

"They wanted you to think he was here to lure you in. And, as you said, you didn't really think he was still alive, anyway. You had an instinct. It's part of your job to have instincts like that."

He smiled, a brief twitch to the side of his mouth. "It's also part of the job to question my instincts. I didn't with Simon—"

"Naturally."

"But you seem real in a way that Simon wasn't."

"Doesn't mean I'm not." I'd already checked that Gavin was Gavin.

"I'm going to have to trust that you are you. For now, at least. You are here because of me. This is a trap and I'm the bait."

"I know." I knew it was a trap, but I didn't know why they wanted me. Maybe I'd made a good impression on the King. "I came here of my own free will."

"They'll know you're here, surely?"

"I came in the back way. They might not know." If I said it often enough, I might start believing it myself. I glanced at Agnes, but she looked back, disinterested, and shrugged. She did that a lot. I didn't know what had got into her since we'd reached the Kingdom.

"So now what?" Gavin asked.

"Now, we get out of here."

"What if they catch us?"

"I have a surprise."

"What is it?"

I showed him the sunshine bomb in my bag.

"But we're not dealing with vampires."

"I know but—"

A discreet cough interrupted us, so I turned.

"Good afternoon, madam." My jaw fell open. There, behind the reception desk, was Lucas, the central protagonist of *Hotel Hellada*, the man every woman wanted to sleep with, even if men weren't their cup of tea. "How can I help?"

In my reality, Kostas Filo played Lucas, the centaur who had defied Zeus, but here, in the Kingdom, he was just an illusion created by the King. I forced myself to remember that. He was still gorgeous. I could see why the show had such huge ratings. I could barely keep my eyes off him. Gavin was besotted.

"Thank you," I said, struggling to improvise, and trying not to stare. "We're just on our way to the bar to meet a friend."

I marvelled at the level of detail in the illusion. There were things here that I would never have noticed on television. Vases of flowers. Cups of coffee. The overstuffed chairs you only ever find in hotel lounges.

And they were doing all this for me? Amazing. When were they going to pounce?

"What a lovely cat," Lucas said. She'd jumped up onto the desk and was letting Lucas scratch behind her ears. "What's his name?"

I opened my mouth to give my usual answer that he was a she, that she doesn't have a name, that she was a free spirit and answers to the wind, but my mouth, on its own, said, "She's called Dione."

Where did that come from? She has a name? Was I becoming part of this illusion? Was that how they were going to grab me?

"An excellent choice," he said. "So regal."

Dione purred.

"Excuse me," I said. Agnes – the new impatient Agnes – had wandered off.

"Agnes," I said, in a stage whisper, although I didn't know why. The inhabitants of the illusion weren't listening. "Wait for us."

She stopped short and turned, irritation written on her face. She pointed deeper into the hotel.

"Why?" I asked.

She tapped her bare wrist. Whether that meant we were short of time, or this way was quicker, was unclear.

"I hope you know what you're doing," I said. "Come along, Gavin. Dione."

My cat, with her new name, turned to me and lifted her head to catch my eye, just like she had on the ferryboat. A familiar presence looked out at me, one that I didn't want to believe was there, although it made a weird sort of sense.

***

"Where are we going?" Gavin asked, distracting me from thinking about … What had I been thinking? Something about my cat.

"Agnes is leading us out," I said. "Apparently."

"She's right, you know," Lucas said.

"What?"

"Your guide is correct."

His current storyline had him flirting heavily with Sophia Kyriakidou, one of the housekeepers and, in the way of soap operas since the dawn of time, his secret half-sister. Neither knew they shared a father, and it would not end well. "I would leave that way," he added. "It's quieter."

Why was this illusion of Lucas trying to help me escape the Kingdom? It made no sense. He was an illusion created by the King, and the King wanted to keep me here, didn't he?

"Are you sure?" I said, standing in front of him again, and staring him in the eye. "I thought I knew—"

I wasn't sure what I really expected to see in his eyes, but what

I saw was a surprise. What I heard was even more of a surprise.

Help us. The words were barely audible. I could hear them when I looked into his eyes. That's when I understood.

This wasn't an illusion of Hotel Hellada. At least, it wasn't in the sense that I thought. It wasn't a duplicate of the hotel created from my memories in a bizarre attempt to trap me. It wasn't populated with simulations of characters I knew and loved.

This *was* Hotel Hellada, and the guests and staff that surrounded us *were* the characters I knew and loved. It was filmed here.

More than that, those characters weren't just *played* by escaped non-mythical demigods. They were living here as the characters. This was as real to them as a trip to the shops to you and me. Perhaps this illusion wasn't just for my benefit after all. If I looked at Lucas with more senses than just my eyes, I could see Kostas, the centaur. It was a struggle. My eyes watered from the effort. And you thought Magic Eye pictures back in the nineties were tricky. You should try this.

See us, the voices said through him. *Help us.*

I looked around the crowded reception area, using my eyes and other senses. There were centaurs, satyrs, trolls and even a sphinx. It was smaller than you might think. That one in Egypt was not to scale, but they got the head and the weird nose spot on.

"I'm sorry, madam?" he said. His eyes were still Kostas, while the rest of him was Lucas.

"I thought you were someone else," I said, lamely.

The characters were the problem, of course. The illusion was watertight. The characters believed in their world and in each other. More importantly, so did the millions of adoring viewers. As we know, belief was everything with this lot. The Kingdom had been very clever in persuading the centaurs and the satyrs and the other people to come here and 'act' in *Hotel Hellada.* The collective belief of their global audience powered the illusion and kept them trapped in their characters. Clever.

Kostas had had enough belief in him to be able to resist Zeus and his lightning. He was that strong. Imagine how strong all of them were, with the world behind them.

And the Kingdom had them in thrall.

But why? It's a neat, self-sustaining illusion, yes. The Kingdom pisses off the gods by stealing the demigods, yes. They make the said demigods suffer, yes. What does the Kingdom gain by all this?

A nagging doubt started tickling the back of my mind. There was something I was still not seeing. My thinking was too foggy. It was better than it had been on the river and I seemed to have become used to the Kingdom a bit, but I was still fuzzy.

I had prepared spells to protect me from the worst of the Kingdom's ability to confuse me. They were embodied in totems in my pocket. Nothing special; small cloth bags filled with herbs. I had a couple of them.

"Miaow."

I turned at the noise and found Dione in Gavin's arms. How had he picked her up? Why weren't his clothes hanging off him in bloody, tattered shreds?

"I think she wants us to leave," he said. "Let's go home, Mags."

Gavin gestured at Agnes, who smiled and pointed again. I didn't move. Something didn't feel right. It all felt too easy.

Gavin waited for me to move but alternated looking at me with looking at the suggested exit.

"Miaow."

The cat seemed to make up Gavin's mind, and he took a step forward, and then another.

"You should listen to your cat," Lucas said.

Gavin took another step, and Agnes beckoned him forward. She made a gesture for me to move as well.

I clutched at the totem in my pocket, willing my eyes to cut through the illusion again. Lucas disappeared, and I saw Kostas, his horns and all four of his hooves. His laugh told me he knew I could see him properly.

"The Kingdom's illusions aren't nearly as good as our transformations," he said, as if making conversation in a bar.

TALES OF AN URBAN WITCH

"They're good enough," I answered.

"It's just a trick. When we change, we really change."

I shrugged.

"What's going on?" I said.

"Your cat knows."

"My cat?"

Dione had jumped out of Gavin's arms and sat next to me, staring up at Kostas, but instead of demanding scratches, she was hissing. More than ever, I had the feeling that she wasn't just a cat. She wasn't looking at Lucas either. She was seeing Kostas.

"Surely, you know who your cat is?"

"I…" I thought I knew who she was, but I was just not allowed to remember.

"You know the name, Dione, is a big clue, right?"

Whatever was stopping me from recognising the real identity of my cat was also stopping me from thinking about her name. I looked down at her, but her eyes were fixed on the centaur.

"Let me give you another clue," Kostas said, his appearance changing. He gained a large bushy beard and big eighties-style hair, both of which flared with static. He glowed with a familiar godlike aura. "You know, all of those fans of *Hotel Hellada* just love me. I am the star. I am their god."

The aura intensified as he spoke.

"I am as powerful as old daddy Zeus used to be. If only he were here now to see me fry your cat."

"What? No—"

I could do nothing. Not that throwing myself in the path of a bolt of lightning would have helped. Poor Dione didn't stand a chance. Kostas threw bolt after bolt at her and the spot where she sat glowed white hot.

She hadn't even screeched. She didn't have time.

The glow faded. I was the only one seeing it. The hotel guests stood in their groups as if nothing were happening. Agnes and Gavin stood with vacant expressions on their faces, waiting for me.

"Are you finished, Kostas?" The patch of glowing air asked in

ROBERT WILLIAMS

James Mason's voice. "Did you think that would kill me?"

The centaur laughed. "Oh, majestic father Zeus. What a surprise. I am underwhelmed."

If Kostas wasn't surprised, I certainly was. "I should have known." I think I'd worked out that Dione was one of the Greek gods, when I'd been allowed to think about it, but I would never have guessed she was Zeus. I should have though, because it was so *him*. In all the ancient myths, he delighted in pretending to be other things. Money, bulls, dragons. Why was a cat, and a female cat at that, so unexpected?

And now the cat was out of the bag – every pun intended – I remembered that Dione was the female form of his name.

"You cannot kill me," Zeus continued. The glow had faded. Zeus was dressed in his traditional robes.

"I can kill your body," Kostas said, smirking. "Painfully."

"But—"

"It will weaken you so much that it will be centuries before you can return. You are weak, old man. How many followers do you have? A handful at most."

"The other gods, all of them, have put their faith in me."

"And none of them have had much experience at worshipping, have they? Shall we see how they measure up against me? With the whole human world in love with me?"

"Bring it on," Zeus said, sparks beginning to flare in his beard. "Gladly."

The lightning appeared so quickly that I couldn't tell who threw the first bolt, but both figures were quickly cocooned in glowing white strands of electricity. Through breaks in the bombardment, I could see Kostas, laughing with the cruel merriment of someone who knows he has the advantage. He had the might of countless little old ladies in love with Lucas.

Zeus, on the other hand, was grimacing, his eyes glowing and his hair standing on end. He was flinging bolt after bolt at Kostas, but they weren't having the same effect. He was suffering.

Suddenly, over the noise of the thunder, there were voices.

TALES OF AN URBAN WITCH

Quiet voices that were barely a whisper, but were clear to me, nonetheless.

Help us.

What? They were still there? Why were they still asking for help when Kostas was winning? *Help us help him.*

They wanted to help Kostas? He didn't need any help. I frowned.

Help us help our father.

I looked at the other creatures, the demigods. They were still stuck in their roles as extras in *Hotel Hellada*. None were overtly looking at the battle going on in front of them, but they were all skirting around Kostas and Zeus, and were carefully avoiding the lightning.

Why weren't they rooting for Kostas?

There wasn't time to analyse this. Zeus wasn't going to last long. They could help him … and I could help them.

I reached into my pocket for one of my totems and threw it into the air. I was intending for it to go roughly in the centre of reception, but it hit Kostas on the head. He didn't notice amidst the lightning, but it was still satisfying. It also did me a favour as the energy vaporised the totem, allowing the illusion-busting spell to spread around the room, and free the handful of demis who were there. It didn't reach Gavin or Agnes, more's the pity.

The change was immediate and was like a switch had been thrown. Each of the creatures turned as one to look at the battle between Zeus and Kostas. They were unnoticed by the two combatants.

I didn't know how this faith thing worked for them. For humans, faith and belief are expressed in worship and love, like people loving the character of Lucas and, by extension, Kostas. The public's belief in him gave him the strength to resist Zeus, but would a handful of demigods have enough faith to overturn that?

"Kostas," one of the centaurs said. "You brought me here and promised me respect and a fair life, but this is worse than the restaurant. I choose Zeus."

261

ROBERT WILLIAMS

"You told me I'd have it easy," said a satyr. "There would be an endless supply of virgins and I wouldn't have to work. All lies. I choose Zeus as well."

All the extras in reception said their piece. Then the cameramen and assorted creatures carrying clipboards muttered agreement and turned towards Zeus.

With each one, Zeus stood straighter, and his lightning strengthened visibly. Kostas looked much less cocky.

I looked around reception. Gavin and Agnes were standing in awkward silence, their illusion interrupted, on pause, but not broken. The laws of the Kingdom not letting them see the fight, but also not completely ignoring it.

There were a lot of demigods here, but nowhere near the numbers we knew were missing from the assorted pantheons. Presumably they were still lending their support to Kostas.

So why was he looking so weak so quickly? And why had the demigods moved their allegiance so readily to Zeus when they had been ready for full-blown rebellion?

Among the lightning flashes, I could see Kostas was confused. Zeus was grinning like a toddler at Christmas.

"Yield!" he shouted and flung a bolt that hit Kostas squarely in the chest.

The centaur staggered but stood his place.

"Never!" he gasped and flung another one back. Zeus laughed at it.

I counted the creatures I could see in the set. There were about twenty. I found it hard to believe that they were making so much of a difference to the battle. Zeus had done nothing to win them over. Why change their minds so quickly?

And besides, Kostas should have been winning. Even if all the missing creatures had somehow linked up together and believed wholeheartedly in Zeus, Kostas should still have been winning. He had the entire world on his side. Everyone watched *Hotel Hellada*. Everyone loved Lucas, even me.

"Yield!" Zeus shouted again.

"Not while I have breath in my lungs, old man. I have power

enough to beat you."

"Are you sure about that? It doesn't look like it to me."

In response, Kostas flung a thunderbolt at Zeus, but it smashed uselessly on the floor, scattering sparks like splashes of water. And with that, the battle was over.

"Why have you..." he started in his centaur shape, looking up. There was despair in his voice. He finished in his human form, "... you taken *his* side?" He looked at the other creatures in reception.

The transition from centaur to human was different. When I'd seen Jake become Chiron before, he'd been Jake and then Chiron, but in both forms, I'd had the sense that he had always been that form. He was Jake, but had always been Jake, and then he was Chiron, but had always been Chiron.

It had been the same with Kostas when I had seen him change before. He was human-Kostas and had always been so, and then he was horsey-Kostas, and had always been so, but this time, the transition was different. He was Kostas the centaur, and then he was Kostas the man, but I didn't have that sense of *always* that I'd had before. He was Kostas with four legs, then Kostas with two, but the feeling of him having four legs lingered. There was a *wrongness* to him having only two legs.

I looked around the set again. The others were flickering between their proper shapes and their human shapes as well. These human shapes weren't their 'natural' human shapes, the ones that they adopted that allowed them to move around in our world without people pointing fingers. These were illusions, a psychic misdirection, to make the unwary think they were seeing something they weren't. The flickering was like a television with a poor signal, flipping from one station to another. The Kingdom's illusion was trying to re-assert itself, but it was struggling.

With Kostas, however, the switch had been sudden and strong. The Kingdom had tried harder. Why? Why was Kostas different? Why was the Kingdom trying so hard to hide the way Kostas looked? Or was it hiding something else? Like what he'd been about to say? Or to whom?

"Come on, Mags. Time to go." Gavin had dropped out of whatever illusion had been holding him in place while the battle had been fought. Zeus remained as Zeus, however, and was looking as smug as you'd expect. He'd just beaten a rebellious centaur into submission and regained control of several pantheons' collections of demigods. He'd also spent a long period of time as a cat, so the smugness level was off the scale.

"I..." I couldn't say what I wanted to say. I didn't know what I wanted to say. I gripped my remaining totem tighter still and looked at Kostas. Instead of the man, I saw the centaur, and he looked crestfallen.

Zeus nodded, and the demigods took this as a cue for them to file over to where he, Gavin, and Agnes were standing. More of them filtered into reception.

Still, something felt wrong about this tableau. It had all been way too easy.

Gavin, Zeus, and the demigods, with the exception of Kostas, stared with joyous eyes at the corridor behind Agnes, as if it really were the route home.

"Come along, Mags," one of the centaurs said. "You have done well to get us all back together. We can all go home now."

But what had I done? I had followed Gavin as bait into a trap, but I realised now that I wasn't the prey. The Kingdom wanted me there, but only because my cat had come with me.

I was just the bait in an even bigger trap for Zeus.

They wanted Zeus. The Kingdom wanted Zeus. All of this was for him, Gavin luring me here, me coming with Dione, and Zeus battling with Kostas.

But why?

And how had they been so sure that Kostas would lose?

"Yes, come on Mags. Let's get you home and put the kettle on." And that, if I needed it, which I didn't, was the nail in the coffin for the whole circus, because that had been Agnes speaking. You remember Agnes? Friend of mine? Big knitter? Not fond of speaking? Yes, her.

This wasn't Agnes, not the real one. I'd left her on the ferry, knitting. This one was someone else. Cursing myself for not doing this earlier, I clutched my totem tightly again and the glamour surrounding 'Agnes' slid away. I could see her for who she really was.

"Hello, Dorothy," I said.

***

Back when she'd lived in our world, and had been my friend, Dorothy had been a strange woman. I don't mean the headaches or the messing around with time. I just mean she was ... odd.

You know people like her. We all do. They are the people that never fit in. They try, but it's as if they received a different version of the *How to Human* manual to the rest of us. They laugh at things a second after everyone else, and clap along to songs out of time with the rest of the audience.

I don't suggest that all those people are changelings. It would be very worrying if they were. They all had their reasons to be different. It was just that Dorothy's reason was rather more outlandish than most. Literally.

Like Clark Kent, she had been brought up human, with morals and values that were completely at odds with her Kingdom nature. While she'd been my friend, she'd been a simple soul who didn't have the hang of being duplicitous. She could never have worked in any job where the truth was a somewhat flexible resource. Politics was never an option for her, and neither was sales. And acting was obviously out of the question.

No offence intended to salespeople or actors.

She could cast illusions, but had no idea how to lie.

After I greeted her, I could see conflicting emotions chasing themselves across her face, her mouth opening and closing a few times. She wanted to tell me a lie, to perpetuate the myth that she was Agnes, but she didn't have the first idea of how to do it.

"Stupid girl." Her father's voice appeared to be everywhere. "I told you not to speak."

"I'm sorry, father. I was trying to get her to join us."

Gavin, Zeus, and the demigods continued to look towards the corridor, ignoring Dorothy and her father's voice. He appeared beside her, still the most beautiful man I had ever seen. I looked away to avoid being bewitched.

Kostas continued to hold his ground.

"You will come with us, Kostas," the King said.

"No," the centaur answered. His voice was weak, drained.

"Yes. You will join us. You are needed."

"But you need me here."

"No longer. You have served your purpose now. Join us."

"You need me to—"

"We do not."

"But—"

"You will not argue. Join us."

Kostas shuffled forward. He was reluctant, but he was beaten. He couldn't resist. It was as if all the strength he'd possessed had been drained away.

Of course. That was how Zeus had beaten him. The belief of the millions of viewers was still flooding in, but the Kingdom had siphoned it away.

"You did it," I said. "You left him weak."

The King laughed. "You are so dim-witted to have only realised that now."

I knew the belief in Zeus from the other gods and the demis hadn't balanced out the love of Kostas from his legions of fans. The King had drained it, and he'd slapped on an illusion to stop me from hearing Kostas ask him why he had done so.

Had he also been responsible for the sudden change of heart from the demigods, or had that been real?

"What of Mags, father?"

"The witch has served her purpose as well. We have Zeus now," the King said. "We know he is not just a cat. Kostas confirmed that."

"But why do you need Zeus?" I asked, still looking away. He ignored me, so I turned to him and asked again. "Tell me. Why do you need Zeus? What are you going to do with him?"

"It's none of your business, witch."

"Oh, I think it is. You used me to get him here. You should at least tell me why."

The King turned to me, and his eyes captured me. They were pale blue beacons of will and impossible to resist.

"It is none of your business," he repeated. "And you will give up trying to find out. Come with us."

I stepped forward. Why had I questioned him? How could I ever question my King? I would follow him anywhere. I nearly had before, but then my traitorous friends had stopped me. They had jabbed me in the arm with a steel needle. I remembered it. There was the tiniest memory of a twinge.

"That's it, Mags, love," Dorothy added. "Come with us. It will all be better."

I followed eagerly. The remembered pain from where the needle had been in my arm was a tickle. I took another step forward.

"Come on, Mags, we need to be getting back."

Her words stirred something at the back of my mind. The tickle became a prickle, the memory stronger.

"Silence, daughter."

The prickle became a stinging, and a larger portion of my mind focussed on it. Unconsciously, I rubbed my arm as I took another step.

Why had the King shut her up? What had she said to warrant him wanting to keep her quiet?

I took another step. The pain in my arm felt as bad as when I had been jabbed with the needle. I could feel the metal in my arm as if it were still there. It was agonising.

But it brought clarity. I could think again.

Dorothy had said something important. We. Need. To. Be. Getting. Back.

Back? Back where?

And the cameras. How did cameras work in the Kingdom? They needed cables and electricity and iron.

Oh, my ... Not only was this a studio, but it was *in our world.*

ROBERT WILLIAMS

It must be lined with foil. We weren't in the Kingdom. Somehow, we'd left it. There was a portal in one of the corridors and we'd passed through it without me noticing.

Or perhaps I had. It had been when the endless tight corridors had suddenly ended, and they'd opened up into the bright busy Reception set. We'd left the Kingdom at that point and slipped into my world.

That's what she meant by back. She wanted to lead us back to the Kingdom. No, she wanted to lead Zeus back to the Kingdom. They'd just needed him to show himself, to make sure they had him and not just a cat.

I needed a distraction. I had something – a couple of somethings – planned. I just hoped I was close enough. I had prepared, but Hades, and the Kingdom, had messed with my mind. Even though we were in the real world now, there was enough 'Kingdom' radiating out from Dorothy and her father to cause me problems, but the memory of the pin had helped clear my head.

One of the things I had prepared was the other totem in my pocket. It had been amazingly useful, but I was about to destroy it. I needed it for my distraction.

Last time, Zeus and Kostas had provided the energy to vaporise the totem, but I didn't need it. Overlaid on top of each totem's reality-grounding spell was another, or rather most, of another spell. It was something called an expansion spell, and I only needed another word to complete it.

I threw the totem at Zeus and shouted after it, "Expand."

The totem disintegrated in a puff of smoke – I'm old-fashioned – and the smoke expanded to encompass Zeus, Gavin, and the group of demigods. And me, thank goodness. None of this would work if I was unable to resist the King.

The smoke dissipated quickly, but I could feel the spell working on me already. I could see the demis in their true forms again. Kostas looked sullen. A massive portal hung in the air behind Dorothy.

The King laughed. "What was that meant to achieve, witch? I

TALES OF AN URBAN WITCH

am unharmed by your trifling spell. Daughter, usher them into the Kingdom. We have dallied here too long."

Dorothy looked at Zeus and the demigods in fear but didn't have time to answer her father.

"And who are you?" Zeus asked the King, sparks of anger in his beard. He was seeing him for the first time. "Where do you think you are taking my people?"

I swear I saw the King jump. He wasn't expecting to be seen by Zeus and the others. Now that I knew the spell was working, I set to work with part two of my plan, keeping half an ear on the conversation. I took my bag off my shoulder.

"Your people? Your people left you."

"You tricked them into playing out some silly little hotel fantasy."

"Instead of working in your restaurant."

Zeus glared at the King, and his aura started blazing.

"Zeus," one of the satyrs said. "I want to come back. I really do."

There was a chorus of "and me" from most of the assembled demigods. Perhaps their change of allegiance had been real, after all.

"Kostas?" Zeus asked. "What about you?"

The centaur, as ever, had a sour look on his face. That's probably why it had taken me so long to recognise him as Lucas. Lucas was always smiling.

"I don't want to serve mortals."

There was a general muttering among the others. It sounded like agreement. Oddly, some of the muttering came from people who'd said "and me". Sheep.

"There! You see? Your people don't sound like they want—" the King said, but Kostas interrupted him.

"I also don't want to be in the Kingdom."

"You are the star of *Hellada*," the King said. "Think of the power it gives you."

"It's power I only see when it suits you. You were quite happy to throw me – us – away when we'd served our purpose."

"And that was getting me into the Kingdom," Zeus said.

269

"Why?"

The King laughed but didn't answer.

"Oh, come on, Zeus," Kostas answered. "Why do you think?"

The aura blazed again, but he got it under control quickly.

"I have it now," I said, my preparations finished. I'd also worked out what was going on. "You were going to become the new star of *Hotel Hellada*. You were going to be adored by the world over. You're a god, not a centaur. You know how to accept adoration and you would have had more of it thrown at you than at any time in your life."

Zeus looked shocked. I could see him thinking about what he was rejecting.

"And you would have seen none of it," I added hurriedly. "The King was going to steal it away from you. No, worse than that. You would have given it to him gladly. They wanted you to power their return to our world."

"But that was why I was there," Kostas said. "Why we were there."

"It wasn't enough. You only gave them a toehold," I said. "Then they built on it. Had you in *Hotel Hellada* to build up your following. And your strength."

"Zeus will return us properly to this world and we will take our rightful place as its rulers."

"Will I? Will I, really? You still think I'll do that?"

"The witch's spell is fading." He wasn't wrong there. I could already feel the subtle tendrils of their glamour coming back. I would have to work quickly. "You will soon join us. Willingly. You will have no choice in the matter."

"Well, no," I said, and pulled the sunshine spell out of my bag.

"You will stop us with that? A sunshine spell? That will work on vampires. I *am* the Kingdom."

"I told you that. It worked for Augustus," Gavin said, then added after a heartbeat, "And Simon."

"Yes, thank you, gentlemen, for that display of mansplaining. I am fully aware that I'm not working with vampires."

Gavin and the King rolled their eyes and shared a look. I would have words with Gavin later.

"I am also fully aware that people in the Kingdom have a distinct aversion to iron and, because of it, to radio waves."

"We know you are not carrying one of your abominable communication devices," the King said. "We had you throw yours in the river when you set foot in the Kingdom."

Clever move. I hadn't even noticed. I wondered if losing a phone in the Styx was covered by the insurance. Did I even have phone insurance these days?

"I know how to construct a sunshine bomb," I continued, "and to charge a sunshine bomb, and most importantly, I know how to tune a sunshine bomb."

"Tune?" the King looked genuinely puzzled. "It will play music?"

Bless.

Dorothy, for once, understood before her father and started edging towards the portal.

"Oh no. Not music. Nice idea. Maybe I'll do that next time. No. Tuning, in this case, means that I have been able to isolate and amplify part of its electromagnetic spectrum. Specifically, I've limited it to radio waves."

Gavin laughed, the temporary bromance between him and the King over. "Mate, I'd start running now, if I were you. This is gonna hurt."

Sunshine bombs don't need fuses, but as I didn't want to actually kill the King, the bomb I'd made had one. It was a short one, however, and he only just made it to the portal before the bomb exploded. Enough of the blast caught him to make him scream before the portal closed.

***

Given we'd returned to our world without me noticing, we could have been anywhere, but it turned out that we weren't that far away from the estate. We were actually in the old bottle factory on Helston Road. I'd wondered who'd bought it from Harris and Hall. Now I knew.

The Kingdom had done their whispering trick on Kostas and

ROBERT WILLIAMS

had him buy the factory – those ancients were *loaded*, even the demis – and then line it with foil and open a portal.

I took Gavin home and let him stay in my spare room for a few days to recover. He hadn't spent as long in the Kingdom as I had feared. A couple of days and he would be as right as rain. If nothing else, it would give me time to cook up a protection spell for him. The Kingdom wouldn't get to me through him in the future. Not that I thought they would try. They were clever enough to see my bomb as a warning. I had no plans to do so, but they had to know that I could send another much bigger modified sunshine bomb through a portal if I chose.

Once I had Gavin settled, I checked the date. As we all know, time in the Kingdom was a funny thing. Seconds could elapse in there, but centuries go by outside. I was willing to bet, however, that the entire business with *Hotel Hellada* would have to have meant that the Kingdom would be in sync with our world. I felt like we had only been away a few hours, and luckily, that was the case. Today was still today.

Over the next few weeks, things returned to normal, or as normal as they could be in the circumstances. Zeus and the immortals all returned to their homes around London, but in Greektown, Little Rome, Asgard, and the others, there were differences.

For one thing, it seemed that Zeus had been listening to Kostas. The gods still ran restaurants and taxi companies and nail bars, but they employed humans to serve other humans.

And they cooperated more. Greektown was no longer a bitter rival to Little Rome. There were still two restaurants – there was room for both – but there was no need to have two rival taxi companies, or two nail bars. Other establishments filled the gaps, community libraries appeared popular on both sides of the street, and were well attended, nearly exclusively by the demis, when they weren't busy elsewhere.

And elsewhere, was of course, *Hotel Hellada*. Zeus took it over as a going concern and the demis were employed as actors, proper actors this time. Zeus was a natural as a director, which

272

made sense, I suppose, and the Muses made an outstanding job with the scripts, as you'd expect, even Polyhymnia.

Zeus got himself and a fair few of the other gods on screen regularly. The idea of the world worshipping them again was too tempting to pass up, even if it was only part-time.

"I love working in Greek again," Calliope told me over a gin and tonic at the *Werewolf and Tin Mine*. "Much more lyrical."

And it occurred to me then that I still didn't know why they were here. That I hadn't been allowed to even ask. I still couldn't. That made it a very important question.

Why exactly were the ancient gods in London?

ACKNOWLEDGEMENTS

Many people helped me work on this book over the years. So, I say thank you to …

… everyone in Bromley Writers for providing a nurturing, creative space.

… all of my fellow South of the River anthology editors, for helping me hone my writing skills.

… all the friends I coerced into reading the stories for the useful comments.

… Richard for being a Mags fan from the very beginning and for convincing me I had a story to tell.

… Ray and Alison, for all the encouragement, the endless proofreading, looking at my covers, but mostly for persuading me I had a novel after all.

… David for being so patient while I worked on this.

SOUTH OF THE RIVER COLLECTIVE

The South of the River Collective launched in 2023, with the aim of linking writers of all abilities across South London and Kent. SOTR Collective's aim is to enable writers and poets to share skills such as editing, and to request feedback from beta readers.

Authors can also request permission to use the unique South of the River Collective logo for their self-published projects, and publicize their work via the website.

All use of the Collective's skills is completely free.

Publicity via the website and use of the SOTR logo is also free, dependent upon the author producing a piece of work of sufficient quality. This is to encourage self-published authors to achieve excellence in all aspects of their work.

SOUTH OF THE RIVER ANTHOLOGIES

SOUTH OF THE RIVER

South of the River is the first collection of the best fiction and poetry from the Brixton and Bromley creative writing groups. Some authors were previously published, others are showcasing their work here for the first time, but they all have one thing in common; imagination. Romance, history, murder, sci-fi, sex and horror – it is all here in this marvellous collection.

JOURNEYS

The word 'Journey' can mean a literal path from one place to another or, by extension, a pathway from one stage in a person's life to another. The writers featured in this anthology have used the word in both senses to inspire them to write stories, poems, essays and a radio play. We have a train journey with a sinister twist, time travel, romance and much more.

THE OTHER SIDE

The Other Side. What do those words conjure up? The other side of the road? The other side of the mirror? The other side of a marriage? All of these interpretations and more are explored in this anthology of stories, poems and essays.

COMING SOON

Look out for these titles from members of the collective in the next few months:

The Creative Writing Group
Ray Little

Remembering the Night
[working title]
Robert Williams

Printed in Great Britain
by Amazon

95b80df0-c62b-49a4-9f00-81db5c3d1341R01